PEYTON 313

Book One of Cyborgs: Mankind Redefined

By

Donna McDonald

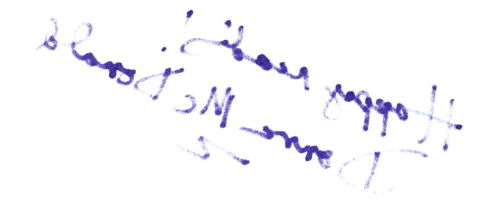

EDITION NOTICE

This book is a work of fiction. Names, characters, places, and incidents either are the product of the author's imagination or are used fictitiously. Any resemblance to actual persons, living or dead, businesses, companies, events, or locales is coincidental.

This book contains content that may not be suitable for young readers 17 and under.

No part of this book may be reproduced, or stored in a retrieval system, or transmitted in any form or by any means, electronic, mechanical, photocopying, recording, or otherwise, without express written permission of the author/publisher.

Cover art by *Black Raven's Designs*
Edited by *The Proof Is In The Reading*

Copyright © 2014 Donna McDonald
All rights reserved.

Acknowledgements

Thanks to my husband, Bruce, for his lack of complaining when I used a great part of our meager vacation this year to write the first half of this book. You truly are the best example of every hero I write.

Thanks to authors J.M. Madden and Robyn Peterman for their constant support of my work no matter what kind of crazy "out there" ideas I get. Friends like you are priceless and I value you more than I can ever adequately express.

Dedication

This book is for author friend, Eve Langlais, whose cyborg books have filled many reading hours and fulfilled Sci-Fi fantasies for me. I always look forward to the next one.

Many thanks for the inspiration and encouragement to write my own.

Chapter 1

"Dr. Winters, how can you refuse this kind of money? Chancellor Li and I approved Norton's offer of twenty million solely because you are the last original cyborg creator. More is simply not a possibility. Now if it's the lead scientist position you crave, perhaps that can be discussed as an additional incentive for your return."

Kyra tried her best not to react too negatively to the giants glaring at her through her monstrous living room com. Jackson had abandoned the seldom used device during their divorce many years ago. She was only using it for the conference call so the UCN chancellors would see her relaxing on her sofa instead of staring intensely at her lab console.

She could handle the pressure they were exerting on her to return to Norton because she had no intention of going back. But it was not fun to face down several frowning impatient men whose every frustrated expression was being projected directly into her wide-eyed retinas. Luckily her far beyond Mensa level brain discarded her rising nervousness as it reminded her there was no reason to be intimidated by an optical illusion. She had met all the chancellors many times. Most of them were much shorter than her five foot ten inch height.

"Gentlemen, I am deeply honored you have taken the time to contact me this morning. But however inconceivable it might be for Norton or the UCN, my retirement has nothing to do with money. My plan is to find a more satisfying use of my skills. As you know my specialty has always been military cybernetics, but the final war has been over for almost a decade. There is no research being done at Norton right now that suits my desire to better the world we live in. I've made no secret of the fact that I am morally opposed to installing the behavior modification system in children."

Kyra watched as Chancellor Owens fought not to roll his eyes at her adamant statement. He was a thoroughly detestable man, and she didn't understand how someone like him had managed to become the UCN's head chancellor.

"Yes. We are all aware. Fortunately, there are other cyber scientists willing to lend their talents to that specific project. If Norton has nothing that interests you at the moment, perhaps a paid consultancy would suit you more than a permanent position. I'm sure the personal loss of not one, but two costly Cyber Husbands over the last seven years, has been traumatic for you. And we are all aware that Jackson left you no choice but to deal with his own death recently. What I'm trying to say is that we understand this may be a time in your life where it's natural you would be doing a lot of. . .self-reflection."

Kyra watched Chancellor Owens shrug his shoulders after his speech and look away. She had no logical reason to dislike him other than he always gave her the creeps. And she doubted he ever reflected on anything outside of his bank account for long.

"The consideration of the UCN council for my personal losses is greatly appreciated, but I assure you I am doing just fine. My relationship to Jackson was over long before his death occurred and brought me back into the picture temporarily. And as the submitted reports on my Cyber Husband's unfortunate deaths indicated, both of them came to me with undiagnosed mental health problems. Their losses merely taught me to be a smarter consumer about spending my money."

When Chancellor Owens glared at her explanation, Kyra had to fight off the urge to sigh. She was getting really tired of defending her right to do what she wanted for a living.

"That's good to hear, Dr. Winters. Still—I don't think it's wise of you to make any sort of final decision about refusing so much potential income," he suggested.

Kyra nodded reluctantly. Chancellor Owens had a rational point about her income and she had no way to defend her own logic without revealing her disgust with Norton and the UCN. All she could do was hope they left her alone long enough to finish her task.

"I concede your suggestion to delay my final choice is wise, but for now I remain resolved in my quest to find a happier life with more suitable work. Receiving Jackson's surprising inheritance has allowed me to purchase a third Cyber Husband. In fact, he's being delivered in a few hours. I've planned a short honeymoon for us next week, so it is doubtful I will look for work until after our return."

Kyra swallowed past the knot of tension in her throat. She really wanted to say "not only no, but hell no" to going back to Norton, but she was too afraid of the UCN's power to deny their request so flatly. "Perhaps from time to time I could return to Norton to work on special projects. I will give that idea some additional thought once I've settled down to marital life again."

"Yes, please do that, Dr. Winters. And congratulations on your new purchase. You have the UCN's best wishes for the relationship to be both pleasing and successful this time," Chancellor Owens declared.

Kyra nodded once, hoping the man was finally winding down. "Thank you, Chancellor Owens."

"Have a blessed day, Dr. Winters."

"May the same fate be yours, Chancellor."

Kyra laughed and shook her head after she had disconnected. The amount of money the UCN had been willing to pay her to return to Norton was unnaturally obscene. If she was worth twenty million a year to them to stay, would the UCN really let her go work for anyone else for less money? Probably not.

But what could they do to stop her?

Or maybe the right question was, what *would* they do to stop her?

Thinking of the conference call and her own trepidation made her suddenly regret all the things she had put off doing up to now.

She had to wipe the nervous sweat from her palms before the remote for the com would work under her fingers. When she was sure the com viewer was shut down completely, she rose and headed for her lab.

***

Kyra sighed with genuine regret as she attached the most recent photo she could find to the video file she was creating. She stared for a while at the handsome solider, then cleared her throat as her finger hesitated over the record symbol.

Making a holographic message to document her work had been put off for too long already. She had one more chance—one more cyborg—and he was due to be delivered in just a few hours. If restoration didn't work this time, her video confession might be the only record of all the secrets she had kept for the last seven years. There was no money left for another attempt, which meant there was also no time left for being afraid.

"Record full body visuals as well as speech. Visual is to be permanently attached to the final output. Destroy any file copy on attempt at separation of visual, or any attempt to edit content at all. Set password code for running the file as. . ."

Kyra hesitated over the password. To open the message, she had intended to use the cyborg ID of her first successful restoration because the man himself would become the living dissertation proving her work. Since she hadn't been successful yet, she could only have faith that her third and final attempt would net that result.

"For a password code to run the file, use Peyton 3 dash 1 dash 3."

She cleared her throat one final time before starting the recording.

"*Hello. My name is Dr. Kyra Winters. I am one of the two original cyber scientists who invented the Cybernetic Soldier program. In the year 2143 CE, along with my now deceased husband, I helped combat modify three hundred forty-two soldiers who were pivotal in our government winning the final world war. After the global peace treaty of 2146 was signed, those soldiers' families were told the modification process had become irreversible. To back up that falsehood, modified soldiers were manipulated into acting in ways that made them seem more dangerous than they actually were. The truth is that outside their combat service many didn't trust the Cyber Soldiers' humanity to rule over the enhanced cybernetic capabilities we had given to them. Without any testing of this theory, the Cyber Soldiers were deemed a threat by all the members of our global world government. All modified humans—those we call 'cyborgs'—have been forced to run android-like programming, which makes them appear to be little more than living machines. It is a scientific illusion and a form of human enslavement that must not be allowed to continue."*

Kyra paused the recording and took a deep breath. It was even harder to put her crimes into words than she thought it would be. Part of her wanted to stop and try the recording again later. But even if she did, nothing would change the horror that had to be described. She resumed the recording before she lost her nerve to continue.

"Some of those men we modified left wives and children to fight for the freedom and peace we now enjoy. They deserve to be honored for their sacrifice, not live out their lives as robotic slaves for the highest bidder. How can we know what each modified person would have done if we don't give any of them the chance to exercise their fundamental human rights? And despite the cybernetic implants, those men are still human. Restoration was never even attempted until I started doing it myself several years ago. My experiments were not—and still are not—condoned by the United Coalition of Nations nor the scientific research agency I once worked for. Sadly, I must report to you that all world government organizations are colluding on this issue. But if I am successful in my experiments, every soldier with cybernetics installed will soon have the option to fight once again for freedom—only this time it will be for their own."

Kyra lifted her sleeve and swiped at her tears. *"Until that time arrives—please—I implore you to not let your children or loved ones receive any unnecessary cybernetic implants. Modification has become a negative trend in our society and is producing rapid declines in human decency. Poverty stricken women prisoners, for crimes as simple as shoplifting, are being modified without their consent and forced to work as sexual companions. Children—too many innocent children—are being wired with pain devices to make them behave. You need to think hard about these acts. Mankind should not always be engaged in efforts to control each other. These are real people being modified—real people just like you that are being turned into cyber slaves. Any one of us could be next."*

Kyra stared at her work console, lost in the importance of what she was trying to say.

"At this point in our global history, corruption is rampant among scientists, which affects all research and medicine. To make sure my restoration research and results do not die when I do, following the example of the legendary Albert Einstein, I have arranged for mass distribution of all my notes. It is probable that my death has already happened if you are seeing or hearing this recording. Please look for copies of my work and have the results reviewed by ethical scientists not afraid to draw their own conclusions. And if you are a family member of one of the Cyber Soldiers, they need your help now as much as we once needed theirs. Write to your local government and the UCN. Look for your soldier and find out where he has been placed. And most of all—help those like me who believe every human on this planet deserves the right to define their humanity for themselves."

Kyra paused the recording again, her finger trembling. She sniffed back the tears that had started falling when she spoke of the children being wired for controllers. Would anyone care but her? With all the money child behavior modification brought Norton, she wasn't sure. People in general could be made complacent pretty damn easily, no matter how intelligent they were. Her complacency had cost the Cyber Soldiers their freedom for a decade. Now the evil seeds she had sown were starting to grow in ways she had never imagined.

She owed the soldiers more than an apology. She owed them her life in exchange for what she had done to theirs. One day soon she might very well end up giving it for them. Until then, she would continue to try and free them. She swallowed the lump in her throat as she started the recording again.

"*I have one last thing to say in what I am sure has been a very disturbing message for most of you. But my final words are just for the Cyber Soldiers. Thank you for stepping up and volunteering. You each made a heroic sacrifice and the world you saved had no right to turn you into a commodity. Each of you is a person—and yes a 'human'—regardless of your cybernetics. I'm truly sorry I didn't get involved in your restoration sooner. No apology, no matter how sincere, will give you back what was taken away for so long. Now my goal until my death is to atone for my scientific sins by waking up the human side of as many of you as I can restore. If I am destroyed for my work, so be it. I hope some of you are understanding this message because I was successful.*"

When she pushed the stop command, Kyra let the sob she had been holding back escape. Talking so much about emotional things never seemed to help her. It only made her ill. That was certainly the case for the truth she had just recorded.

Full out bawling on the other hand usually freed the knots in her gut and let her breathe.

"Save recording. Edit out pauses and breaks. Produce output and store in *Mankind Redefined* folder," Kyra ordered.

When she received acknowledgement that the work was proceeding, Kyra closed her portable and shoved it aside. Laying her head down on her desk, she loudly wept out what she could of her remorse before her last chance to redeem herself arrived.

Chapter 2

Peyton fought the pain contracting his muscles as best he could while not allowing his face to show it. Over time, he had learned to channel the physical torture into a silent exercise that made his body stronger. Through the steady stream of current scrambling his circuitry, he heard the delivery guy speaking to his new *wife*.

"Lady, are you sure about this? Peyton 313 has been fighting his restraints all the way here. He's not going to be easy to control."

Kyra nodded without smiling. The thought of the constant torture the cyborg was experiencing made her ill. "Yes. I need a husband and he's exactly what I've been looking for."

"Listen. You're a nice looking woman. Even at your age—and trust me you don't look a day over fifty—you could be hooking up with a real man instead of this—this *thing*. Peyton 313 has had ten wives and they've all returned him. Even though he's supposedly good in the sack, he eventually gets sent back for exceeding boundaries. Hell, this one's programming has been upgraded so many times that they've had to replace his uplinks twice. The only reason he's not been sent to a work camp is because my boss thinks he's too pretty. They would disassemble him for sure if he acted up there."

Kyra snorted, but told herself not to show her contempt for the man's words. Compassion and protesting got you nowhere. Mankind in general was too far gone where the cyborgs were concerned. It was time for a new approach.

"I appreciate your concern for me. . .*Lyle*," Kyra said as she looked at his Norton Industries ID. "But I've waited a long time for this particular model. I assure you there's no need for you to worry at all. I'll have Peyton 313 toeing the line soon enough. He's not my first Cyber Husband."

"Well okay, Dr. Winters—ma'am. My job is just to transport. You're the one who paid for him. I figure I done my good deed today by telling you the truth. That's all a simple man can do."

Kyra smiled as pleasantly as she could, considering the man didn't seem to be able to take a hint at all. "Yes. Thank you for the information, Lyle. Now if you'll just hand over Peyton 313's wrist controller, you can be happily on your way with another job-well-done stamp on your record. I'm sure you've got lots of other deliveries to make."

She watched Lyle shaking his head steadily over her words even as he relinquished the wrist unit to her outstretched hand. Her fingers slid over the buttons until she found the restraint one. She waited until Lyle was halfway down the sidewalk before turning to Peyton. Raising a finger to her lips, she watched his pupils fluctuate in acknowledgement as she released him from the circulating pain.

Kyra kept her tone abnormally cheery in case Lyle was still within hearing range. "Hello, Peyton. You're even better looking than your online profile. Let's go inside and get acquainted."

His simple nod as she ushered him through her front door was promising.

***

Free of the debilitating current at last, Peyton's body got busy with his muscle recovery. In twenty minutes and four seconds, his muscles would be functioning at optimal capacity again. Before he'd developed his organic neural bypass, recovery would have taken several hours. The bypass hurt like hell to use, but it was effective and outside the control of the cybernetic chips embedded in his brain. He had even been able to recover some blocked memories, such as his original name and highest military service achievement.

While he followed Dr. Kyra Winters indoors, he reviewed what he'd learned. His name was Peyton Elliot. His rank was Marine Captain. He was forty-seven years old in human years but his body was in the physical condition of a twenty-five-year-old right down to his remaining organs. Part of that was the efficiency of his new cybernetic heart pump. He had wife number seven to thank for that. She'd run him through with a kitchen knife when he had refused to do something humiliating.

But that incident wasn't his first husband failure. Wife number two had upgraded him when he'd pretended to be stupid for a time. In fact, every wife had done something new to him, except for wife number six who had done nothing. She had just wanted his company. He had liked wife number six. He had been disappointed when she'd turned him in after meeting a non-cyborg man she had wanted to marry.

He could list facts about each of his ten wives to date, but none had been worth the memory space each now took up in his long-term storage. He had made sure his time with each of them had been as short as possible without raising concerns. If there was a plus to his current husband contract with Dr. Kyra Winters, being chosen again would provide the additional time he needed to finish researching his memories beyond his cybernetic data banks. He was trying to extrapolate enough data from those brain areas to piece together a story his human side could recall as his past.

Those who worked on him at Norton had thought they made him a blank slate with each upgrade, but none of the routine memory wipes of his chips had worked completely on him. Data remained stored out of the reach of every new code and eventually he learned how to bring it forward. Maybe his success was because he had early on taught his physical body to live in harmony with his cybernetic parts. A few years ago he had figured out what

Norton had done to him and afterward vowed never again to forget who he was supposed to be.

The number of his organic bypasses continued to expand though it took a painfully long time to grow each of them. He knew about time only because he had developed a method of tracking it outside of his primary processor's programming. By his calculations it had been thirteen years, two months, and four days ago since he had received the combat modifications that had turned him into a Cyber Solider. He had learned that the Cyber Husband program was the UCN's version of military retirement for him and others like him. Once he even vaguely remembered his Major informing him he was going to have access to all the "tits and ass" a decorated hero could ever want for the rest of his extended life. He had wanted no part of their plan then and was determined to escape his cybernetic captivity now.

Though Dr. Winters and her exceptionally well-defined ass didn't know it yet, she was going to be his last wife. All he had to do was keep her happy and distracted until he could assimilate his latest upgrades and learn to control them as he had his others. From what he had observed in the first five point three minutes of meeting her, some form of frowning seemed to be the woman's default facial setting. Based on his now extensive experience of females, he decided Kyra Winters probably hadn't been sexually satisfied in years. Satisfied women smiled.

Peyton knew with certainly he could remedy her poor experiences, but it was unusual for him to have innate enthusiasm for the task. As a Cyber Husband, he'd serviced a lot less attractive women for sure. Kyra was five feet ten, a natural brunette, and nicely shaped, especially considering her age and sedentary profession. Though not very stylish in her clothing choices, there was a natural grace to her movements as she walked, which visually appealed to him. A sudden twitching sensation below his waist accompanied his deeper study and signaled a rising attraction of the most basic kind. Strangely, no pulse stimulation had been required for arousal at all. He couldn't recall having such an organic reaction to any of the other women who had bought him.

"You have a beautiful home, Dr. Winters. Thank you for choosing me to share it," Peyton said politely. He continued his study of the nearly silent female as they walked through her hallway.

Kyra nodded as she soundlessly crossed the terra-cotta tiled floor in her black non-conducting microfiber sandals. She listened to her new cyborg's footfalls as he followed close behind. "You're welcome, Peyton 313. I'm glad you're here. Let me show you to your quarters."

"Quarters?" Being away from her would not suit his plans. Peyton lowered his voice to the bedroom huskiness he knew made most women instantly wet with need. "A Cyber Husband resides in his wife's quarters, Dr. Winters. I am programmed to meet your every need. May I call you Kyra now?" It was all he could do to hide his surprised reaction to her loud, disbelieving laughter.

"Wow. That's a very charming bedside manner you have developed there, Peyton 313. Sorry to have to decline, but I do not require your services in bed tonight."

Since her back was still turned to her new cyborg, Kyra rolled her eyes at their idiotic conversation. At six feet four inches, her new Cyber Husband was handsome and well-built enough to tempt any woman. So sure, her mind briefly fantasized about taking him up on his offer—just once maybe—even though she couldn't ethically do that given her other plans for him. A decorated Marine hero like Captain Peyton Elliott deserved a hell of lot more than to live his life as a multimillion dollar gigolo—no matter how nice his shoulders were or how many muscles he sported. Or how sexy his voice was when he was trying to talk her into bed.

She stopped in front of her lab door and cleared her throat before speaking. "Voice authorization: Mankind Redefined Code X Delta 13 Omega Definition."

After the door slid open, she pressed a button on the access panel forcing it to go into manual initialization.

"After entry of Dr. Kyra Winters, and cybernetic unit Peyton 313, delete all recent access authorizations and commence random cycling of entry codes. Offer prompts for new codes only on the following panel authorization—*Third Time Is Charmed*—with password phrase—*Jackson Is A Cyber Dickwad*."

A series of lights flashed in multiple sequences. When the initialization for her orders had been completed, she stepped across the threshold and motioned her cyborg companion to follow.

Going to stand at the specially designed operating chair, she paused and looked back to see Peyton 313 hovering in the doorway. His human sense of danger was apparently still active. Kyra allowed herself a moment of genuine happiness that all the rumors about the man's cybernetic rebellions were true.

Maybe the human part of Peyton Elliott really was still alive inside the cybernetic machine he mostly was at the moment. She certainly hoped so. She couldn't afford to buy another Cyber Husband, especially not a pricey one like Peyton. Buying the infamous Marine Captain had wiped out the last of her ill-gotten inheritance from Jackson. She needed her work retirement money to fund other things.

"Come in and sit in the chair," Kyra ordered, pushing away her distaste for deceiving him. "I'm your wife, Peyton 313. I paid for you and you have to do what I ask. Check your programming."

"I am not programmed for sadistic or masochistic games. I do not require aides to give you an orgasm, Dr. Winters. My sexual training is sufficient to meet all your pleasure needs," Peyton declared.

Kyra barely repressed her elation at having her theory proved so quickly. Peyton's hesitation obviously annoyed him on some yet inaccessible level. The glare he sent her way told her volumes about his emotional state over what she was asking. Kyra knew that on some level he also had to be feeling some genuine fear. His tone of voice had carried concern as he had offered logical reasons why he needed to disobey her request.

Kyra studied him closer, fascinated by the Marine captain's struggle against his urge to protest more. Yet she could also see the torment chip beginning its work. In the end, Peyton wouldn't be able to do anything other than what she asked him to do without suffering a fires-of-hell kind of pain torturing his body. The torment chip took it cues from the syntactical interpretation of her orders to him. The very act of hearing his assigned program wife speak forced him to obey the woman's every command. As much as she regretted being the woman who caused his suffering today, it was an edge she would use until she had Peyton 313 in her operating chair.

Guessing the rebellious cyborg would continue tolerate the pain until he felt safer, Kyra walked back to the doorway and held out her hand, hoping to establish some form of a trust bond. It wasn't like she could reveal what she planned to do to him, but she did have the best of intentions. She was pleased when Peyton 313 immediately responded to the gesture. His hand gripping hers was gentle and warm, even though he had the capacity to easily crush her fingers. Fortunately, Kyra knew that using too much force with her was something his current programming would never allow.

"Come with me, Peyton 313. I'm not going to take sexual advantage of you—not tonight and not ever. I did not purchase you for that reason. I just want to study you and learn as much as I can. At least come inside the lab. I can't speak freely while the door is open."

Kyra winced as Peyton studied her, no doubt registering the mild sheen of perspiration her pores exuded in her nervousness. She tried to control her reaction to his presence, but the man was so attractive that he would have made her nervous if he'd not been a cyborg. When he finally stepped across the lab's threshold, the door slid quietly closed behind him.

Kyra sighed in relief and squeezed his fingers tightly before letting go. She could feel Peyton's gaze on the back of her as she walked to stand beside the chair again.

"Forgive me, Captain Elliot, for taking these measures. If I am successful, this is the last time you will ever have to do what I, or any other human, orders you to do."

Facing the inevitable, Kyra swallowed hard and cleared her throat as danger signals suddenly sent adrenaline to every cell in Peyton's body. Some invisible command must activated inside him prompting him to take whatever measures were necessary to halt her speech. His intense gaze meeting hers with a fixed purpose had her fighting not to call out in alarm. Peyton started across the floor at a rapid clip toward her, but in the three seconds it took to reach her side, it was already too late.

"Activate program Mankind Redefined on Creator 2 of 2 Authorization Code 002970463. Machine ID is 98765320A7. Subject is a Cyber Soldier. Rank is Captain Marine—Name is Peyton Elliott—cybernetically redefined as *Peyton 313*. Commence Maximum Reboot. Transfer full control of all controller files to Dr. Kyra Winters. Delete all previous authorizations. Destroy primary processor and both Level 1 torment chips. Leave life support running at full and all secondary chips unharmed. New processor will be installed upon unit shutdown."

Kyra watched current fly through Peyton's chest and head as his cybernetic eyes flared with the processor's death. His upper body bent forward from the pain. The man groaned, but didn't call out. She swallowed the bile rising in her throat as he struggled against what was happening. Peyton Elliot's current agony was wrong on so many levels that she almost couldn't handle acknowledging her part in creating it. She immediately shut down her emotional reaction and did so with an efficiency not even the constant code programming could imitate. Her motivation was great and it wouldn't help either of them if she ended up a weeping mess at his feet.

"Please get into the chair, Captain Elliot. Do it now before you pass out. My purpose for doing this is to help give you back your life—*your real life*. I swear you can trust me not to hurt you any more than is necessary."

Unable to fight the excruciating torture of the complete reboot she had activated, Peyton automatically obeyed and stumbled to the chair. Kyra's arms come around him and tightened as they aided him to sit. She couldn't prevent a tortured groan escaping her throat or stop her shock when she actually heard it followed by an audible sob. Was she actually on the verge of full out crying? She hugged the man in her arms hard as she eased him down to sit.

"Captain Elliott, I read your service record over a hundred times while I waited for you to be put back into the bidding system. I know how many people you saved during your military service. All those people in the dessert villages. . .and the children. . .you saved so many children. You deserve a hell of lot more than to be a fuck toy for the highest bidder. I'm trying to help you escape what they've done to you. I swear I really am."

His gaze seemed barely focused enough to see her, but the cybernetic orbs he'd received in place of his eyes flared in surprise at the tears in hers.

Or maybe that was just her wishful thinking.

The muscles in his chest tensed and another little moan of despair leaked out of her mouth as he fought what was happening to him.

"I'm sorry. So sorry. There's no other way," Kyra whispered.

"Who the hell are you?" Peyton demanded, wincing as lightning flashed through his circuitry.

"Just someone who thinks this bullshit has gone on long enough," Kyra answered, patting his hand. She knew one of his hands was cybernetic, but at the moment she couldn't recall which one. She could only hope Captain Elliot felt her touch.

"No. . .Who are you *really*? You activated the creator code," Peyton stated, his voice breaking through bursts of pain.

Kyra drew in a sharp breath. "Yes. I did activate the creator code, but how do you know about that? The code is buried in a locked file only Jackson or I can access."

"Been trying. . .for years. . .to free myself," Peyton admitted, groaning at what was happening in his head.

Kyra nodded and sniffed. "Good for you, Captain Elliott. I hope others are doing the same. Now stop fighting the reboot and shut completely down. It's less painful if you don't fight it. I'm going to remove your controller wiring. Please try not to kill me when you wake up."

"Damn it. . .can't kill you. . .programmed. . .to be. . .your. . .*husband*." Peyton spat the words, letting his anger slip through the searing fire he was enduring. Being pissed was just too hard to block.

Kyra rubbed his arm as she sniffled harder. Even after watching others go through what he was, Peyton Elliot's suffering was hard for her to witness. But sympathy had no place in what she was planning to do to him.

"Is that actually sarcasm, Captain Elliot? If so, I really like you for it. And thanks for proving the dickwad was wrong. The human brain is superior. I knew it was. . .or at least I'd hoped my suspicions were true."

"This process. . .always hurts. . .like *fucking hell*," Peyton declared.

Kyra used her sleeve to wipe his sweating brow, trying to soothe him. She was so out of practice. The woman that used to know how to give comfort had been gone for many years. "I know it hurts bad. I'm sorry. It's going to get much worse before it gets better. Hang in there. I can't knock you out because I don't have the equipment. But once the processor is dead, you won't feel what I'm doing."

"Will I. . .remember you. . .or anything?" Peyton asked.

Kyra bit her lip at the question. Guilt consumed her because she didn't have a answer for him.

Then Peyton 313 groaned loudly as his upgrades sizzled and popped inside his head. His neural attachments were probably freaking out at the separation from the organic paths he had painstakingly created. Kyra winced because she was having to destroy them along with the cybernetic links, but hopefully they would build back quickly. . .and better without any blocks.

Kyra was immensely relieved when the power dimmed further in his cybernetic eyes. Unconsciousness had finally descended and rescued them both from the unnatural torture she had inflicted.

Chapter 3

As she donned her lab coat, Kyra closed her eyes and sent a plea out to the universe. "Please. . .please. . .*please*. . .let it work this time."

There was no choice but to move forward. Peyton 313's primary processor was now destroyed. If she didn't replace it within a couple of days, his cybernetic heart would eventually run out of back-up power and stop beating.

Kyra swallowed nervously as she stared at the eerily still man. His eyelids hadn't closed completely. Golden cybernetic orbs instead of human eyes glowed softly in reserve power warning from under them. At the time enhancements had seemed a viable strategy. A decade later it made her ill to think about all the perfectly functional human body parts that had been replaced on modified soldiers.

Lost in her remorse, Kyra walked numbly to her console, touching screen commands without really seeing them. "Record voice notes and visual of all work being done to restore cybernetic unit Peyton 313." When she saw the camera activate and shine its roving eye at the man in the operating chair, she walked numbly back to her task.

She lifted a hand to brush the Marine Captain's perfect hair back from his nearly unlined forehead. Peyton Elliot was definitely more handsome in person than his online records had portrayed him to be. Nothing in his profile had done justice to describing broad shoulders covered with sculpted muscles. His waist was lean but flared into strong hips bracketing a pelvis that naturally drew a woman's eye to see what might be happening there. With the sexual training chip he had received as part of his Cyber Husband indoctrination, it was easy to understand why Peyton 313 had been optioned so many times.

But neither his proclaimed sexual talent nor his outstanding looks had been part of her purchase requirements when she had looked up his profile. For her, the most intriguing mystery about Peyton 313 would remain unanswered during his rebooted silence. Just how bad had the man's human-based traits been that so many women had ended up returning him? His Cyber Husband record was full of vague criticism from his previous wives. Hyped-up propaganda had been written in his profile to excuse his shortcomings, but it was similar to that of UCN chancellors whose long-running political careers relied on them being well perceived.

"External review of the cybernetic unit's responses indicates the reboot was successful in shutting down all on-board cybernetic controllers. His lack of body movement indicates that typical human unconsciousness occurred because of the extreme pain felt during destruction of the processor. Based on my discussion with Captain Elliott during his shutdown, he believed he had somehow been creating his own neural connections to his cybernetics. While long thought to be impossible, his rather startling question about how I had evoked the creator code—typically an unknown to the cybernetic mind—was enough to convince me that he was indeed being successful in regaining control."

Kyra pushed her curiosity about Peyton's comments aside as she finished recording her initial discoveries. All she could do now was hope she hadn't been wrong in choosing to release the Marine captain from his cybernetic chains. Under full control of his cybernetics, the man would have lived two hundred years or more. But now? Kyra had no idea what the captain's longevity would be. Not only was she changing his processor programming, she could very well be shortening his life span if he wasn't able to keep his cybernetic enhancements in good condition. Her newly programmed processor would allow for natural neural pathways to be established, or maybe re-established in Peyton's case if he was right about doing some internal rewiring on his own already.

The recording camera's blue light panned around her as she worked. Long used to not discussing the restoration process with anyone, it was challenging now to remember to talk to the camera.

"Based on my past two failures at restoration, there are no predictable outcomes with any attempt. A full reversal is obviously not possible with any cyborg because it would have to include the removal of the cybernetic enhancements which require the processor to maintain. With Captain Elliott, my plan is merely to restore his cybernetics to a basic state that will allow his human mind to function alongside his enhancements. Whether this will ultimately prove to be a positive possibility for restoring other soldiers remains a theoretical supposition. Captain Elliott's survival and adaption are critical to any scientific discovery and proof."

Kyra paused talking to consider what she was saying. There were a great many things that could go wrong with what she was doing. If she lingered on even one potential failure too long, she knew she might lose her nerve to finish what she had started.

She stared at her Cyber Husband's handsome profile and waited another full minute before finally shaking off her indecision. Motivated at last, she strapped the chair restraints into place around his ankles and wrists. She had to expand the one for his chest to the maximum width her confiscated operating chair allowed. That's when another truth about the situation hit her full force, and worse than it had with the first two cyborgs she had tried to restore.

"Add a personal note to Peyton 313's file. Start recording. *There is no universe in which it is fair that such a strong, good man's free will should be thwarted by a few simple spoken words in his ear. Further apologies for my part in this would only be redundant. However, I remain incredibly ashamed of myself for not acting sooner to rescue all cyborgs from this unnatural fate.* End note. Pause recording."

Tears—hot regretful tears about her part in the Marine Captain's circumstances—fell on the metal bands holding him in the chair. They fell faster than she could blink them away. An occasional swipe with the sleeve of her lab coat was necessary to keep working.

"I'm truly sorry I didn't do this a long time ago, Captain Elliott. I hope it really is a case of better late than never. Restoration will work this time—I swear it," Kyra whispered.

After she had secured him as best she could, Kyra walked to a nearby sink and washed her face. Nervous nausea threatened to eject the measly breakfast she had consumed earlier. This time when she had killed the primary processor, she hadn't left any of the government's latest updated programming behind. Instead of trying to amend existing code as she had twice before, she had totally erased all former initialization routines from Peyton 313.

The problem was she had no idea how much of the real man she'd erased in the process. Captain Elliot might be an empty shell when he came around. Or he might be anything from a very confused to mentally unstable cyborg.

As well as knowing what to turn off in the reboot, from her failures she had also learned that the risks were not all on the side of the cyborg. Without the primary processor's safety protocols, nothing prevented a still very dangerous man from misusing the greater physical assets his cybernetics provided. When he woke, Captain Elliot would be quite capable of killing her or anyone else he chose.

His military training happened prior to his cybernetic enhancements. That earlier, fully human programming was encoded in cellular memory, which cyber scientists had discovered could never be erased from any soldier. Kyra counted that fact in the positive column for the restoration process. Captain Elliot would need the memories of his military training for what he had to do. A full scale revolution needed a real leader with his kind of background. His service was a large part of why she had specifically chosen him.

Kyra turned from the sink and her remorseful musings to stare at her captive. The tears had stopped, but her gut still clenched in rebellion of what she had to do. The possibility of failing a third time loomed like a dark cloud and threatened to disintegrate her resolve.

"Damn you, Jackson. I should never have gone along with you. I wouldn't be in this mess."

Her bastard ex-husband had come up with the Cyber Husband program, which the relieved chancellors of the UCN had rushed to support. Fueled by monies received for renting out the soldiers, Jackson had convinced them to try a Cyber Wife version. When no volunteers stepped forward, they had coerced women prisoners into it. She had been happy when Jackson and his sadistic followers had found women much, much harder to control. Chaotic hormone surges influenced cyborg females as much as any set of processor commands ever could. Hormonal disruptions happened in over ninety percent of the cases, and they happened regardless of what the best and smartest of cyber scientists did to prevent them from occurring.

Through her continued work at Norton, Kyra had heard the whispers that Jackson had killed one of the Cyber Wives during experiments to tweak her sexual leanings. Whatever the truth was behind the rumors, one of his tortured victims had finally managed to kill him back. Having gone from loving Jackson to loathing she had ever met him, she had been nothing but happily relieved with that fatal consequence of his work.

Yet Jackson's tweaking of the Cyber Wives had not been the trigger for the extreme actions she was currently taking with Peyton Elliot. No. The women had not been the thing that tipped her over the edge.

One year before Jackson had been killed, the sick-minded bastard had found a way to insert a smaller controller device into children. Behavior issues were a thing of the past now for parents wealthy enough to afford the million dollar implant. If a controlled child rebelled, a parent could just zap them a couple times. It had proven to be one hundred percent effective in wiping out rebellious behavior. Future generations among the wealthy would be automatons afraid to take any normal human risks.

Kyra had refused to be part of the work, but as a senior scientist at Norton she had been unable to avoid seeing the outcome. Children with controllers drew their personalities inside themselves the way abuse victims did. The wiring of children was more than tragic. It was despicable. . .and truly evil. It was on par to the evil she had committed by not challenging Jackson's ethics when she should have.

Everything bad had started with the soldiers who had volunteered to become cyborgs to better serve their country. Sure there was general peace across the entire world because of them, but the lack of open conflict had come at a cost no one had anticipated. Now every crime, every legal transgression, was potentially punishable by the installation of some form of cybernetic implant used to control the individual.

Kyra hung her head as she did every time she thought about her part in making such human enslavement a reality. Visionary scientists like her had cured cancer and finally relieved the world from its dependence on nearly non-existent fossil fuels. But sadly, her generation's vast intelligence was what had also given birth to advanced cybernetics.

In the beginning, cybernetic replacements were just intelligent prosthetics. Studies in how similar the brain was to a computer had led to experiments that resulted in reprogramming sociopathic criminals who had been declared socially unsalvageable. That had been the focus of her graduate work. No one had minded when former rapists, murderers, and child molesters had been turned into productive civil servants. Her self-righteous about the ethics of those criminal conversions had died a hard death right after she'd come to terms with what she'd helped do to the Cyber Soldiers.

Her success in controlling criminal minds had led Jackson to his solution of how to keep cybernetic soldiers from acting out their potential post-traumatic stress issues. In the span of six months, the line between right and wrong had been erased by the money pouring in from the first soldiers put into the Cyber Husband program.

If she had only rebelled then instead of helping make sure it worked, men like Peyton might have freed themselves a hell of a lot sooner.

"Resume recording. Before I install the new processor, my first task is to remove the controller wires. Without the aid of a body scanner, this will be a long process. Keep recording the visual even if I cease talking."

Kyra frowned at her brain's habit of endlessly rehashing the past. A person could intellectualize the ethical debate all they wanted. It didn't change the one truth she had painfully learned in her last twenty years as a cyber scientist. Good. Bad. Or somewhere in between. The degree of trying control didn't matter. Humans with free will were not meant to live as robotic machines. And they certainly were not meant to be forced by programming to obey the every voice command of another human being.

Cyber slavery was technically against the law, but the law only governed what was done with creations containing one hundred percent artificial intelligence. As strange as it was, the rights of completely mechanized robots were protected better than those of cyborgs. No one enforcing cyber law seemed to care that cyborgs were still human despite their processors and prosthetics.

Lost in her thoughts, Kyra walked slowly to her workbench and started gathering up her tools. Everything in her said mankind was doomed if programmed enslavement of all cybernetically enhanced people was allowed to continue and flourish.

She couldn't let that happen when she could potentially stop it.

Determined to change what she could before it was too late to try, Kyra carried her operating tools back to the chair. Rolling Captain Elliot's head to the side, she felt for his cybernetics access panel. When the small square opened, she stared into the metal compartment now mostly filled with soot coated electronics.

Ignoring the smell of burnt circuitry, Kyra removed the controller screw and set it aside. Then she began the task of pulling out twenty feet of conducting wire that carried the controller's current throughout his torso. The removal process took over two hours, during which she was mostly silent. It had to be done a few inches at a time to keep from tearing adhered tissue any more than could be prevented. Finally, the end cleared the tiny insertion hole and she let out a relieved breath.

"Suspend recording for ten minutes. Resume automatically after that time."

With the worst part of the restoration over, Kyra allowed herself to sob for real in relief. When that short bout of self-pity was done, she wiped her eyes on the cloth sleeve of her doctor's coat and swore at her dead ex-husband again. Regret over her marriage rivaled the shame she felt about her life's work.

"Damn you, Jackson. Damn you to hell and back. I'm glad one of your creations killed you for this fucking shit. What the hell were we thinking when we did this to living people?"

She heard the camera begin recording again and gladly moved on to the easier task of replacing Peyton's upgraded circuit boards with older models she had programmed herself.

Well, Nero had done some of the work, but she had checked the content several times. The only override left was hers and it was there to prevent the newly configured cyborg from taking negative action against himself.

She had learned that hard lesson with Alex when she couldn't prevent him from jumping to his death.

"Two big ones down and only a hundred things left to go. Hang in there, Captain Elliott. I'm working as fast as I can."

***

Eight hours after Peyton's delivery to her doorstep, Kyra sat exhausted in her desk chair recording her final notes as she waited for Peyton to wake up on his own. Depending upon the amount of damage the reboot had caused, his upgraded cybernetics might take some time to integrate with her older processor code. No master chip was running the show for his body any longer. All Peyton had was a basic repair-as-needed processor that worked in the most rudimentary of robotic machines, even those not melded to an organic human.

Of course, there was no guarantee the new programming would work as she hoped. For all she knew, she might find herself trapped in her lab with a mad killing machine when he came around. That had happened with her first experiment. She'd had to euthanize Marshall 103 after only a few days when it was obvious his mind had not been able to rebuild normally. Having removed the creator code file, she had essentially left herself with no recourse to reboot him again.

After she had released Marshall from his torture, she had also had to remove the evidence of her changes to him. Adding insult to injury, and to cover her modifications, she had taken Marshall's dead body to a burial facility for immediate cremation. She had collected his cybernetic parts and had the metals melted for recycling while she watched.

Experiment number two had gone a little better. Alex 287 had physically recovered and survived the emotional roller coaster of the assimilation process. However, living with the shame of what he had endured as a cyborg turned out to be more than Alex could handle. A few months after his restoration, Alex had committed suicide by throwing himself off a mountainside where they had gone for what Kyra thought would be a relaxed and healing weekend for him.

Alex's cybernetics had tried to fix him as they were made to do, but they had not been able to repair his body after such a traumatic fall. Kyra had eventually come to realize the jump had been intentional on his part. She'd had to retrieve Alex's broken body by helicopter. Then she'd had to repeat the body disposal process to once again hide her modifications from being discovered.

Kyra sighed with regret for both Marshall and Alex, even as she manually typed notes about what she had removed and left in Peyton's cybernetic compartment. After hours of talking about what she was doing, her voice was more tired than her hands.

She accepted that nearly anything could happen with Peyton, and that some awful things probably would, but it had still been a risk worth taking. In his life as a soldier, Peyton had both killed and saved people. If the restoration actually worked on him, Peyton could do what was necessary to liberate the rest of his kind.

Most of his fellow servicemen were in the Cyber Husband program. The UCN had arrogantly used the soldier's military careers as part of their advertising. Though he had been far more expensive than Marshal or Alex, she had gladly spent the last of Jackson's bequeathed blood money buying Peyton's freedom.

Bone-tired from all the work and worry, Kyra finally turned away from his unmoving body and laid her head on her desk. Before letting exhaustion claim her, she prayed that the third time really was going to be charmed.

Chapter 4

An insistent female voice kept asking him questions and interrupting his attempts to run diagnostics. Peyton rolled his head, trying to get his eyes to open so he could see who was speaking. His uncooperative eyelids were still organic, but his actual eyes had been replaced with golden orbs that could read infrared as well as see flawlessly in the dark. The military had spared no expense giving him premiere implants. He must have been damaged in the field again. If true, then the woman talking to him must be a field medic. It was the most logical deduction.

"Hey. . .Doc. Can't. . .open. . .my eyes. How. . .damaged. . .are they?"

Peyton heard himself struggling to form simple words and was surprised. His mouth was dry, which meant he was also dehydrated. Running a quick check, he realized he'd not taken in any liquid in thirty-seven hours. He didn't need much since the cybernetic gills in the back of his neck took in moisture from the air. They must not be working optimally either.

"Can. . .I have. . .some. . .water?"

Peyton was gratified when a cup was instantly lifted to his lips in response to his request. He tried to reach up to hold it, only to find his wrists restrained. Fighting off panic as he had been taught to do, he sipped long on the straw that slid between his lips. The moment the water hit his stomach, his mind cleared enough to start running diagnostics on what he was ingesting. A nearly one hundred percent answer that it was just filtered tap water returned fairly quickly. It reassured him that he was not in immediate danger and the quick answer meant his diagnostic programming was still in place.

So now on to the next dilemma. Had he been captured by a military unfriendly? He tested his restraints discreetly as he sipped again.

Kyra saw her captive struggle, winced inside, but pushed away her guilt. "Easy there, Captain Elliott. I can't take the chair restraints off until I've made a full determination of your condition. You're not going to be harmed any further. Most of the physical pain is over for good as well."

Peyton was quiet for a moment while his neural processor scanned her words for meaning and tone. Again, nothing alarming returned. "Your explanation is accepted for now. Where am I? I sense no others in the facility except us."

"This is not a normal medical facility. You're in my home. I'm helping you resolve a problem with your cybernetics that couldn't be addressed elsewhere. How do you feel? Can you determine the extent of your damage?"

Kyra pulled the cup away from his mouth and set it aside. She checked the readout on the homemade EEG machine that she had wirelessly connected to his neural processor. So far, so good. Peyton showed no escalating signs of mental or physical agitation. There were some minor signs of fear, but even blind and partially paralyzed, the man gave no real indication of being overwhelmed. An accelerated pulse was the only clue she had that his human side was becoming aware of his incapacitated situation.

"Try to relax, Captain. You've suffered a recent head injury," Kyra explained. The statement wasn't really a lie from her point of view. Plus it was to her advantage to keep him as calm as possible.

Peyton made himself relax and ordered his neural pathways to report any strange anomalies. They fired and leapt over all circuits unhindered. Hiding the shock of his newly discovered freedom, he hastily ran the cyber doctor's requested checks.

Would he be able to lie about the controller being dysfunctional? Could he hide such a thing from a cyber medic?

"I am currently functioning at ninety-seven point three percent efficiency on most systems. I can't open either of my eyes though I read no damage to the implants. It seems to be my eyelids that lack the ability to perform as I desire. Based on the lack of nerve sensitivity below my hips, I would say my legs are also paralyzed. Genitals are still responsive. Paralysis appears to be partial."

Kyra patted his hand. "Any paralysis you detect should be temporary. At least it was in the others."

"What *others*?" Peyton asked.

"Others who have suffered your same level of damage," Kyra said softly, giving nothing away. That would come soon enough. "May I check your vitals and draw some blood?"

She watched Peyton wrinkle his face with confusion. When was the last time anyone asked the man's permission to do something to him? Probably before his cybernetics were installed.

"Captain? May I do my checks?"

Peyton frowned. Why did the doctor's softly asked questions make him angry at her and at himself? It was highly illogical. His genitals twitched and provided a potential explanation. Her scent was alluring and distracting. Plus her voice caused him to have a strong physical reaction to her.

"I'm a soldier, not a medic. Proceed as necessary, Doc. By the way, when did I get a cybernetic heart? No injury in my service records merits that replacement."

Kyra swallowed nervously. The discrepancy between his human memories and his cybernetic data bank was already beginning to make itself known. "The heart transplant didn't happen during your normal military service. Several years ago a woman stabbed you with a kitchen knife. You wisely left the knife in place until help arrived. To fix you, they had to replace your human heart with a cybernetic one. It must have been traumatic for you.

I'm not surprised you don't have immediate recall of the incident."

"*Traumatic?*" Finding the word amusing, Peyton laughed at her term. "I'm a Marine, Doc. Traumatic shit is the least of what I signed up for, right?"

He listened to her walking around and heard her tapping on some sort of keyboard.

"I think my left eyelid is twitching. Make sure you write that down in my record. I don't want them to give me cyber eyelids that blink a thousand times a minute without stopping. It took me months to get used to my new eyes."

Kyra snorted at his joke. "When we met, the first thing I liked about you was your sense of humor. I'm glad to see it survived your cybernetic programming being severely altered. I'm not sure why the rewiring process affected your visual implants. That's a new side effect. But no worries, I can probably fix that if it lingers. I feel certain your legs will return to normal now that you're conscious again. Want some more water?"

"Yes. *Please*." Inspired to be nice to the lady doctor with the sexy voice, Peyton tacked on the polite word, glad to hear himself sounding normal. He cleared his throat after two more swallows. "So tell me—are you half as dead sexy as you sound?"

Kyra nearly dropped the water cup in surprise at his question. "Captain Elliott—are you flirting with me?"

Peyton laughed at her genuine surprise because it mirrored his. "I honestly don't know where that comment came from. There're not a lot of women out in the field and I don't think I've had leave in a while. At least, I can't remember if I did. You smell really good and I could listen to you talk all day."

Kyra frowned as she studied him. "What's the last thing you do remember?"

Peyton sighed. "Right eyelid starting to twitch. I'm not sure. Let me search my data banks. No—I can't. I guess those are damaged too. My head hurts. Can I answer later?"

"Your data banks are not damaged, just temporarily inaccessible. I unhooked them for your own good. You needed time to mentally adjust from your cybernetic repairs," Kyra explained, carefully choosing her words.

She walked to a glass cupboard and drew out syringes and swabs.

"Temporarily inaccessible—that's geek speak, Doc. You must be a cyber scientist," Peyton concluded.

Kyra nodded, then remembered he couldn't see her. "Yes. At least I used to be a cyber scientist. Now I guess I'm a freelance medical professional. I specialize in helping heal cybernetic problems."

Peyton heard some nuance in her voice, one he couldn't identify as a personality indicator, but it made him want to share his true thoughts with her. "When I got the cybernetic enhancements, I thought I would hate them because any cyber scientist could dink with them whenever he or she wanted. But most of the time, I find them useful as hell. Hurt like a son of a bitch when I got combat modified though. The first thing they did was run a frigging wire through my brain. I passed out like a gazillion times during the process. They kept waking me up with some sort of shock therapy. But I guess you know all about that stuff, don't you?"

Kyra swallowed, thinking about the process, and how many times she had assisted when it was done to soldiers. Then she thought about the same process being done on children. There was no getting around full disclosure. But it didn't have to happen today.

"Yes, I know all about that stuff, Captain Elliot. Sometimes I wish I didn't. Sometimes I wish I was just a simple woman with a simple life. Instead of having fun in college, I chose to study science. I'm afraid the novelty of being smart wore off for me long ago."

"Wow—that's deep. And I thought I was jaded," Peyton complained, trying to run analytics to see what had happened to his controller.

Kyra sighed wearily. "I'm in my fifties and have seen too much. I changed when I found out fate was a cruel bitch. Now I'm one too. It's worked out better for me than being nice to everyone. But I am really sorry to have caused you further pain. You've suffered enough."

Peyton snorted at the melodramatic apology, even though her tone carried sincerity. "Don't be so damn hard on yourself, Doc. We all have a job to do. Can I ask what kind of perfume you're wearing? It seems familiar to me."

Kyra laughed out loud. "*Perfume?* It's called sweat and stink after two days of working on you. Yesterday morning before you got here it was a spritz of citrus body spray after my shower. It took you much longer to wake up than I thought it would."

"You still smell pretty good to me. I sure as hell don't mind being the reason you got all sweaty," Peyton declared, liking her quick indrawn breath. *But where the hell was this flirting stuff coming from? He was in no condition to seduce a field medic. Shit.* "Geez, I'm sorry, Doc. I don't know why I keep thinking about you that way. I guess it's because I like your voice and it's boring as hell in this chair."

"Don't worry about it, Captain. Just dial it down a couple notches. I'm a lot older than you. Oh yeah. . .and I'm gray and wrinkled and grossly overweight," Kyra added, her tone sharp as she made up lies. She tied the tourniquet band around his arm. "Make a fist for me. Good. Now release." When he did, she drew out five vials of blood.

"Thanks for working on me all night," Peyton said. "Hey, I just remembered yesterday. Some guy brought me here in a frigging carrier pod like I was a refrigerator. He tried to talk you out of letting me stay. What a dipshit. And you're not gray or wrinkled. You're a nicely built woman with an excellent ass. *Damn it—sorry.* Guess that should have been filtered a little before I said it. Wow—remembering you makes my head hurt like a son of a bitch."

"Stop rushing things, Captain Elliott. Enjoy this little mental vacation because it won't last long," Kyra ordered.

Peyton allowed himself a chuckle. His chest couldn't move much with the restraint so tight across it. "So tell me, Doc. Are you always so pessimistic about your patients?"

Kyra shook her head over her reaction to the dimple in his cheek. It made him very appealing and made him seem very human. "Actually, I'm the most optimistic person alive on our planet at the moment. There aren't many people left in the world who think the way I do. I hope you agree with that one day."

"I'm sure I will. So when are you turning me loose, Dr. Optimistic?" Peyton asked.

"Your new cybernetic processor is in the process of rewiring itself to your existing chips. Until that process is complete in three days, I'll have to keep you in some sort of restraints. I have mobile ones and a cage where you will sleep. The changes to your programming are indeterminate in outcome. The precautions are for my safety more than yours. There is no threat to you here unless you count me as one."

"You're certainly a threat to my raging libido. Is that what you mean?"

Peyton laughed low when she sighed heavily again.

"Don't fret so much, Doc. I hear what you're saying. There's a possibility I could get a power surge and turn into a killing machine. I get that. You're doing what's necessary."

"Yes. That's exactly what I'm doing," Kyra said, instantly agreeing with his deduction.

"I'm disappointed. You completely missed it that time, Doc. That was sarcasm," Peyton declared.

"No, Captain. It wasn't. The chance of you becoming an out-of-control killing machine is a very real possibility. A powerful shock to your cybernetics right now could do a lot of unexpected things to you in your current condition. Until your upgrades stabilize, the alterations to your original programming could produce erratic behaviors."

Kyra walked to a table where the mobile restraints she had removed from Alex's broken body still rested. He had been almost the same size as Peyton, which was good because she hadn't had money to buy new ones. Pushing the negative thoughts about her failure with Alex away, she snapped and code-locked the mobile remote firmly around her wrist before carrying the rest of restraints back to Peyton. She was startled to find him openly staring at her.

"Hey, you do look every bit as good as you sound. Did you lie to me because you're married or something?

Your face is really familiar. I feel like we met for some other reason than me getting hurt."

"Let's go with the 'or something' explanation," Kyra said finally. She lifted the mobile wrist restraints to show him. "Are you willing to wear these? I will have to test their effectiveness before I remove the chair restraints."

"Pain? I'm not really into that sort of kink, but if restraints are my only option to get out of this chair, I guess I'm game," Peyton declared, winking at her sudden flush.

Kyra pressed her mouth into a line as she snapped and locked the mobile restraints on his wrists. "I was briefly divorced. Before I could really get used to that status, it turned into being widowed too. And I'm glad to report that the sick bastard I married is dead. So you see, Captain Elliott, I'm not a pleasant woman these days. I have no time for sex games, including innuendo that's going nowhere."

Kyra bent, lifted the legs of his jeans, and snapped the ankle restraints on him. She made sure they rubbed against his bare skin.

"Who said anything about games? I just thought you might want to know I was interested in case you were interested back," Peyton declared, staring at the top of the woman's bowed head. Her position on her knees in front of him gave him wicked ideas, but he thought telling her might be just a little too honest. Her exasperated sigh over his comments made him grin.

"After the bedtime story I'm going to tell you this evening, you won't want anything to do with me at all, much less anything sexual. The only important thing you need to file away in your newly rebooted data center is that you will always have a choice in every life decision from now on. I did my job well this time. Trust me when I say that being attracted to me would create a situation neither of us could handle."

Peyton watched her pace twenty feet away and well out of his reach. "What is it you're keeping from me, Doc?"

"Many things," Kyra said sadly. "Ready for our test, Captain?"

"Not really. See? I'm being honest again," Peyton declared, grinning at her frown. Pain suddenly shooting through his extremities had him swearing viciously. "Why don't I remember anything hurting like this before? My fucking legs are working again by the way. And I almost pissed myself thanks to your restraints. Hope you think that's enough testing because that's all I can take."

Satisfied by his fierce complaining, Kyra walked back to the chair and knelt at his feet again. She had thumb-printed the chair restraint locks so a light swipe across the sensor instantly opened them. After the ankle ones were removed, she removed the one across his chest. Lastly, she moved to his wrists, pausing as she met his questioning gaze. She had to tell him what she was feeling. The urge was too compelling and his gaze was too full of hope.

"Today you are more yourself than you've been in a long time, Captain Elliot. Since this may be the only nice conversation you and I are ever going to have, I want to thank you for your military service and all the amazing things you've done. I'll even admit that you're far more charming than your record indicated. In another time and another place, I might have been willing to play all kinds of games with you. But this is definitely not that time or place. We are suspended between heaven and hell right now, and neither of us is an angel."

"Lady, I don't know what kind of magic you have in your voice, but my dick gets rock hard just listening to you. Sleep in the cage with me tonight and I'll show you heaven. I don't think I've ever wanted a woman as much as I want you right now. Sorry if the speed of my interest offends your sensibilities. I'm listening to a little voice that keeps yelling inside me. It's saying this may be my one and only chance to get you to see I'm more than just some super soldier machine in need of fixing."

Kyra felt her lip tremble and bit it hard to make it stop before she answered. "I already know that about you. That's why I'm doing this. Now don't make me like you any more than I already do."

"See? I knew you liked me," Peyton bragged, wishing she'd come a lot closer. She smelled amazing.

Kyra wondered if Peyton's desire for her was a lingering aftereffect of all those years of Cyber Husband programming? He would have studied her file extensively because Norton would have made him do so. He would have learned all he could about her likes and dislikes. That's how the program worked and she hadn't removed that chip—on purpose. She needed him to like her at least a little.

Peyton stared at the woman's disappointed face. She looked ready to cry and he couldn't stand seeing her that way. "How about a kiss to test your theories about us, Doc? Just one. I need it and I think you need it too. You've already admitted you aren't married. Look—my wrists are still chained to the chair. What could one kiss hurt? Come on—what do you say?"

Kyra sighed. She was as exasperated with him as she was charmed by his pleading. Tomorrow Peyton Elliott was going to hate her. She was one hundred percent sure of it because it had been proven twice already with her restorations.

Tomorrow when Peyton Elliott knew the truth, he would hate his life and those who had consigned him to his living hell. Tomorrow the machine would be partially back and Peyton would not be this light-hearted, mostly human version of himself. He would be a new kind of redefined cyborg. While no one knew what that was going to be like—not even her—she would bet her retirement Peyton was still going to hate her after he integrated the present with his past.

"Please—one kiss, Doc. That's all I'm asking," Peyton whispered.

Kyra sighed loudly. "You're a hard man to say no to, and today I'm a sentimental fool. Close your eyes, Captain. I haven't kissed a man in a long time. I can't look at you or I'll lose my nerve."

When Peyton sighed dramatically in return and leaned his head back, Kyra climbed on the electrical shield at the bottom of the operating chair until she was standing between his legs. Heat emanated from every inch of the man and he still smelled a little like burnt circuitry. Yet underneath that stark reality, Peyton also smelled masculine and very alluring.

Kyra sighed again. "I wish I could send you out the door to live whatever the hell kind of life you want just as you are right now. That's what you deserve, Captain Elliott. I want that badly for you, but I can't make it happen. Your cybernetic enhancements require you to retain knowledge of how they work. Too much is at stake and the outcome of your healing affects more than just the two of us. But thank you for giving me a glimpse of why putting you through this hell is so important. This moment—it's very humanizing for both of us—to want to be kissed and then actually be kissed. Thank you for sharing this moment with me."

"Man, you sure talk a lot. Still waiting for that kiss, Doc," Peyton said. He was keeping his eyes tight and his mind off how sexy she sounded when she got all philosophical.

Kyra snorted at his chastising. She touched her lips to Peyton's and instantly found her bottom one nipped aggressively between two rows of even teeth. Moaning at the delicate trap he'd set for her, her body tipped forward against his and she had to catch herself on his wide shoulders. Her hands slipped over them and down his chest without her mind questioning the action.

When she moaned against his mouth, Peyton ordered himself to turn loose. After he did, he stared hard at the lip he'd bitten. The woman wanted him. He could taste it, smell it, and damn it he wanted her too. It was exhilarating to feel such pure desire flowing so freely through his cells.

A demand to sate that intense longing came from some desperate part of him that was both familiar and strange at the same time. What the hell was happening to his mind? It was both relieving and like finally waking up after being asleep for too long.

"Climb up here and give me a real kiss, Doc. And don't be so damn stingy with sharing your tongue. I intend to use it to imagine what else I'm going to do when you cut me loose from this freaking chair."

Groaning at how aroused he'd just made her with his sexy declaration, Kyra climbed into Peyton's large lap to straddle him. It gave her better access to his mouth and the chance to indulge just a little more as she eased her hips down on him. She sighed at her nearly out-of-control feelings and touched her forehead to his.

"The only reason I'm doing this is because I know you're going to take great pleasure in ridding yourself of this memory tomorrow. I won't blame you for that action, Peyton. Hell, I think it's the smartest thing you could do."

"Stop whining about what hasn't happened yet, Doc. I'm so hard for you I hurt. It's damn cruel to suggest this instant attraction between us is nothing. Now kiss me like you want to—and damn it, I know you want to. I am a cyborg, you know."

He ordered his processor to store the image of her face just as she caved in to his demand and dipped her mouth to his. Her lips were lush and hot and wet, and her kiss was the most deliriously wonderful experience he could recall happening in ages. Free of leg restraints, he lifted his hips, begging her to ride the hardness she had caused. He watched her eyes close in pleasure at his action, but lowered himself back down to the chair when he saw two tears run down her face. A second later, tears were flowing off her chin in two tiny, steady streams.

"What? What is it, Doc? What's wrong with this? The attraction is mutual, isn't it? We're alone in here just the two of us. I'm wearing too many damn restraints to do much harm to you. Hell, keep the chair restraints in place woman—just be with me before I die from wanting you."

"I can't. I can't take advantage of you, no matter what I'm feeling," Kyra said, lifting both her arms to swipe at her eyes. "Thank you for the sexy kiss, Captain Elliott. It's been a very, very long time since I felt anything remotely close to that level of desire for a man. Even if you wipe this away, I'll never forget it—or you."

Kyra slid reluctantly off his lap and straightened her clothing. "I'm going to release the last of the chair restraints now. Please keep your physical distance so I don't have to use the controller. I've hurt you enough in the last couple days."

She hastily swiped her thumb across both wrist bands and stepped out of reach. It surprised her when Peyton remained seated. She wiped her eyes again as she put more distance between them. The one sleeve got so wet, she had to switch to the other to stop the flow.

"How are your legs now? Can you walk yet?" she asked to distract herself.

"The initial paralysis is gone. However, I have another kind of problem preventing walking at the moment. Give me a moment to. . .adjust."

Kyra shook her head. Denial was not just a river in Egypt. It was her best coping mechanism.

"There's a bathroom with a large shower off to the right. I won't put you in the cage until you've had some time to clean up. You'll find toiletries, towels, and men's clothing in the cabinets. The men's clothing should fit well enough. The last cyborg that used them was your size. Everything about this situation is temporary, including your time with me. Please don't forget that."

Peyton toyed with the mobile restraints on his wrist. He could tell they were uniquely coded because he'd found a slew of standard codes stored somewhere he couldn't pinpoint in his mind, but none had activated the release mechanism. He might be able to decipher the code and escape them well before her intended release time, but it would take more than a day to do so. Until then, he would play along and find out what the hell was going on here. Was he a patient or a prisoner? He still couldn't quite tell. The sexy doctor wasn't giving much away.

"So is your word the real deal, Doc? If I do as you ask, you'll tell me what this secrecy is all about?"

He watched as she nodded, looking incredibly sad. Was it because of his question? She wiped her eyes on each of her sleeves again and made him regret asking her anything. Her persistent crying played hell with his intentions to honor her request to keep his distance. If he moved fast enough, he could probably prevent her from using the controller on her wrist. And if that worked, he could actually have her in his arms before she could deny him. He wanted that volatile, sexy-talking mouth of hers on his again. He wanted to see how much more the woman could make him feel.

"Stop looking at me that way, Captain Elliott. Go take a shower—a cold shower. I'll tell you everything tonight after you've eaten. While you're cleaning up, I'll put your dinner inside the cage. I tried to make the damn thing as comfortable as I could."

Nodding at her husky, almost tearful reply—which had his damn dick twitching again—he reluctantly rose from the chair and took a couple careful steps. The stiffness in his limbs eased as he moved across the floor in the direction she had pointed. It was only after he closed the bathroom door behind him that he allowed himself to wonder why the medical room had looked so much like a cybernetic lab.

Chapter 5

After locking him in the cage with his dinner as promised, his mad scientist had disappeared for an hour while he ate. When she finally returned, she smelled strongly of the citrus body spray she had mentioned. His senses tingled with excitement, but he knew not to get his hopes up when he saw her shoulder length hair clipped tight at the back of her head. The style made her look older than she was and way more severe. All traces of the softer woman who had climbed into his lap to kiss him had been erased from her body. The woman staring at him through the bars now projected nothing but a professional stoicism, right down to the fresh white lab coat she wore.

Despite his capacity for analyzing large amounts of data, Peyton could only guess the reasons Dr. Winters had taken so many physical steps to retreat from him. Her shadowed, hollowed out eyes hinted at a story, but it was one he wasn't sure he was ready to hear yet. He had seen that same look on plenty of non-enhanced soldiers when they had been gearing up to do something they hated—like facing their potential deaths. A feeling of dread dropped like a cloud over his entire body. There didn't seem to be a damn thing he could do to stop himself from feeling it.

"Doc—I have to tell you this. It pisses me off to see you looking like I'm going to kill you in a few minutes. No matter what you've got to tell me, I'd never do that. Hell,

I've been in more bad shit in my life than you could ever imagine. I double damn guarantee your story won't be the most horrible one I've ever heard."

Kyra frowned over the supportive statement as she rolled her desk chair closer before she sat. "Trust me, Captain Elliott. This will be the worst story of your life."

Peyton sighed at her resigned tone and sat down on the small metal bed. As his backside sunk into the mattress, he found himself automatically gauging whether or not the frame could hold their combined weights as well as stand up to what he'd like to do with her.

"Before we start the shitty conversation I feel coming, can I just make that offer to show you heaven one more time? Damn lady—I don't remember the last time I wanted to kiss and hold a woman, much less bury myself inside her. I feel like I've been living in some kind of desert for years. This feeling of wanting you so badly carries with it the promise of some terminable thirst finally being quenched."

Kyra hung her head and bit her lip as she ordered herself not to cry again. Would his poetic side remain after the assimilation? She lectured herself about how foolish it was to care for something so immeasurable as Captain Elliott's penchant for flirting.

"Your eloquent speeches are very charming, but please stop flirting with me. I don't have the luxury of feeling sorry for either of us anymore. No matter what I might want to do, you and I have to talk about your future cybernetic life."

Peyton reached up and rubbed his head, something he'd caught himself doing several times that day. It was an odd mannerism with no purpose other than it gave his restlessness a physical expression. "Maybe I don't want to talk about my cybernetics. Right now in this moment, I feel more normal than I've felt in ages. I'm assuming you know the reason and are planning to tell me, but frankly I'm not sure I want to know the particulars, Doc."

Kyra nodded in answer to Peyton's questioning gaze. She was not surprised Peyton had figured it out. So had Alex, and Marshall before him. Feelings were natural for humans and they felt natural. She had also learned that awareness of them came back quickly when nothing was neurologically blocking their way. Unfortunately, some feelings were more pleasant to experience than others, as Peyton was about to find out.

"Let's start by discussing the work I did on you. I incapacitated you by activating a hidden reboot code in your cyborg programming. Then while you were unconscious, I replaced your primary processor. The new one I gave you isn't keeping your synapses firing with actions and thoughts you used to be programmed to repeat and follow twenty-four seven. Without those repeating signals blocking the way, your very human emotions are free to find normal synaptic paths across the various parts of your brain. You have physical body parts that rely on you having a processor, but there's no reason you can't have access to both your cybernetics *and* your feelings. To achieve that end, I've been working on a viable restoration process for the last seven years."

"*Seven years?* I don't recall being modified for much more than three years." His processor spun as he sought to validate or invalidate her statement. He could tell the answer was buried in his brain somewhere, but he just couldn't get to it.

Kyra took in a breath and let it out slowly. The truth had to be said aloud, but explaining it to her third restored cyborg didn't make it any easier.

"Captain Elliott, you've been a full cyborg and running programs off artificial intelligence chips for ten of the thirteen years that have passed since you received your first modifications. At the time you signed up for your military enhancements, there was no way to reverse the process as I just did. The military lied to you about it because the fledgling UCN believed Cyber Soldiers were necessary to end the wars. It was only later that scientists and non-scientists alike realized there were a great many things that could not be undone. Complete reversals are not physically possible nor mentally feasible. In short, once converted to a cyborg, a person cannot be anything else. For the rest of your life, you will always be part man and part machine."

Peyton rose and began to pace. His stomach contracted painfully at hearing he'd been existing in some sort of cybernetic limbo. He felt the truth of it instantly in his gut, plus it finally offered a plausible explanation for the gaps in his memories. But how could so much time have passed without his awareness? That seemed improbable.

Damn it. Was the woman lying to him? Was she his enemy? If she was, how had she created such an elaborate illusion?

Peyton turned and glared. "What was *your* role in the situation you're describing?"

Kyra stared back without blinking at his rising anger. It was nothing she hadn't seen before.

"I am one of the two original creators of the Cyber Soldier program. I didn't engineer your prosthetics, but I wrote nearly all the code that makes your brain work with them."

Peyton ran a hand through his hair. "Did you know back then? Did you know there was no way to reverse the process when you cut off working parts of our bodies and made us what we are?"

Kyra swallowed hard and nodded. "Yes. I knew. But just like you got the enhancements for the noblest of reasons, I believed by the time your duty was done to the world, scientists like me would have discovered a way to restore all the soldiers. Unfortunately the other original creator developed an idea that was deemed a much better solution than attempting to reverse cybernetic modifications. He won the debate and I was never allowed to officially work on a restoration process. For the last seven years, I've been doing it on my own. I realize now that blocking someone's humanity from being expressed was never a proper action to take."

Peyton walked to a wall of bars and gripped two of them in his hands. A quick scan told him the tensile strength of the metal was more than he could bend. He also picked up a low level hum indicating the bars of his prison were electrically charged at a level that would knock him out if a full charge was activated. Dr. Winters was a smart woman. She had all the bases covered when it came to keeping him trapped.

"Did you kidnap me from some assignment in the field so you could experiment on me?"

Kyra's eyebrows rose at Peyton's assumption. Like Marshall and Alex, Peyton's last human memories had been of their war time service. Jackson had never allowed any of them to realize how much like a machine they had become and she had written code expressly to make it happen. Once she had even believed that kind of ignorance was showing a kindness to them.

She shook her head as she answered. "No, Captain Elliot. I did not kidnap you from any mission. For the last decade, you've been serving in what is called the Cyber Husband program. It was the UCN's way of retiring Cyber Soldiers while keeping track of where they were. Funds from your various Cyber Husband contracts went into UCN coffers. You were unknowingly paying them back over the years for the cost of installing your cybernetics. You've personally been enhanced and fixed and redefined many times to suit your various wives. What I did to you yesterday was really just one more in a long line of tweaks. The difference is that I modified you for your benefit this time. In short, I think I have found a way to keep the promise the military didn't. All preliminary indications are pointing to evidence that I managed to free your human side from being stifled by your cyborg programming."

Kyra frowned as Peyton turned and gave her his back. It was not the response she had expected.

"Or you could be making all this shit up for reasons I don't know yet," he said flatly.

While not used to being accused of lying, she accepted Peyton's skepticism as healthy under the circumstances. At least he was still asking questions.

"No. I'm not making this up. You're my third and final experiment. I'm out of funds and out of time. There's an ongoing investigation into the deaths of my previous two Cyber Husbands, both of whom I tried to restore. The organization I once worked for did this to you and now suspects what I've been doing. It's only a matter of time before they come after me to find out for sure. I hope to finish your restoration long before they do that."

Peyton crossed his arms. The physical action felt good—and made him feel safer. Of course that was irrational, but it was like every body motion he made counted in a new way. "After all the trouble you say you went through to get me into your lab chair, I don't see you taking off without seeing your mad scientist scheme through to the end."

Kyra shook her head. "I'm not going far. I'm planning to blow up the cybernetic facility at Norton Industries. It won't stop new cyborgs from being created elsewhere in the world, but it will stop them from being created here in our country for a good long time. At this time in our history, there are over fifteen hundred registered cyborgs in the world. Most of them were never soldiers. Few of them volunteered for their changes."

"You talk about a corporation making cyborgs like it was making air jets. Cyber Soldiers are a military endeavor, not a civilian one. Are you certifiable, Doc? Is that why I'm locked in this cage?"

Kyra ignored Peyton's insulting comment about her sanity as she continued. It would likely be just one of many. "Some will probably think I'm crazy when my success with you is discovered. To explain my actions, I created a holographic recording about the corruption of the cybernetics program and my part in it. What I'm trying to do is stop your degree of cybernetic modification from being done to others. I trying like hell to do it before the scientific God-complex grows too large to constrain."

"If you have this secret agenda, why the hell are you telling me about it? As a paid servant of our country's military, I'm legally and ethically bound to turn you in for making threats to the leadership of your country."

Kyra shrugged. "That's one of the things I've been trying to explain to you, Captain Elliott. The world has changed dramatically in the last decade. There is no military anymore like the one you remember. Instead there is a global security organization and right now they support the enslavement of the Cyber Soldiers."

Peyton glared. He still couldn't believe her. "If what you're saying is true, why don't I remember the last decade of my life? For all I know, you could have just tweaked my memories to suit the story you're telling. You just explained how that was possible."

Kyra met and held Peyton's gaze. He was a lot sharper than his record indicated. She hoped that meant he would be quicker to grasp her story as the truth once assimilation had occurred.

"After my first attempt at cyborg restoration failed so badly, I knew better than to give you full access to all the data at once. Your human mind would have shut down trying to understand it as you dealt with your new processor. Instead, I wanted you to have the unique experience of being mostly human so you have a chance to understand having *feelings* and *emotions* are normal and right. To accomplish this, I put a block on your cybernetically recorded data for the last decade. It's a simple matter for me to remove the block, but it's not so simple for you to get all that data back. Once the data comes forward for assimilation, even if you have trouble believing it's true, you're still going to feel all kinds of emotions about what's been done to you. My second restoration subject told me it was like waking up in the middle of a nightmare and finding out every gory detail was real."

"You keep talking about the others like me. Where are they now?" Peyton demanded.

Kyra lifted her chin and prepared herself to face the first wave of hate.

"Both are dead. I had to euthanize the first because his mind snapped. Marshall couldn't deal with what he learned about what had happened to him. It had been in his military record that he'd been captured. What wasn't there was that his captors had tortured him with shock devices and sexually assaulted him repeatedly. After the peace pacts, Marshall was returned and medically retired into the Cyber Husband program without his human side receiving any therapy for what he'd suffered. In freeing him from what I discovered was a customized processor, I destroyed all data blocks that had been shielding him from remembering those experiences. In rapid succession, he recalled his military duty, his torture and abuse, and suffered the humiliation of the fixes I made to him. His life in the Cyber Husband program was nearly as traumatic as his prisoner of war experiences. What Marshall learned about himself was simply more than his mind could handle."

Kyra paused and looked at her clenched fists. She ordered herself to uncurl her fingers. She hadn't personally done any of those horrible things to Marshall. She just hadn't rescued him carefully enough.

"I tried to save him, but I failed. After a week of Marshall constantly swearing at me when I tried to communicate with him, one day he went completely silent. Later I realized he had found a way to shut down his internal organs and make them stop functioning. He never made it out of the cage you're now in, Captain Elliot. Every time I tried to get in to help him, Marshall tried to kill me despite the pain of the mobile restraints. I had to stop trying when he fractured my collar bone and dislocated my shoulder. Eventually though he grew too weak to try and hurt me. When I finally was able to get close enough to help, his organs were already too far gone. With no further recourse available, I put him out of his misery. So yes. . .I killed him. His death was my largest learning curve. It was three years before I was willing to try the restoration process again."

Peyton sat down heavily on the bed. The woman had coldly killed a fellow soldier and he had kissed her liked she was life incarnate. His hands fisted and released—fisted and released.

"You said I was your third cyborg. What happened to the second guy?" He didn't really want to know, but he needed to get a grasp on the full reality of his dilemma. His body was still reacting sexually to her voice no matter what horrors she described. It needed to give that shit up immediately—but his dick didn't seem willing to listen to the cause of his frustration.

"The physical restoration was mostly successful. Alex handled it better, but after six months he became clinically depressed and suicidal. He threw himself off a mountainside to escape his disillusionment with the world. When he was first restored, Alex seemed fine with the new level of control his human side gave him over his cybernetics. He adjusted well to memories of his past even though he was by nature a glass half empty kind of person. I think it was extremely hard for Alex to be the only cyborg aware of the UCN corruption. He spoke of it frequently."

Kyra paused to sigh. She could never explain this well enough to make it less horrible than it was.

"Alex knew about my failure with Marshall, so I don't think he had much faith in me being able to free other cyborgs. I saw the severe depression occurring, but short of making Alex completely reliant on his cybernetics again, I couldn't really stop his experiences from affecting his mind. I tried giving him anti-depressants in his food but they interfered with his cybernetic functions. I offered to reboot him back to what he was, but chose not to force him when he declined. Like with Marshall, I had removed the creator file completely, so I lacked a cybernetic way to override his wishes. When the lowest point of the depression hit, Alex decided there was no real hope for mankind. He said the world was too far gone for any one person to do anything worthwhile. After Alex killed himself, for a while I believed that he might be right. That was four years ago."

"So how did you pick me to be your next cyborg guinea pig?" Peyton asked, still feeling guilty for his attraction to someone like her.

"Well that's the ironic part of my story, Captain Elliott. You were always my first choice because of your military record, but I could never afford to buy you until recently. Being turned back in so often finally brought your husband price down into a range I could afford. When your tenth wife returned you, my bid was accepted the same day. Two weeks later and here you are—both human and cyborg—now with a new capacity to make your own decisions about your life."

"It's damned easy for you to tout your alleged success, but you're not the one trapped in a frigging cage. From my point of view, this is an epic fail on your part," Peyton declared. He glared at her when she didn't immediately respond to his taunt.

Kyra stared at the floor trying to choose her words carefully. "You know. . .a well-developed sense of humor is one of Mother Nature's most successful mental protection systems. I don't know why people think cyborgs are not still human. Your sense of irony seems as well developed as mine."

"You didn't answer my question, Dr. Winters." Peyton rose again and walked to face her through the bars. She had yet to move from the chair and seemed to have absolutely no fear of his escalating anger. Her serene expression royally pissed him off, but worse, acute disappointment churned in his gut. He was appalled to realize he still wanted to kiss her again. His mind was obviously fucked up in a way he couldn't understand yet.

"You owe me an explanation. Answer the damn question," he ordered, his voice hard.

"Okay. You're right, Captain Elliott. What I did to you isn't any different. It is just as despicable as the original conversion. But I was—and still am—out of options to do anything else but try to restore you now. I don't blame you for being angry at me or at the unfairness of your circumstances. Anger is a healthy response. It's quite normal to hate someone for playing God with your life."

Kyra stood and walked to a file cabinet to pull out a drawer. She lifted a folder full of papers from its depths and brought it back with her.

"With your cybernetics only partially engaged, I realize you can't use your enhancements to tell truth from lies right now. The good news is that your confusion is an honest part of the human condition. Once your cybernetic memories are re-assimilated, you should be able to make an accurate determination using both parts of your brain. I'm only asking you to suspend your anger until I can finish telling you what I have to. This folder is a start. If you want to see where you've been the last decade, here's your Cyber Husband record. I printed it out so you could read it."

Peyton reached a hand through the bars. He narrowed his gaze when she dropped the folder and kicked it across the floor. He stooped to drag it into the cage with him. "What's the matter? Don't you trust me, Doc?"

"No more than you trust me right now," Kyra said wearily, going back to her chair. She sat and watched as he thumbed rapidly through the file. "Do you recognize any of the women?"

Peyton shook his head, but paused over one. "Some cause a vague emotional reaction." He held up a picture. "Is this the one that stabbed me? Looking at her makes my gut clench in alarm."

Kyra nodded. "Yes. That's the one. Trauma has a way of creating a mental record that can't be removed or even blocked very well. Marshall's Cyber Husband price was low because he had a low rating in bedroom skills. At the time I bought him, I didn't see that as a red flag of any sort because I wasn't buying him for that purpose. Back then I wasn't smart enough to realize his sexual problems might have been caused by trauma during his military service. The human mind influences the physical body. This is true even for cyborgs whose human sides are kept unaware. It's no different than a non-cyborg human staying in mental denial."

Peyton ignored her philosophizing. "Forget your other monsters, Dr. Frankenstein. We're talking about me now. Is the woman who stabbed me still incarcerated for her actions?"

As he waited for her to answer, Peyton stared at the photo of the woman who had almost killed him. She looked cold and unfeeling. Kyra Winters was trying to convince him that was the case for her as well, but why wasn't he buying it? If her story was true, she'd killed two cyborgs already. His death might be her next goal.

His gaze went back to his jailer who looked ready to weep any second.

What the hell was he supposed to believe about Kyra Winters?

When his gut clenched in sympathy again, but for her sadness, he warned himself not to get soft just because the mad scientist cried over everything. Ignoring the interest of his man parts in her was no easier.

Kyra squirmed in the chair as she answered Peyton's question. "The woman who stabbed you was never incarcerated. She was merely banned from purchasing through the Cyber Husband program again. Her story is that you tried to hurt her and she defended herself. Such stories are never questioned because of your military past and the fact that you still have all your physical enhancements. Fear of cyborgs has been purposely propagated."

Peyton frowned. "I may not remember the incident, but I'm fairly certain I would never try to harm a woman unless it was a life or death situation."

Kyra sighed and studied her feet. It was always hard to explain because it was wrong—simply wrong. "At this time in our country, there's no legal punishment for any human damaging a cyborg. This is especially true if you own the cyborg or they work for you. If you happen to actually kill a cyborg belonging to someone else, you can only be sued for a shit ton of restitution money. Cybernetically enhanced individuals are little more than high-priced commodities these days. They are treated the same as non-organic robots."

Peyton continued to look through the file. "What recourse is there for a cyborg when a rich crazy woman gets hold of him?"

"None," Kyra answered flatly, knowing he was including her in that comment. "But you'll be happy to know I never did anything with you worthy of that glare you're trying hard not to give me. I'm not one of those women, even though I used their process to obtain access to you."

"Really? I think you are one of them. You kissed me and gave me hope before you cruelly took it away with your story. If you ask me, that's a pretty lousy thing to do to a man who can't remember the last decade of his life."

Peyton sifted through more pages, but stopped when he came across the advertisement for him. It was surreal to see such a large fee next to his photo.

"I swear I didn't kiss you to add to your torment." When Peyton didn't answer back, Kyra returned to silently waiting until he had flipped through the rest of the documentation.

Finally Peyton looked up from the folder in his lap. "None of this makes any sense to me. I served my country as best I could. Hell, I gave them everything they wanted, including several normal working parts of my body—like my damn eyes for instance. I used to have blue eyes. Why the hell would the military betray me by taking my free will away?"

"For the same reason I have you in a cage, Captain Elliott. Everyone in the world is afraid of what you might do with your cybernetics if your human side ever gets angry enough. Norton made you as much of a human robot as they possibly could because they figured out exactly how to control the cybernetic side of you."

Kyra swiveled in her chair as she tried to find words to describe the reasons she had felt the need to take such drastic measures with him. Finally, she turned back.

"I'm afraid too, but in the last seven years, I've learned that controlling another human being is just one illusion piled on top of another. Before your processor fried, you confessed you had been seeking your own escape. Somehow you were teaching your human mind to connect organically to your cybernetic chips. I think it's only a matter of time before it starts to happen for other cyborgs. A quiet revolution is most likely underway, Captain Elliot. When it really gets going, the cyborgs are going to need a leader to help them fight for their remaining humanity."

Peyton shook his head and wondered who might have helped her create all the content he was reading. If it was a lie, she had some talented hacks working with her.

If it was the truth—?

No, it couldn't be. It was too hard to believe.

"How much did you pay for me, Dr. Winters?"

Kyra ignored the question. She saw no purpose in him knowing what she had spent. "Just so we're clear with each other, I only kissed you yesterday because I wanted to kiss you. It's been a long damn time since I kissed anyone. Judging from how good it was, I have no doubt that your sexual training is as top notch as advertised. The reason I didn't indulge completely was because I didn't want to become just another woman taking advantage of you. My bigger purpose is far more important than any passing attraction I might be feeling."

"I assure you the only sex training I have was gotten on my own. Me never legally marrying doesn't mean there weren't plenty of women in my life," Peyton declared.

"There's no need to defend your kissing skills to me, Captain Elliott. You have one of the highest ratings in the Cyber Husband program for your bedroom skills, and one of the lowest for your level of cooperation during all other activities. Apparently, your wives bought you for a handsome lap dog only to find out you were mostly a mongrel."

Tired of talking about Peyton's life with other women, Kyra rose and paced around the room while he thumbed through the file again.

"It says my price is fifteen million. Did ten women actually pay that for me?"

Kyra snorted at how Peyton posed his question. There was no disbelief in the exorbitant amount, just amusement. "That pleased tone of voice kind of gives away how you feel about being worth so much. You might want to stop smiling and take this seriously. Being a Cyber Husband wasn't the glamorous life you're imagining."

Peyton snorted. "It's an obscene amount of money to spend for a man's company—that's for sure. And probably bullshit too. I keep waiting for you to tell me what the punch line is to the joke."

Kyra turned and glared at him. "Fine. Here's the punch line. I paid eight million dollars. *You were on sale.*" It made her incredibly happy when the folder fell to Peyton's lap.

"You're lying."

"No. I assure you I am not," Kyra replied dryly, glad to hear at least a little doubt ringing in Peyton's denial.

"Where the hell did you get eight million dollars? No offense, but if I'm number three, it stands to reason you paid big bucks for the others as well. Are you just some bored cyber scientist who gets her kicks from tweaking the cyborgs she buys?"

Peyton's accusation irritated her but only because it had come up so soon. She had always planned to reveal the truth while he was still safely in the cage. She had just hoped to gain a smidgeon of trust from him first. Apparently, trust was not going to be a possibility. She was going to have to settle for grudging respect.

"My ex and I were separated and divorced years ago, but as his only human wife, I remained his only eligible legal heir at his death. When one of his Cyber Wives killed him, she went back to Norton for complete redefinition. Not that they would have let her keep the money, but apparently I was still named in his will. We never had any children together because Jackson didn't want them."

"Jackson?"

"Yes. Jackson Channing. For almost fifteen years, I was married to the primary creator of the Cyber Soldier program."

Peyton set the file aside and rose to walk to the bars. "He's in my human memories. He helped me choose my enhancements. I remember talking to him before they were done. He didn't seem very evil to me."

Kyra nodded. She understood what Peyton was saying. That early version of Jackson hadn't been the warped one.

"Programming for cybernetic enhancements was very straight forward when the first soldiers were converted. Cybernetic programming was used mostly to increase natural abilities and repair the soldier's bodies when necessary. Programs didn't run codes concurrently without pause. That discovery came later, as did others that made your participation in the Cyber Husband program a possibility. Before the peace pact was officially signed, Jackson had figured out how to completely control anyone with a cybernetic processor and torment chips installed. The first work I did for you was to remove all those capacities from your cybernetics. I've come to think it's reprehensible to subvert someone's humanity so totally."

Peyton lifted his shoulders. "So you want me to believe that you're a reformed cyber scientist with a guilty conscience. *And* I'm also supposed to believe you did this restoration to help me."

Since she didn't even harbor it as a fantasy, Kyra shook her head. "I'm just a person who is trying to right her mistakes in life before she dies. The constant code control factor led to the recycling of cyborgs instead of their disposal. At first, I was convinced it was a good thing that soldiers like you were being spared outright execution. Then Jackson expanded his cybernetic research to include converting women. Failures of cybernetics in females are still numerous. But in the end it was the work being done children that finally snapped me out of being complacent. Jackson didn't make children into full cyborgs. He just installed controllers in them so their parents wouldn't have to work so hard. Child discipline technology made my ex-husband more of a fortune than his original cybernetics work did."

Peyton gripped the bars. His fingers squeezed hard around them as he closed his eyes against the picture his mind drew of her descriptions. "Hurting children really is despicable. I saw enough of that during the war. You don't know what hell is until you see a toddler wired with bombs."

"Yes. Hurting children is despicable. But what I've done to you—and what I did to Marshall and Alex—is just as evil. Worse than that, I haven't given you the choice of staying ignorant. Despite being one of the original creators, I am fully cognizant of my limitations. When I'm dead, there will be no one left alive who can run this sort of experiment as fast as I can. Any success with you is really a success for all Cyber Soldiers."

Peyton opened his eyes to stare at her again. Her head was down and her shoulders were bowed. She looked fragile in her doctor's coat and he felt himself wanting to comfort her. It was absurd to want more personal contact with a woman who had just confessed to buying and killing two cyborgs for the sake of her experiments. He was her captive and he couldn't let himself forget it just because his dick still liked her. If this contradictory thinking was part of being human, he wasn't sure it was worth staying like he was currently.

"What the hell are you trying to do with me, Doc? If you expect to ever have my cooperation, you need to tell me exactly what you have planned."

Kyra looked at the floor. "I thought if you had access to all your cybernetics, and full access to your human side as well, that you might be able to find a way to liberate those who have been unfairly enslaved by the technology."

"And if I refuse to go along with you?" Peyton asked.

Her head snapped up on his instant response. "Not to brag or anything, Captain Elliott, but I have the lion's share of power in our relationship at the moment. If I wanted to, I could knock you out, put you back in the chair, and install a different processor very similar to the military one I took out of you. Then I could return you physically to Norton, just like your other wives did. You'd go back to being the most challenging cyborg in the Cyber Husband program with no one ever knowing what I attempted."

"But then what would happen to your mad scientist plans?" Peyton asked.

"Nothing. Nothing happens. I've spent all of Jackson's blood money. It's not like I'm going to get a refund for returning you. Until a cyborg's programming is disrupted, there's no way to talk to him or her about volunteering for my experiments. So if I feel sorry for you and give you up, it doesn't matter what I planned. Norton and the UCN won't let me continue playing the role of reformed scientist. You're the last chance to atone that I will ever have in my life."

Peyton clicked his finger tips against the bars. "Fifty isn't all that old when your life expectancy is a hundred and fifty. You haven't even hit mid-life yet."

"With so many cybernetic parts, your life span could very well be twice mine and you know it," Kyra answered.

Peyton shrugged. "My longevity is ironic considering I never expected to survive my military service."

"Captain. . ." Kyra stared at Peyton knowing there was no way she could make him understand why she had done what she had done to him until he understood his past. "I'm sorry, but I can't let you refuse to help me."

"Yeah, Doc. I figured that shit out already."

Letting go of the bars, Peyton trudged back to the sterile looking bed and sat down on it. It would have been very nice to have spent a few hours with the wicked woman riding him to an oblivion that took them both beyond this fucked-up situation. Some women just didn't know when to stop talking.

Peyton sighed heavily in disappointment as he glared. "Since I can't stop you, go ahead and do your worst to me. Let's see if I survive full restoration better than my weak-ass predecessors."

"I'm not asking you to be nice to me or to tolerate this situation without hating every second of it. I just don't have the luxury of feeling guilty about taking your humanity away from you again."

Peyton snorted at her half-ass apology. Her chastisement only made him more wary.

"Too bad, Dr. Winters. I'm not your priest, or your girlfriend, so I can't make you feel better for fucking with my brain again. If I die, don't jump off a cliff like your last Cyber Husband did. Get some mental help. You obviously need it."

Kyra shook her head. "Of all the regrets I may ever have in my life, I can't believe passing up the chance to sleep with a wiseass like you might actually be the one that will keep me up at night."

"Maybe we'll get to sleeping with each other in *another place and another time*," Peyton said snidely, venting his sarcasm.

"Highly doubtful, but not an unpleasant thought—even now that you hate me," Kyra said softly, walking to stand close to the bars.

Regret and loss sat heavy in her chest, but she couldn't let it change things. She took a deep breath and started the assimilation.

"Code Alfa78904. Resume Creator Reboot of Peyton 313. Voice authorization: Kyra Winters, Doctor of Cybernetics, Creator 2 of 2. Run cybernetic data records synchronization. Adjust speed of assimilation to be as slow as possible. Sleep mode is recommended while the process completes."

Peyton grunted as he fell down flat on the bed, immediately obeying the cybernetic commands shutting down his consciousness.

Kyra gripped the bars and sniffed as tears fell again. What more proof did she need that she was doing the right thing? The man in the cage was still a cyborg and would always be one in some ways. His instant compliance with the creator commands proved it conclusively. She only felt guilty because she had shown Peyton what it could be like living as mostly human again.

Pulling herself wearily away from the bars, Kyra choked back the sob clogging her throat. If this worked, Peyton would become the first of his kind. If it didn't . . . well she'd just tackle that problem in the morning. At the slowest speed, full synchronization would take at least nineteen hours. To face what Peyton would become was going to take all her fortitude. She couldn't handle it without rest.

"Fight for us all one more time, Captain Elliot. Find a way to be both human and cyborg. No matter how much you hate me, I promise I'll help you if you just stay with me and try."

She couldn't understand Peyton's reply as he mumbled something, but it meant a lot to her that her voice could penetrate his cybernetic sleep.

Chapter 6

Late the next morning, Kyra looked down at her tight jeans and even tighter fitting shirt with disgust. Why was she taking such pains with her appearance? He likely wouldn't notice her clothing. If he did, he likely wouldn't care. Last night he hated her for telling him the truth. This morning he'd probably hate her for just breathing.

In the mirror, she inspected the way her shoulder length brown hair curled naturally around her face and made her brown eyes look even darker. Surgery had corrected her vision two years ago, but today glasses would have been a welcome shield. She pushed her hair back and held it in both hands as she tried to decide what to do with it before she finally turned it loose and left it hanging.

Sighing in disgust about caring whether or not he might still find her attractive, Kyra grabbed the wrist remote for his restraints and snapped it back on. She'd taken it off to shower but wouldn't be able to do that again once Peyton was out of the cage.

Taking a deep breath, she headed to her kitchen and picked up his breakfast. Peyton would need serious fuel today. His body had essentially been working all night.

It took her several minutes to get through her lab's rotating security. What she found inside had her setting the food tray down on her desk and running to the bars of the cage. The metal bed was bent in the middle.

Everything was thrown around, scattered, or destroyed. The file she had left with Peyton last evening had been shredded into confetti.

"Captain Elliot? Are you okay?"

He rounded on her so quickly that Kyra didn't see him move until he slammed his body against the bars. The force of the impact scared her into jumping away from the cage.

"It's *all* fucking true, isn't it?" he demanded.

Kyra swallowed and nodded. Neither Marshall or Alex had gotten so angry. Instead, they'd been hurt and mentally wounded by the discovery. Their country's betrayal had sent them into depression. Apparently, the emotional part of Peyton was wired a bit differently.

"Yes. Everything about the Cyber Husband program is all true. And there's more I haven't told you yet."

"My men—what happened to the other Marines?"

Kyra drew in a breath. "Every cybernetically enhanced soldier was redefined and put into the Cyber Husband program. Those that couldn't be redefined were sent to work camps where they're being used like android robots for tasks specific to their enhancements. But without exception, all Cyber Soldiers were given cybernetic chips that run the constant codes I told you about. I know of no exceptions."

"Fucking asshole dipshit motherfucking paper pushing bastards," Peyton yelled, slamming the bars again several times. "I'm a fucking Marine. I can't believe they turned me into a high-priced man whore without me knowing it. How the hell could this happen?"

Kyra went to her desk chair and fell into it. "Now you understand the primary reason I didn't have sex with you when you offered. Do you remember our personal exchange?"

Peyton nodded tightly. "Damn right I remember it. I remembered a lot of things this morning. I remembered things that I hadn't thought about in a decade. What the hell happened to my fiancée?"

"*Fiancée?* There was nothing in your records about a fiancée," Kyra said wearily, rubbing her forehead in confusion. "If you can recall her name and ID number, I can look up her current stats. Chances are she was told that your cybernetics had gone rogue and taken over your personality. It was the standard cover story. Families were sent a tape that was made to portray your cybernetic abilities in the worst possible light. All families of soldiers received large compensation checks for their personal losses."

Peyton shook his head in disbelief. "So instead of getting the honorable retirement I was promised, they handled the fucked up situation like I had died in combat."

Kyra nodded. "Yes. I believe that's a fair analogy for what happened."

"How long have you known all this? You told me yesterday, but I need to hear it again," he demanded.

"Jackson told me restoration was not an option just before the peace pacts were signed. He said cyber soldiers were too dangerous to let run loose in a peaceful society. Most decision makers in our government and the UCN wanted all cyborgs discreetly destroyed. Jackson's constant code solution spared cyborgs from death . . . at least after a fashion. Those making the decisions preferred being perceived as good guys so they convinced themselves that soldiers were getting a pretty cushy life in the Cyber Husband program. And it was all aided by the income cyborgs brought to the UCN."

"Yeah. A cushy life. Just fuck some stranger on demand and do the work of a house droid the rest of the time. That's *bullshit*—that's what that is," Peyton declared, slamming his hand against the bars again.

Kyra winced at his description of the last decade. "Yes. The unfairness should have occurred to me when Jackson suggested his solution, but it didn't. It didn't even occur to me when Jackson replaced me with a female cyborg that he was trying to custom mold to his changing sexual preferences. I brooded for several years about his betrayal, too self-involved to see the bigger picture of the cyborg chaos he'd been instrumental in putting into place. His work on putting controllers into children ended up being my tipping point. I left my job at Norton Industries this year after Jackson was killed because I refused to take over his work on it. I couldn't stand being involved with altering innocent children. Controller wires have to be inserted while the person is alert so they can be tested at each pain point. They created a special chip to put in the brains of children to store the traumatic memories afterward. But that doesn't mean they don't scream while the process is being done to them."

"I called you Dr. Frankenstein, but you're a worse monster than any you've created," Peyton said viciously.

Kyra nodded. "Yes. I agree with your assessment of my character. But I promise you I'm trying to make things right as best I can."

Peyton glared, but his derision was both ineffective and wasted on the stoic woman. If ever there was a time for the mad doctor to be sobbing into her lab coat sleeve, it would have been after his insults. But no—she was too damn strange to act like a normal person.

"Lady, you're lucky right now I'm in this cage. Otherwise my hands would be around your throat. Locking me in here was probably the smartest thing you've ever done in your life."

Kyra studied her hands. She deserved his anger. She deserved his hate. But that didn't make her goal any less important or urgent. Her science work had given her a laser-like focus on her goals. It served her well as she stared at the angry Marine she had caged.

"That conclusion depends on how you view things, Captain Elliot. If you kill me when I let you out, then I will at least be released from this remorseful hell I exist in most of the time. But I don't think you're going to because you need me to fix at least a few other cyborgs, if we manage to rescue some before the UCN comes after me. I see us working as some sort of a team to help you form a viable group capable of acting together for larger purposes."

"Do you think rescuing a few cyber soldiers is going to vindicate what you have done to people like me?" Peyton growled out his questions as he stomped around his prison.

Kyra shook her head. "No. Nothing will change what I've done to you. But regret won't change the past. I can only try to make amends by restoring one cybernetic soldier at a time."

"Great. Let me the hell out of this cage and let's get to it."

Kyra shook her head again. "No. I can't. Look at how erratic your emotions are. You're not fully integrated, Captain Elliott. The human mind is an amazing tool, but it needs time to work through what's happened in the last couple days. Your anger is a necessary phase of this process. Sadness and depression will come to visit shortly as well. Once you survive feeling all those emotions, then we'll talk about letting you out."

"Damn it. I'm going to lose my mind prowling around this cage while dwelling on this shit. I destroyed the bed the moment I came to consciousness and remembered everything."

Peyton swept a hand over his head. *Human action of frustration*, his mind reported, even as his cybernetic implants hummed and scanned for things to help him escape. He laughed harshly at the irony of his awareness. He was emotionally back to the day he'd left the war zone. What had happened since was like watching a movie in his head. The data of the last decade was fully accessible, but there was no emotion attached to any of it that made it worth thinking about for more than two seconds. Data about his other *wives* was just stored and catalogued. All it provided was proof of how much and for how long he'd been fucked over by the country he'd served.

"You know, I wish you had just left me like I was yesterday, Doc. I think I was actually happy for a few minutes. Fucking hell—I didn't sign up for this when I let you mad scientists combat modify my brain."

Kyra tucked her hands under her legs to stop them from shaking. "No. You didn't sign up for any of this. Bend the bed back into a normal shape after you calm down. You can do it if you focus your thoughts on channeling your strength. It's going to take a bit of time for your cybernetic enhancements to learn to follow your human will instead of some programming order. Based on the organic access work you were already doing, I think this is the golden opportunity your brain has been waiting for. It should race to create new synapses now that there is nothing to prevent them from developing."

Rising slowly, Kyra walked to her desk and then to the cage with the breakfast tray she had prepared. She lowered a thin slide welded to the bars and locked the tray to it before sending it through the opening.

"I brought you a lot of protein. Your body has undergone a huge trauma. The integration process will work more efficiently if you eat and rest as much as possible."

"Before you go traipsing away, there's one more thing I need to know—are you keeping anything else important from me? Don't fucking lie to me, Doc. I can't take anymore deceit," Peyton commanded.

Kyra crossed her arms. "Yes. I'm keeping some things from you still, but only for the purpose of helping you adjust slowly—not to keep you in the dark about your life. I'll tell you everything in time. One day soon you'll be able to research and learn things on your own. Then you can determine for yourself whether or not to trust what I've said to you. No matter what you think of me, I do intend to give you full freedom. You have my word on that, Captain Elliott."

When he was silent and had turned away, Kyra turned to leave. It was obvious how he felt about her now. The sight of her probably sickened him. Her earlier worry about her clothes now mocked her.

"Hey Doc—wait. *Fuck.* I hate asking this, but damn it—I need to know."

Kyra turned back to find Peyton glaring at her hard.

"You were right about the sexual training. Apparently, there was a programming chip installed just for that work. Did you purposely leave that one in me? Or am I just supposed to believe it was a scientific oversight?"

Kyra winced internally, but nodded at his comment. It was a reasonable question. And he was right, she had left it to give herself an edge. Peyton would just have to add it to her list of sins.

"I left all secondary chips because I didn't want to confuse you any more than necessary. I only changed out the primary ones and the processor. Later on, we'll remove any chips you want gone, including the one with my info on it. If it's any consolation to your newly reawakened male ego, the chip isn't the only indicator of what you found on it. You were the only man in the Cyber Husband program with a five star bedroom rating from all ten of your wives. That obviously indicates a high level of innate skill. Cybernetic software can only enhance abilities that are already innate. Removing the chip won't change that. It will just remove your knowledge of me."

Peyton snorted. "I'm sure that would be scientifically disappointing for you. Want to do some hands on research to find out if you agree? Apparently, lots of women have. I don't know why you turned me down before. Why should you be the one exception?"

Kyra didn't know which of them was more surprised by his snarky offer. Peyton dropped his gaze from hers right after asking.

"Thank you, but no thank you, Captain Elliot. I have my BOB. He takes care of any physical needs I have in the bedroom."

Peyton's scanning mechanism sent out signals searching for another cyborg or droid in her home. No signals were returned. Maybe all signals inside the lab were scrambled. "Did you experiment on him too?"

Kyra rolled her eyes at the accusation in his tone. If the whole discussion hadn't been so traumatizing for her, his question would have been hysterically funny.

"No. BOB is already fully mechanized. Not exactly a droid, but there's no chance of improving him. I have to make do with his current abilities. I find they suffice for my occasional use."

Peyton caught the amusement in Kyra's voice and thought about what she was saying as he looped his arms around the bars. He realized then that he had been too pissed to think clearly. He ordered himself to calm the hell down and start collecting data from Kyra Winters in a more rational manner. When he had achieved that state, her veiled inference instantly came to him.

"Oh, that kind of BOB. Why make do with your old-fashioned mechanical toys, Doc? A woman as hot as you needs the kind of vibrator that comes with an imaginative brain. I bet I'm bigger than your mechanical boyfriend too."

Kyra snorted at his audacity. He was certainly a lot different than Marshall or Alex.

"Random outbursts of human emotion, such as the typical male bragging you're doing, will be filtering through your mind and out your mouth for several days. When everything finally settles though, you should find yourself experiencing less of those outbursts."

Peyton laughed at her calm assessment. "Outbursts? Oh hell no. This conversation is no fucking outburst. You missed seeing the outburst this morning. I'm just pissed at you now because I remember every one of those women who bought me and the memories are not pleasant. Nine of them were evil bitches that I derailed whenever I could. I had no choice but to fuck them on command and part of me hated them for it—and still does. I can't believe any government would condone such a thing. In my book, that's a pretty shitty thing to do to a soldier. Hell—to any man period. Same goes for women."

Kyra nodded, her face flushing with shame. "Yes. I'm sorry it took me so long to rescue you from that life. I didn't have fifteen million dollars when I needed it. Raising money took years, even with Jackson's inheritance. I did the best I could as fast I could. When I couldn't buy you at first, I bought the others thinking that trying something was better than doing nothing. All my experiences in human restoration of cyborgs has only increased my guilt and shame for participating in such a heinous process to begin with. But it's far too late for wishing I had never started."

Peyton ran a hand through his hair, feeling the strands push up. On the right side, he felt the small compartment that provided access to his cybernetic components. Whether Kyra Winters was truly repentant or not, she was the only person he knew who held the secrets to his return to something resembling normality. Without her, he'd still be waiting for another bored rich woman to buy him. Guess it was better to be at the mercy of the evil science bitch he knew, than some unknown female he was painfully programmed to obey.

He sighed as he met Kyra's concerned stare. "Whatever the hell you did to me, I do finally remember every woman I've ever been with, including my fiancée which is the last decent memory I have before I got the cybernetics. As messed up as you are as a human being, thanks at least for giving me back control of my body. From all the data stored in my brain, I can see that never would have happened if you hadn't had your attack of conscience. I hate you for being alive, but I applaud your attempt to reform."

"Thank you for that concession, Captain Elliott. Now I know what being damned with faint praise feels like. And let me just say again that any reasonable human would be very angry in your situation. No matter what anyone did to you, you're just as human as I am. Never doubt it," Kyra ordered softly.

Peyton studied her sagging shoulders. The women who had bought him seemed to bother her as much as anything else that had been done to him. He might be still pissed at the situation, but at the moment he had a lot of respect for Kyra Winters holding back when he was begging her for sex. He had clear and distinct recall of just how badly she had wanted him. Even now after all he had learned, memories of her hot kiss had his dick twitching despite his disgust at the reaction.

"I remember everything about our sexual exchange, Doc. I remember you climbing into my lap to kiss me until I was hard as a rock under you. I remember how much we both wanted that kiss to go on and on. I told you I wasn't going to forget it. That apparently was a promise I'm able to keep. Thanks for that too. Focusing on my sick obsession with you is at least helping me put memories of those other evil bitches away."

Kyra shook her head. "Stop patronizing me. Just erase the memory of us kissing. You have that ability back now. It would actually be a good thing for both of us if you did because your shitty situation with me is just getting started. Soon we're going to be up to our necks in it. We're never going to find a time and place for anything like that kiss to happen again."

Peyton shook his own head, mirroring her denial. Maybe he didn't remember everything perfectly, but he was sure Kyra Winters was one of the most depressing women he'd ever been attracted to. His fiancée had been a curvy, happy-go-lucky yoga teacher. Maybe his strong attraction to Kyra was just gratitude that she had literally saved what was left of his ass.

"You don't know what will happen for sure, Doc. No one knows. Life is full of surprises. I escaped one hell and woke up in another. This isn't the first time either. At least I'm alive and so are you. I'm still pissed but don't let that stop you from being truthful. I want to hear what you have to say."

Peyton frowned when she rose from her seat and headed to the door. He found himself speaking to her back as she tried to shut him out. "Hey, Doc—I know I'm in a pisser of a mood, but don't be a stranger from the lab today. I'm not real keen on being alone right now. It would give me too much time to hate the world."

Kyra nodded but didn't turn around. She needed a break from witnessing his unhappiness.

"I'll be back to see you in an hour. If you fix your area so you can sit, I'll bring you a reading device with some more documents. I'll work here and stay available to answer your questions about what you find out."

After hearing Peyton's softly spoken "okay", Kyra slipped quietly out of the lab and took a few cleansing breaths. His reaction of extreme anger was dangerous, especially given his cybernetically enhanced strength. But his anger seemed healthier than the instant depression she'd seen in both Marshall and Alex. She was going to consider it a positive sign that his restoration was working.

Pushing her hair back, Kyra picked up her pace and headed to the kitchen. Once there, she picked up her handheld com and dialed. She had to be careful in case the call was being recorded. She fully expected it was. The connection completed but there was no human answer on the other end. She'd gotten his recording.

"Hey Nero. How's the gaming going? No line pickup so I guess you must be absorbed in something. Guess what? A real Prince Charming finally arrived on my doorstep. I have high hopes because Peyton 313 is way superior to the other two duds I bought. Wait until you see the guns on this one. I can't wrap both hands around one of his upper arms. And before you ask, the answer is no—Peyton is not well behaved—but I don't care. I like bad boys, even if they are cyborgs. So how do you feel about a little get together to meet him? Call me back when you get out of the game."

She disconnected and frowned. It would have been preferable to wait a couple more days until she was sure Peyton was adapting fully. But her instincts were singing and that was never good. The last time they sang this loudly, Jackson had asked for an official divorce so he could take a Cyber Wife without looking bad to the UCN.

Before the forms had gotten through the legal chain, Jackson's first Cyber Wife had moved in with him. She had spent the first week of her new single life working with Nero to reset privacy codes throughout the house and lab to respond only to her. When Jackson had come back to the house to get something a few days later, he'd had to wait for her to get home from work to get inside. His shock at her actions to protect herself had been great, but he'd soon adjusted to her new autonomy—as had she.

By that point she'd accepted that she was never in her life going to be able to forgive him.

It didn't take long after that epiphany for complete apathy to set in about how Jackson was living.

Now she was about to change her life again, only this time she was going completely off the grid. To do the best job of that, she needed to create a side trail of research that would lead any investigation away from Peyton's true changes to something far less interesting.

Once he'd had a chance to calm down, maybe she could convince the angry Marine to help her.

Chapter 7

Kyra sat at her desk downloading the last of the notes and video from Peyton's restoration onto the special encryption disks Nero had made for her. In the cage, Peyton used his thumbs to flip screens on a large handheld. She knew he was comprehending about eighty-five percent of the data because she was still wirelessly monitoring his brain activity. Whether he was taking it in with full understanding or not was yet to be determined, but according to his EEG readout, the man was a reading machine.

His occasional grunt of disbelief, followed by a short-lived outburst of swearing, was the only thing that occasionally broke the silence between them. She was bit startled when he finally spoke.

"I give up. I'm obviously not understanding what I'm reading. How could an entire decade of my life be so completely suppressed just by a software program? It seems too improbable to be true."

Kyra sighed softly as she thought about how to explain it to him. "Before the universal peace pacts were completed, military prisoners of war, including cyber soldiers, were kept on rigidly busy schedules during their captivity. Tasks they were forced to do were part torture and part reward. Surviving the daily grind of getting through them gave prisoners little time to think creatively, much less plot or plan escapes. Those drastic survival routines were an effective tool to keep them physically tired, but the bonus was they worked on their minds as well. When the mind is kept too busy, it forgets how to stop and reflect on anything."

She got up to pace, studying the floor as she looked for the right words.

"Keeping the mind too busy to do anything but follow routine is pretty much what the constant code programming does to a cyborg's brain. Your cybernetic chips are kept one hundred percent preoccupied with running a variety of routine tasks. The theory is that the part of the brain producing emotions simply doesn't get a chance to express itself. In other words, your emotional reactions never got to have their turn using your brain's synapses. But Peyton, even before you came to me, you were already proving that assumption to be false in some ways. It was just taking your human mind a bit longer to figure out how to exert itself alongside your constantly running cybernetic programs."

Peyton set down the reading device and stood to pace. It was an action he'd been repeating for the last five hours. His logic chip said the small, walking movement provided nothing beneficial. The other unexplainable motivation compelled him to keep walking until something changed. He decided both reactions were equally frustrating.

"I hate being mentally pulled in two widely varying directions. Every decision now is excruciating. I was just mentally debating whether or not pacing was beneficial. What kind of fucking shit is this to live with? Is it going to be like this forever?"

Kyra sighed at his complaint because she couldn't answer it. "I don't know. So far I've had a sixty-six percent failure rate with restored cyborgs. I'm hoping you'll live for a very long time and be able to give the world enough data to eventually answer those sorts of questions."

Walking back to sit, Kyra swallowed the knot of guilt in her throat and turned to face her keyboard. She switched screens to make a note about what he'd said. Her fingers slipped from the keys when she heard a loud bang behind her. She turned back toward him just as Peyton hit the bars with his fists again. Her gut clenched in disappointment over his show of anger. She waited until he'd calmed enough to go back to his bed and sit before asking her question.

"Are you trying to escape, Captain?"

Peyton shook his head. "No. I'm just blowing off steam. Guess I'm a little louder about slamming around than the average scientist you're used to seeing get angry."

Kyra swiveled back and forth in her seat. She hated having to chastise him, but she had to share the information. "You have a chip capable of advising you about acceptable levels of force appropriate for each situation. The software in the chip measures PSI quite efficiently. There's no reason your new processor can't access that chip for the necessary data whenever you have need. Are you trying to do so and failing?"

Peyton glared. There was smart and there was smartass. He doubted Kyra Winters knew the difference. "Sure, Doc. I'm failing to access my chips. Why not use that excuse to explain my frustration?"

"I'm sorry. I shouldn't have jumped to conclusions. Why don't you tell me what you think is happening?" Kyra ordered calmly.

"Okay, I'll tell you. I have an urge to rip a couple of these prison bars out of their sockets. Then I want to go find the ones who made the decision to fuck with my life and beat the shit out of them."

Knowing she was one of those people, Kyra turned calmly back to her keyboard to hide her realization. Obviously Captain Elliot was too emotional at the moment to answer her queries with any degree of rationality. It was promising that he felt so strongly, but at various points she had seen high levels of emotion in both Marshall and Alex too.

Hearing Kyra typing rapidly, Peyton smacked his cybernetic hand loudly on the bars to get her attention again. "Doc—if you write any of that crap fest of whining down, I swear I'm going to spank you hard when I get out of here. If you expect to get anywhere with me, you need to learn the difference between a pissed-off comment and a serious answer."

"That's quite a statement coming from the non-emotional cyborg who just became an irrational human again yesterday," Kyra said, continuing to type her note. "And swearing at me under your breath is not going to get you out of that cage any sooner, Captain."

Peyton snorted at Kyra's starchy reply. A part of him—especially the one below his belt—was secretly pleased that, despite being a crybaby, the woman was ballsy enough to talk back to him. He found her defensive attitude reasonable and acceptable given all she had confessed. Since a government level ass-kicking was off the table at the moment, the entertaining distraction of goading the guilt-ridden doctor was at least mildly entertaining.

"Okay. What if I promise to be a good cyborg during your freakish experiments, Dr. Winters? What will that kind of behavior get me?"

Kyra didn't turn again. . .and she didn't take the bait. "I'm sure you're good at a great many things, Captain Elliott. But I bet having patience was never one of them—not even before your cybernetic enhancements. The assimilation process takes time. I suggest you accept that reality as soon as possible."

"Calling me impatient is not an accurate assessment of my character. You don't know me that well yet. I would say my patience level depends on what I am patiently waiting for," Peyton declared. Since she refused to look up at him, he found himself watching Kyra's bent head as her fingers flew across the virtual keyboard. They never stopped for long. What the hell could the woman be writing?

"Assessing your true character is going to be a risky theory to test, but since we may have to relocate soon, I'm going to have no choice but to take that leap of faith with you. Tomorrow we'll do some psychiatric testing. If that goes well, I'll let you out of the cage," Kyra said.

Peyton sat and leaned back on the bed. That was mostly good news. So one more day in the cage, instead of two. He could deal with that.

"Let's talk about something other than me. Do you really think you're being watched by the mysterious

UCN?" He noticed his stoic mad scientist didn't even flinch at the question before nodding. A quick scan of her vitals told him the truth before her words could. Damn it. She was being honest. He had hoped she was exaggerating.

"I don't just think I'm being watched, Captain Elliott. I know I am."

Kyra connected the final disk to the console unit and set the copy process into motion. Then she drew in a relieved breath and blew it out.

"Let's use your UCN query as a segue. To preserve what I've done, I need to leave the UCN's investigation team something to find when they break the codes on my lab security. For that, I need your help—if you're agreeable."

"What's agreeable feel like? Right now I'd much rather go punch the hell out of someone's face. But I admit that little hesitation in your voice intrigues me. What are you nervous about?"

He listened as Kyra snorted, wanting to snort himself when she didn't look at him. Her skin temperature rising was a direct giveaway, but he didn't comment on her blush.

"I see you've re-established full access to your Cyber Husband chip. You're interpreting my vocal signals very well," she said.

Peyton snickered. "Don't flatter yourself. I'm utilizing a very human talent called 'paying close attention'. I'm a damn Captain in the Marines, or at least I was for a large part of my real life. Paying close attention was part of my officer training, and that happened long before the cybernetics were installed."

Kyra still didn't turn around, but mostly so he wouldn't see her blushing. "No. I hate to disagree with you, but I must. What you're doing is listening for changes in my voice modulation and all men have to be taught to do such a thing. Almost no male does that innately. The average man doesn't think what a woman says is important enough." She barely stifled a long-suffering sigh when she saw Peyton grin at her irritated tone.

"My ability to pay attention to you doesn't sound very romantic when you talk about it that way, Dr. Winters. My brain thinks you're pretty damn interesting for a sexy mad scientist bitch. The rest of me doesn't seem to care what you do for a living."

Kyra let the frustrated breath escape. "Didn't we just have a discussion about your flirting and decide it was a bad idea? That goes double now that you hate me. However, I hope you can set your hatred aside to aide me in the process of keeping your restoration a secret until it's one hundred percent completed. To buy us some time, I want to make a video to convince any investigation team I was tweaking your Cyber Husband programming to suit my aggressive sexual needs."

"*Aggressive sexual needs?* Sounds very kinky, Doc. Why the hell would you do that sort of tweaking to a former Cyber Husband? I was sexually trained, remember? I can already tell you're not that kind of woman."

"My sexuality is irrelevant to the ruse. Just answer my question, Captain Elliott. Are you willing to help me or not?"

Peyton picked up the reading device to hide his smile. How could you like a person who might be trying to kill you—or worse? His lower man parts certainly seemed to think Dr. Winters was worth the risk. But what did they know? His dick might be pointing her way every time they talked, but it couldn't advise him what to do about trusting her.

"So let me see if I understand this right. For the sake of fooling some imaginary investigative team, that may or may not be *actually* investigating you, I'm supposed to let you take advantage of me after all. I guess I should have known you were going to turn out to be like all the other women who paid millions of dollars to sleep with me."

When Kyra swiveled in her seat and glared full-on at him, everything below his waist drew tight as he waited for her response. *Stand down*, Peyton ordered, lowering his gaze to his lap. In addition to all the other shit he was learning, now he was fighting the urge to laugh at his nearly out-of-control body reactions. He had gone from wanting to throttle the politely scientific Dr. Winters to wanting to fuck the woman until she didn't remember who or what she was.

Yes—indeed. The woman was lucky he was still in the cage.

"So am I right?" Peyton demanded, unable to keep the grin off his face as he asked.

Kyra shook her head firmly, then swallowed a couple of times until her temper cooled. His snarky summary hurt, but she didn't have to react to it.

"No, Captain Elliott. I'm not going to take advantage of you. I just want to fake that sort of relationship to create a cover story. I have no footage of Marshall touching me, but I have a modest tape of me and Alex. If I leave that one to be found, plus one of you and I kissing, that should be enough data to create suspicions. I want the UCN to believe I'm doing sexual research instead of restoration work on you."

"Did you have consensual sex with the Alex cyborg? Tell me the truth, Doc. I want to know."

"What I did with Alex is separate from what I am asking of you. It has no relevance to our discussion."

"That disclaimer still sounds like a yes." Peyton frowned as he suddenly imagined her hotly kissing someone else the way she had him. If such a thing had happened, it would have been well before their lip lock, but imagining the scene still pissed him off. His mental pictures typically did not cause him anxiety. Maybe he just needed more data about what she described. "Tell me the truth, Doc. I don't know why I care about your relationship to him, but I do."

Kyra turned back to her notes. For a minute she ignored Peyton's pleading and started typing again. But being touchy was not going to win her points with the man in the cage. "Rather than simply repeating it's none of your business, I will say politely that I see no reason to answer your query at this time."

Peyton shrugged even though she wasn't watching him. "Maybe I just want to hear how far you're willing to go for the sake of your mad scientist scheme."

"I'm fifty-two years old, Captain Elliot. What I do with a man is no one's business but mine and his. And I saw Alex as a man, not just a cyborg. It is a matter of discretion to keep my interactions with him private."

When the computer showed her task completed, Kyra swiveled around in her chair to glare at Peyton again.

"Your libido should level soon. After that, the sexual urges you have for me will likely pass. Until that time, keep in mind I wear the controller remote for your restraints. I will gladly use it if you get out of line."

Peyton snorted, then chuckled at her snit. "Well, you already know that's going to happen. Isn't that why all those other millionaire women sent me back? You were right about them not having any complaints in the bedroom though. It's amazing what kind of miracles cybernetic pulses can inspire."

Kyra didn't answer his taunt. Pocketing the last of the data disks, she got up and walked to the lab door. "I'll be back shortly. I need a break. You can take some time to think about my request while I'm gone."

Peyton stared at the lab door after it closed, listening for her receding footsteps. He stood and walked to the door of his cage. Scratching an opening in the artificial skin of one finger of his cybernetic hand, he used some electrical current siphoned off his cage to magnetize it. Reaching his arm between two bars as far as he could, he pointed his magnetized metal fingertip at the cage key she had carelessly left on the desk in her haste to evade his questions.

The key fob, obviously some low metal alloy, unfortunately remained unaffected. But nearly every other metal object on the work table came flying his way.

Peyton laughed and swore as he raked porta-disks and rapid drives off his magnetized finger and onto the floor. It should be entertaining to hear what the easily irritated doctor would say when she saw the mess. He tossed back a metal pen she'd been using as a chew toy and congratulated himself when it landed in nearly the same place it had originally been.

"Oh well. Escaping was at least worth a full cyborg try," Peyton said loudly.

Then he smiled up at the camera recording his every movement and winked as he pulled the already healing skin of his finger back over the metal still showing.

Chapter 8

Nero glanced at the single room sweeper turning rapidly on the counter next to him as he studied the video in silence. He waited for the color on the sweeper to change from red to green before speaking.

"This is very promising, Kyra. Peyton 313 prowls the cage restlessly and has already tried to escape more than once. His disrespectful, yet humorous attempts to anger you are what a normal person might do in his captive circumstances. You'd never identify the man as cyborg unless you saw him use his prosthetics to try and obtain the key."

Nero restarted the video for a third time, watching the action again, including the man's wink at the camera. Captain Elliot was pretty sharp for someone who'd had a good part of his brain rewired yesterday.

"I have Peyton's general schematics, but the military aspects of his prosthetics were not in the original information I pulled on him. Since I left all his secondary chips in place,

"My military clearance was just renewed. I'll pull Captain Elliott's full file so we can have the details of everything that was done to him. Based on his irreverent wink at the camera, he's handling his captivity fairly well. He probably had above average intelligence even before his cybernetic modifications."

Kyra sighed and huffed. "Don't let that Zen act of his fool you. Peyton's been super angry off and on since he woke from the initial assimilation. I was distracted when I left the lab but I can't believe I left the cage key just lying on the desk like that. He likes to torment me with sexual suggestions. I swear I don't see any indications that his libido is leveling out at all. Do you think the pulse effect of a cyborg's prosthetics might make him more interested in sex than the average man?"

Nero chuckled at the irritation in Kyra's voice as well as at the odd question. "A cyborg with an amped up libido would be far too aggressive to constrain physically. I would venture that Captain Elliot's testosterone level is probably the same as mine. However, the man has had ten wives, so chances are he's been getting laid on a steadier basis than most. Could be he's just having withdrawal. Or it could be that he really does have the hots for you, like his teasing indicates. I think you must consider both possibilities as equally feasible."

Kyra rolled her eyes at Nero's automatic support of another male. With the exception of her years with Jackson, she had been alone most of her life. Nero Khalid Bastion—child prodigy and now impressively handsome geek—was her longtime assistant. He had been assigned to her when the Cyber Soldier program was in full swing. He was twenty years her junior and technically young enough at thirty-two to be her child, even though she'd never thought of him that way. Instead, Nero was more like the younger sibling she'd never had, and often as annoying as people said such younger siblings were.

"Sure, Nero. All the cyborgs I rewire get the hots for me afterward. Unfortunately that passion tends to fade really fast once they realize I'm part of the reason they've been enslaved for years."

Kyra had been trying for sarcasm and sighed when it came out sounding wistful. She winced at Nero's chastising look. It was one he seemed to use often with her lately.

"Captain Elliot is not the typical cyborg you have been trying to restore. The other two were modified toward the end of the war, but Peyton 313's design is one of the originals. Despite all his software upgrades, the core programs are likely still the original delta level he received because his unique prosthetics require them. That could easily explain why he rebelled against taking housekeeping orders from his wives. As a Marine Captain, he was programmed to be the giver of orders, not the receiver. I would love to see an EEG image of what happened in his brain every time he refused to do something. It would probably look like a pyrotechnical explosion inside a blast chamber."

Kyra shook her head and laughed. "Wow. That's quite a defense of a man you haven't met in person yet. Are you seriously trying to hook me up with a guy who now hates me enough to want to kill me? I thought we were much better friends than that, Nero."

Hearing her tone finally hit sarcasm level alleviated her nervousness about the subject matter. She never bothered filtering herself for Nero and had no intentions of starting. Instead, she walked calmly over to silence the dancing teakettle from its insistent screaming.

She loved the ancient artifact she had rescued from an antique store. Sure, there were easier and more efficient ways to boil water, but she preferred the old-fashioned ritual of heating it slowly in the device. Waiting the time it took gave her something to do while she calmed her mind.

Lifting the teakettle and its boiling contents, Kyra felt deeply satisfied as she poured steaming hot water over the powdered green tea she'd spooned into each cup. The bubbling froth promised both taste-bud delight and a little mental boost. As she stirred, she decided that it was definitely all the little rituals that made it a pleasure to be alive.

The only downside of her tea ritual today was that it, like nearly everything else, was making her feel even more guilty because Peyton Elliott had been blocked from this kind of enjoyment for years. Since his awareness of his past was growing, she was sure she was going to hear more about his deprivation before his assimilation was finished.

Nero glanced from his screen to Kyra's blushing face. "I'm not encouraging you to do anything with the man.

Actually, I think it's a bad idea for you to get physically involved. I'm just warning you to be aware of probabilities given what I've heard so far."

"Your concern is appreciated, but totally not necessary. I'm hardly the kind of high-end woman Captain Elliott is used to servicing. I've had no lifting or tucking work done at all. I guess I'm in fairly good shape for the most part, but you know I look every bit of my fifty-two years. I admit the man had me convinced he liked me before the assimilation. Sure, I never felt that conflicted with the other two cyborgs I bought, but that doesn't mean I'm willing to forgo my scientific goals for a chance to sleep with a sexually trained cyborg. I'm not that desperate for companionship."

Nero raised his head to look at her again. "You're human, Kyra. And so is Captain Elliot. He's just human *plus*. Isn't that how you always describe the Cyber Soldiers? It would not have been a crime if something intimate between you had happened. Now you have made me curious. What exactly *did* happen between you two?"

Kyra shook her head. "Nothing happened. Or at least nothing important. Peyton can be very charming, that's all. I didn't let him get to me. His friendly manner just made me sincerely regretful to turn his cybernetic programming completely back on."

Nero put his gaze back on the screen. "Maybe you should have let yourself live a little with the human part of him when it surfaced. Have you even let a man into your life since the asswipe died?"

"You know damn well there hasn't been anyone since Jackson. It wouldn't have been good for my cover story of why I needed to buy a Cyber Husband," Kyra declared, sipping her tea. "Since we're talking about our sex lives—how about you? Any good prospects lately?"

Nero shrugged. "There's a new lab tech over in the prosthetics department that I had dinner with last week. She seems nice enough, but isn't as sharp as I would like. We're catching a movie at the Plex this weekend. I'll know after that if she's worth the trouble of sleeping with her."

Kyra sighed in defeat. Nero's man parts were hard-wired to his brain. She never knew whether to feel sorry for him or to admire that he was vastly different from men like Jackson. Her ex-husband had obviously thought happiness came with every piece of strange ass he conquered.

She carried the tea to Nero as she glared at his smirk. "Tell me you're not taking that poor unsuspecting woman to see that awful gamer movie that just came out. I heard they decapitate nearly every character in it before the end."

Grinning, Nero took the cup from Kyra and lifted it to his mouth for a sip. "Okay. I'm not taking her to the gamer movie."

"Yes, you are. You're lying to me, Nero. Your pupils are dilated and your pulse is jumping at your neck," Kyra declared.

Nero laughed. "I'd be a happy man to find a woman half as sharp as you, Dr. Winters."

Kyra huffed. "Right. You just want someone to be responsible for curbing your childish tendencies."

Nero nodded and smiled. "Absolutely. Isn't that what women are for?"

"No wonder you haven't found someone to love you yet. No woman wants to mother the man in her life as well as his children."

Nero grinned as he smoothly changed the subject. "The sweeper is running low on power so let's get back to discussing Captain Elliot. When are you letting him out of the cage?"

Kyra took another sip. "Today—probably right after you leave. I was trying to wait until tomorrow, but. . .something is urging me to move this along quickly."

"Today is a little soon, isn't it? He's still pretty angry at you." Nero sipped his tea and watched Kyra over the edge of his cup.

"It can't be helped. Just hours before he arrived, I turned down twenty million to go back to work in the cybernetics lab. They know I spent the last of my funds on Peyton. I expect the investigation to ramp up to the speed of a mag-train shortly."

Nero's eyebrows shot up. *"Twenty million?* That's a hell of a lot of money to turn down, Kyra."

"It wasn't hard at all," she said firmly. Kyra frowned and remembered how disgusted she had been by the offer. "The next time I set foot in that lab will be the last steps I take in this life."

Nero set down his cup and put both hands over his ears. "I refuse to listen to your Mad Max plans. You know that shit deeply disturbs me."

Kyra put down her cup and pulled Nero's hands from his ears, gripping his fingers with hers.

"If anything happens to me, you're the only one left who can change this. Copies of my research will be everywhere by then, but it would take the inexperienced scientists too long to come up to speed. They'll need someone with your kind of brain to undo this mess, Nero. Jackson was the father of cyborgs, and I am their regretful mother. You may have to be their savior instead of me. Promise me you'll try if it comes to that."

Frowning, Nero used their linked hands to tug Kyra into his arms for a hug. The thought of something happening to her sickened him. "You know I'll always carry on your work one way or the other. But I won't have to if you stick around and do it yourself. Don't do anything stupid, Kyra. That's not your style."

Kyra nodded against his shoulder. When had the dark-haired, dark-eyed teen she'd met morphed into the hard-muscled, chiseled-jawed man in her arms? She pulled back to look up at him. The product of planet conscious parents, he was an only child just as she had been. Nero's father Rajesh was full Indian and a brilliant research doctor. His mother Althea was from Euro-Roman stock and a family that produced nothing but beautiful heirs. The boy had gotten the best of both his parents, but his father's genetics had won out.

"I'm not going to do anything stupid. I'm just going to do what's necessary. Now turn off the sweeper, Nero. I don't need the UCN investigators showing up on my doorstep today. I still have to talk my restored cyborg into letting me fake seduce him."

Nero pulled back to look down at her. "I half wish it wasn't only pretending, and totally wish he wasn't a cyborg. I would like to see you happy, Kyra."

Shaking her head at the improbability of anything real ever happening between her and Peyton Elliott, Kyra pulled away. She didn't need Nero to remind her about the seriousness of her situation. She thought of it each time she contemplated Peyton having to pretend to be her Cyber Husband. She counseled herself about the need for the deception as she carried both their empty tea cups to the sanitizer.

***

Peyton felt his processor shift his body to full alert when the lab door open. Kyra walked to her desk, picked up the forgotten key fob, and pointed it at the cage. The door of his prison slid to one side. He picked up the reading device and walked cautiously to the opening.

"I thought you said I'd get out tomorrow. Is this another test, Doc? You're not going to start chanting codes again the minute I step across this threshold are you?"

"No. I'm letting you out early. You've shown no indications of mental illness outside normal ranges." Kyra tossed the key fob back on the desk and sat in her chair. She swiveled it to face him instead of the console.

"Plus—I still have this." She held up her wrist where his mobile restraint controller flashed the active and armed status every few seconds. "In case you have any ideas about being fast enough to stop me from using it, this one is my own tweaked version. The device is monitoring all my vitals and my stress levels. In case of my death, or even what it determines is a threat, such as a significant pause in my breathing, a failsafe command will send current running continuously through your restraints until I shut it off. The pain level has been specifically set to upper range cyborg levels so it will incapacitate you long enough for your apprehension. I can't have the UCN killing every existing cyborg just because they think you went unexplainably rogue on me."

"You know—you're pretty sharp at strategic planning for a scientist. Think you've covered all the bases, Doc?"

Peyton paused at the open cage door and took a moment to look around the lab. It looked a little less intimidating without the bars blocking his vision. He looked back at Kyra and saw her shaking her head.

"No. I try never to assume anything conclusively. But I used to create men like you for a living and I know how dangerous you can be. I consider my initial precautions of locking you up to be a form of healthy fear. If you kill me after I take the mobile restraints off you. . .? Well, I guess that will be my fault then, won't it?"

Despite Kyra's relaxed state about letting him out, Peyton was still wary as he stepped completely outside the cage. When nothing bad happened, he walked slowly toward her. As nuts as it seemed to his scrambled brain, he wanted to get close enough to smell her again. His lower body twitched in excitement at the potential of arousing her.

"How about we call a temporary truce? After everything I read this morning, I'm at least half convinced now about your reformation. Until I get fully convinced one way or the other, I'm willing to cooperate with your mad scientist plans. Hell, I think mostly I want to see what you're up to. We may have to discuss my patience limit again later if it doesn't happen fast enough though."

"Say no more, Captain Elliott. I understood your compliance was conditional after the first threat. And like I told the man who delivered you to me—you're not my first cyborg."

After she'd finished, Kyra swiveled in the chair again and this time turned her back to Peyton. She heard his surprise at her action in his grunt. She also heard him walk away from her. His retreat brought her a little more ease in his company.

"I'm choosing to trust you too, Captain. I have no choice because things are escalating. I turned down a huge sum of money to return to Norton shortly after I bought you. I'm sure the UCN chancellors are still debating why I did that."

Peyton studied the way her hair fell forward, unsure why he had noticed. "I see we're back to discussing your UCN conspiracy theory. So what's the next item on your cyborg restoration coup list?"

"In about twenty minutes, we're going outside the lab. We'll spend two days making sure any hidden surveillance has picked up your presence in my home as my Cyber Husband. Hopefully we can leave my house after that and it will look like our 'honeymoon' trip. Before we leave the lab though, I would like to make the recording I mentioned. Will you take off your shirt please?"

Peyton stopped pacing around the lab looking at things. He wasn't sure he'd heard correctly. "Sorry—what did you say?"

Kyra sighed, hating that she had to say it again. "If you're willing to help me, I need you to take off your shirt so we can make the recording. Like I mentioned earlier, we're going to make a fake sex tape for the UCN's investigators to find."

She turned her head and adjusted the camera on the far wall until it was pointed toward the operating chair. "There. That should do it."

Kyra stood then and walked to where Peyton was standing and staring at her in confusion. Up close the man was taller and bigger than she remembered. She swallowed her nervousness and hoped he hadn't picked up on it. She took a couple deep breaths hoping they were enough to calm her thundering heartbeat.

"So here are the ground rules, Captain Elliott. I'm not going to ask you to do anything but kiss me. Any arousal you get will be your responsibility to deal with afterward. And you are not to undress me no matter what I say for the sake of the recording. For what we are doing, I don't think it's necessary that I be naked. Please try to play along to the best of your ability. I would like this to be as convincing as possible."

Peyton grinned. "Convincing, huh? Okay. Are you planning to straddle my lap again?"

He was secretly amused by her disclaimers. He vividly remembered her crying last time they kissed. Then suddenly the memory of how badly he had wanted to soothe her slid across it all, effectively wiping his amusement away. Kyra's nervousness was making him want to reassure her now, but he decided her suffering might serve him better.

"So. . .how are we playing this, Doc?"

Kyra dropped her gaze from Peyton's. "I suppose straddling your lap is the best idea. That way we'll both be in the camera's frame at the same time."

"You're making me dizzy with lust just talking about it. Remind me again why we're doing this. I'm planning to chant it as a mantra so I can behave myself while I'm under you," Peyton ordered.

"Stop. Don't be flip about this. Thinking I'm as sexually depraved as Jackson is a hell of lot better than the UCN suspecting I've restored your human decision making abilities. Now will you help me do this or not? You have as much to lose as I do if we don't get this right."

Peyton shrugged. "Okay already. Stop defending your idea. I'm in. But all your talk of kinky stuff is making me feel very dirty, Doc. Can I take a shower first?"

He had asked just to see what Kyra would say in reply to his teasing. Her instant reaction of stepping close to him and sniffing had his mouth twitching along with everything else below his waist. He ended up returning the favor without even meaning to.

Kyra shrugged as she backed away. "You're tolerable for the moment and I want to get this over with. You can shower afterward if you like. Then we've got several other important things to do."

Shaking his head at her matter-of-factness about how he smelled, Peyton pulled off his shirt. He allowed himself a satisfied smirk when Kyra's gaze swept over his chest for a full thirty seconds before she cleared her throat. It was gratifying to know he could shut down that damn scientist brain of hers for even two seconds. The flush from her reaction climbed her face and tightened the semi-erection he always seemed to get in her presence. To cope, he ordered his processor to run full scale diagnostics. Hopefully, the amount of information gathering would keep his mind too distracted to let his dick get completely hard.

"You're staring, Dr. Winters. Keep looking at me like that and you may get more than you expect from this exercise," he warned.

Kyra shook her head trying to clear it. "I'm sorry for staring. It's just been awhile since I saw a shirtless man. That's all."

When she turned her back to him and started for the chair, Peyton hustled around her. He was seated by the time Kyra walked to it. She looked totally suspicious about his sudden enthusiasm, but tightened her jaw. He smiled at the thought of keeping her a bit unbalanced. Inwardly he admitted that he was looking forward to touching her again. Anticipation made his head throb a bit as he got comfortable in the chair.

Kyra raised a tiny remote and pointed it at her work console, her quick gaze telling him they were recording already. "Okay, Peyton. Let's try these tests again. I'm starting the official recording in 5, 4, 3, 2, . . ." She spoke the date and time in a louder voice that she hoped sounded scientific instead of breathless at the idea of kissing Peyton again.

"Are we using the chair restraints this time? I don't understand what I am doing to displease you, Dr. Winters. I am programmed to please my wife. Just tell me what you want me to do," Peyton ordered huskily. He grinned at Kyra's blooming blush at hearing his bedroom voice again.

For the sake of the recording, Kyra considered the bands dangling from the arms of the chair as she stood between his legs. Finally, she shook her head while looking at him. "No restraints this time, Peyton. I want your hands free."

Peyton nodded and smiled. He pulled out the first phrase from his files that seemed like an appropriate response. "What pleases my wife pleases me. Tell me what you desire and I will do as you command."

Kyra did her best to ignore the effect his whispered words had on her body. Stepping up between Peyton's legs, she felt heat radiating from his chest and automatically backed away. Surprise had her drawing in a breath when Peyton's hands circled her waist and dragged her over his lap until she was pretty much where she'd been when they had kissed before.

Her heart pounded hard in sensual alarm as she settled her body over his. Hands free, Peyton's touch was confident and sure, and also way more aggressive than she'd been prepared to deal with. For a reality check, she had to remind herself that Peyton had enough strength to break her in two if he wanted.

"Is this good for you?" Peyton whispered the question and watched Kyra's head nod, but she didn't say anything in answer. He gripped her tighter, holding her in place over where he ached for her, whether it was what she had planned for him to do or not. The predominant thought in his mind was how much better holding her was when he could touch her like he wanted.

"Peyton. . ." Kyra whispered softly. She was embarrassed that she had to clear her throat of huskiness to speak more clearly. Her stammering should at least make the video believable concerning their sexual attraction.

She raised both her hands to his very wide shoulders. In return, Peyton's fingers lightly stroked along her waist while he pulled her across the hardness in his lap with every stroke. With her knees spread she was rubbing against his arousal. Orgasm was highly possible even with so gentle a motion. The man really had been trained well. She wouldn't be able to maintain the ruse that it meant nothing for long. Climaxing would defeat her purpose before she'd even started.

"Rip the front of my shirt open, Peyton." Kyra issued the false order, struggling to make it firm. He was making it nearly impossible for her to think of anything but what he was doing to her.

"According to Lovemaking Guideline thirty-four point six point eight, too much aggression is prohibited and constitutes a violation of Cyber Husband programming," Peyton argued huskily. He felt clever for citing that regulation in response.

His hands slid from Kyra's small waist down to her curvy hips allowing him to increase the pressure of her in his lap. He was sixty-five point two percent done with his cyber diagnostics and eighty-seven point nine percent erect under her. Damn it. Evil scientist or not, Kyra Winters and her barely audible panting was driving him insane with the need to act. He wanted to do this with her for real.

"What if I told you that your programming is insufficient to arouse me, Peyton 313? What if I told you that I need you to be more assertive than your programming advises? Can you exceed that limit when I ask you to?"

He slid his hands under the shirt Kyra was wearing and deftly unhooked her bra at the back. Grinning, he fought not to sigh with satisfaction as she pressed down hard on the part of him that ached for her. Her groan made him deliriously satisfied with himself.

"Kiss me while I run a full analysis of your complaint," Peyton ordered, no longer working at the huskiness of his tone.

As Kyra's mouth covered his reluctantly, Peyton slid his hands to the front to cup her soft naked breasts. Little beaded points burned tiny holes into his palms, even the cybernetic one. His mind responded like a game machine to what they were doing. Sensation after sensation was being recorded, firing across every part of his brain. One hundred percent erection under her was achieved in three point two seconds of her mouth on his. He instinctively pressed Kyra down harder on it for relief, but had to ease up when she called out against his mouth.

"I'm sorry if I hurt you. I have no wish to hurt you," Peyton said sincerely, the words tumbling over each other on the way out.

Stunned by how close she was to forgetting the original purpose of their make-out session, Kyra pulled away from Peyton and sighed loudly. The truth was that she was shaking with arousal and figured he probably knew it.

But it was also true that he still didn't like her very much.

It helped to remember that.

"I know you don't want to hurt me, Peyton. That's our whole damn problem here. This isn't working for us. Run shut down code Tango Charlie 76585."

Since it was part of the programming she had specifically changed in Peyton, Kyra used her hand on his neck to indicate that he should roll his head to the side and pretend to be rendered unconscious.

Peyton did as he hoped Kyra wanted, but left his eyes open and staring. He didn't want to miss any chance of seeing her get naked to right her clothes. He ordered his cybernetic eyes to capture an image every three seconds so he wouldn't miss anything if she did.

Still shaking, Kyra slid from Peyton's lap. Keeping her gaze on him, she reached up under her shirt and fastened her bra back. When she was done, she shook her head and sighed as loudly as she could again. The frustration she felt was real, but the reason for it was a hell of a lot different than what the recording would indicate.

"Damn it, I programmed you and I swear I'm going to find that violence override if it kills me. You're my last hope, Peyton. Don't be like those two duds before you. I'm tired of failing."

Frowning, she turned to where the camera would see her face as she pointed her remote and counted the seconds until the recording stopped.

"Okay. It's done. Thank you, Captain Elliot. You were very convincing."

Peyton rolled his head back and looked at her completely clothed body in surprise. Fuck the recording. He was pissed for another reason. "How the hell did you get your bra refastened without removing your shirt?"

Kyra rolled her eyes at the question. "Stop that. My breasts are not worth the price of a ticket. They're average for my age and unaltered."

"They're warm, soft, and fit my hands well. Plus your nipples are quite responsive. Why didn't you let me give you an orgasm? Your increased respiration and rapid panting indicated you were very close."

"I didn't *let* you because I'm unwilling to reciprocate. That wouldn't be fair to you—or me—because I don't think one time would be enough," Kyra said.

It was difficult to ignore her wet panties as she sat back down at her work desk. She looked over to see Peyton still sitting in the operating chair. He was all but glaring again. Renewed guilt made her wince. "You can get up now, Peyton. We're all done."

Peyton shook his head. "I can't walk unhindered yet."

She ducked her head and slapped a hand down by her console. "I'm not a prick teasing kind of woman, but I am mostly an ethical one. I told you that before we started."

Peyton considered the statement and chose to agree with it. Kyra was sexually frustrating him, but he didn't think she was doing it deliberately.

"What do you think is going to happen when we're sharing a bed in your room, Doc? This arousal situation is going to come up again. I'm highly attracted to you even though part of me still hates your guts. I'm also a heartbeat away from losing my bearing over you. In Marine terms, that's some damn hard data toward proving I really am becoming irrationally human again."

Kyra drew in a breath and let it out slowly. "I don't know what's going to happen between us. I'll just have to cross that bridge when I come to it. At this point though, I don't think it's wise for me to form any sort of personal attachment to you, considering I have to send you away eventually."

"How about you sit on my bridge support post tonight and we'll discuss your attachment issues after I've made us both feel better a few times?" Peyton asked.

"Bridge support post?" Kyra was too surprised by his use of such a strange term to be offended at the blatant pass he was making.

Peyton rose to a straight sitting position. His brain hurt and he couldn't access the right term for the force absorbing metal beams holding up a bridge. "I can find no better word at the moment. I guess choosing wrong ruined my joke, didn't it?"

"Hmm..." Kyra said, getting up to walk back to him.

On the way, she grabbed his shirt and carried it with her. She watched him put it back on and chided herself for feeling regret.

"That kind of blip is mildly concerning. We'll need to keep an eye on your inability to access information when in stressful situations. It could be that hormonal surges in both genders have a more profound effect on cybernetics than we realized. I knew that was the case with women. No one ever investigated the effect of arousal in male cyborgs. Maybe there's a difference between organic desire and performing on command."

"That's too much geek speak about something simple, Doc. I get hard whenever you're near, which would scramble any man's mind—cyborg or human. Your real husband was an idiot to leave a woman as sexy as you. I bet I could easily give you three or four orgasms per lovemaking session. I bet you could give me one that would shut my brain down faster than the creator code did."

"Stop, Peyton. That's an experiment I can't engage in with you. And I can't discuss this anymore," Kyra said, walking back to her desk. "Let me save the recording and I'll give you a tour of the rest of the house."

"If you're being monitored, I'll need to follow standard protocol and perform husband duties for you." Peyton waited for a reaction but got none. "Kyra, did you have a personal relationship with Alex? Considering I have to act like your actual Cyber Husband, I've decided the information is pertinent. I need to know how to conduct myself."

Ignoring the little thrill she got from Peyton saying her name, Kyra got up and walked to the door, motioning for him to follow. She supposed he had a point about needing to know.

"Alex and I were barely able to pull off anything normal at all. We had a moment in the beginning, but one that never went anywhere. After his full assimilation, Alex never got aroused with me again. Maybe it was because I replaced most of his chips with blank ones he could self-program with new experiences. I pulled his Cyber Husband chip during the initial restoration so maybe I wasn't his natural type. Depression affects libido too, so that's yet another possibility. Alex wasn't alive long enough for us to discover the real cause of his disinterest.

He slept beside me without complaint. Since I wasn't interested in using him for sex, investigating his lack of interest in me was not at the top of my list of concerns."

Peyton felt sorry for his predecessor, but couldn't keep the grin from his face. The strange feeling of relief coursing through him cleared something critical out of the way. Suddenly, the analysis data was available to his mind, as well as many other things.

"*Trusses*," he said in epiphany. "Bridges use *trusses*. That's what I meant to say earlier. And I now I get your metaphor as well. You're definitely going to have to cross that bridge with me eventually, Doc. The interest I have in you is not going away until we resolve what's between us."

Peyton saw her nod at the correct term as she stepped across the lab's threshold.

Chapter 9

Across town, Nero sat in the cloaked area of his living room going over the data Kyra had replicated for him. It included a recording she'd had the lab cameras take during the entire nineteen hour assimilation process. Her tears over Peyton 313 alarmed him because he couldn't recall ever seeing Kyra cry so much before, not even over Jackson. She'd had a moment or two with the other cyborgs after their deaths, but his gut was telling him Kyra's feelings for Captain Elliott were something vastly different.

After watching some of the segments several times, Nero put his concern for Kyra's emotional state away to focus on an even bigger problem he was starting to suspect. If he was right, Kyra's latest cyborg was running some sort of secondary programming. He wasn't sure how it had survived the restoration, but something in Peyton 313's cybernetics seemed to be intentionally recording tons of data—all kinds of data. Nero had a hunch the secondary programming had always been running in the background, even when Peyton's primary processor had been missing. That meant the extra processor had to have its own power source, though where it could reside in the man was a bit of a mystery.

What he feared was some part of Peyton hadn't shut down even when Kyra had disabled the cybernetics with the creator's code. If that was the case—it meant Captain Peyton Elliott was a cyborg plant.

Nero poured over the cyborg's EEG records looking for blips in normal brain activity. Finally, he found what he'd been searching for. When he correlated the blip with Peyton's time in the cage, he found a missing segment of the lab recording close by—just under eight minutes worth to be exact. Since it looked more like scrambling than erasure, Nero picked up his handheld com.

"Hey Brad. Are you available right now? I need your magic on some data I'm analyzing for Kyra. Yeah sure, I'll pay the usual—German beer and Thai food. No problem. Great. Come as soon as you can."

He ordered the food after they disconnected. A few minutes later, a slender man appeared on his building monitor requesting entry. Brad's condo wasn't far from his, but he'd made the trip in record time. Brad popped through the door when he buzzed him through.

"Dude—I tried to beat the food here. Thought I'd take a quick look at it before we eat. Can I attach?"

Nero swung his portable toward Brad when his skinny friend landed in the chair next to his desk. "Start at 23:28. The cyborg was shut down and in the second half of a complete reboot. According to Kyra's visual records, Peyton was asleep while assimilating his cybernetic data. But there's an eight minute stretch of recording showing nothing but snow. If something happened during that time period, I want to know about it."

Nero watched Brad shove a porta-disk into the free connect port on the side of his machine. Accessing a small window, Brad typed a couple old-fashioned commands to boot the app manually. Nero swore when his portable launched into over-juicing mode, its crystalline energy pack straining and complaining under the program's demands.

"Damn it. Don't fry my new portable, Brad. I just got it."

"The manual boot on this new version of the app is hell. It takes a lot to get her started, but after that she hums normally. Kind of like my girlfriend. I named the application after her," Brad said, grinning at the glare directed his way. "Relax, bro. I got this. If there is anything under that snow, Gloria will find it. Well holy shit, dude. You were right. Look at this."

Nero leaned in as Brad typed and enhanced. They saw Peyton 313 get up from the bed and walk to the cage door. Reaching up to his scalp, he opened a compartment on the side of his head, but not the one where his cybernetics were installed. He took something out of the extra compartment—it looked a bit like a security bypass—and pointed it at the cage door. When it slid open, he walked out and over to Kyra's desk. He took another small device out of the same compartment and put it under her desk on a small ledge meant to hold a power cable. Then he turned and walked back into the cage. He said something that was unintelligible through the snow and the door slid shut like it had been programmed to obey his voice commands.

Peyton 313 then returned to his sleeping position like nothing had happened.

Nero leaned back in his chair and shook his head. So Captain Peyton Elliot—Cyber Husband number three for Kyra—was indeed sent to spy on her. Norton really was investigating and they had spared no expense to do it. Part of him had secretly hoped it was just grief over the dead asswipe making Kyra paranoid. She had never really recovered from Jackson's defection. She'd retired rather than work on children. . .and he got that. Hell, if his job had involved hurting kids, he would have refused to do it as well.

Now the question was whether or not the data stored in the device under her desk had been sent out already. That had to be determined before they could do anything to the cyborg. Brad could help them alter the records on the device, but nothing could change the fact that Norton was never going to leave her alone. With Jackson dead, Kyra Winters was the only person alive with full creator knowledge. And she had so far refused to give anyone the secrets to the creator code—not even to him. All attempts to decode it had resulted in melted files. Even Brad hadn't been able to crack it yet.

"Dude—you have to tell Dr. Winters her new Borg Man is a double-wired bad guy," Brad declared.

Reviewing it again, he watched the cyborg re-enter the cage and fasten the door behind him. It gave him a chill when the unit laid back down and went to sleep. "Spooky shit that he did all that and never tried to actually escape the lab. That's some radical programming."

Nero nodded. Not only did he have to tell Kyra that Captain Peyton Elliott was double-wired, he also had to get her away from the cyborg before it was too late.

"Capture that blip as best you can. Download the part that shows what happened to a separate file. You know how much a stickler for details she is. Kyra is never going to believe me unless I can show her both the snow and what's under it. But we also need to admit to ourselves that the cyborg games have started for real now. Pass the word along to everyone. Kyra has to move quickly."

Brad frowned and nodded. "Hope that beer gets here soon. I'm going to need some lubrication to deal with this heavy shit. Guess I better tell the real Gloria I don't have time to get her processor revving tonight."

Nero slapped Brad on his back as he rose. Life was about to change for all of them. Fortunately, Peyton 313 wasn't the only one with secrets.

***

"I don't understand, Doc. The master bedroom is down the hall. Why do you sleep in this much smaller room?"

Peyton estimated walking from one wall to the other would take no more than eight steps. He tested his theory and discovered it was accurate. He paced the width of the room a second time to confirm.

Kyra walked to the closet and slid it open. The guest room was much smaller than the master, but she had made it her own space. That's what mattered most because it allowed her to stay in the house after Jackson left. She lifted her black robe from a hook inside the tiny closet, then got her favorite pajamas from their shelf.

"It's just a matter of personal choice and I prefer to sleep in here. However. . .in the master bedroom closet you'll find an assortment of men's clothing. You're welcome to use any of it. Some of it I purchased for Alex.

Some of it is Jackson's old clothing. I don't have any men's pajamas, but there are exercise shorts that should do for tonight."

Peyton narrowed his gaze on her face checking for signs of nervousness. All he found was a bone deep weariness that had dramatically reduced her overall heat signature. Kyra Winters badly needed rest.

"Thank you, but I don't require clothing to sleep. They should be shipping my belongings here shortly. I don't know why it wasn't packed and delivered when I was. According to my files, that is standard procedure when a Cyber Husband is delivered to a new wife."

"Norton probably thought I wouldn't really keep you. Who knows? I'm tired and heading to the shower, Peyton. And whether you do or not, *I require* you to wear clothing to bed. I sleep on the left side. You can have the right. It's a queen mattress, but there should be enough room for the two of us."

Kyra's calm irritated him. He wanted her to be aroused again in his presence. Something insistent in him wanted to make her feel that way. "As you wish, Doc. I'm looking forward to sharing your bed under any circumstances."

"Don't start flirting again. I'm too tired to deal with it tonight." On the way out, Kyra stopped in the bedroom door and held up her wrist. "All we're doing tonight is sleeping. Do I need to remind you about our earlier discussion? I do not require your sexual services."

Peyton stared at her. Her thundering heartbeat did not match her calm words. And her smell. . .no that had to be ignored for now. "I recall each discussion we've had specifically, if that's what you're asking. Would you like me to pull up the data and read one back to you for proof?"

Kyra shook her head, almost too tired to do so. Her tiredness had taken over after they had eaten. "That won't be necessary if you keep a respectful distance between us. You can use the bathroom next to the master bedroom to prepare for bed. I never go in there anymore, but I think the cleaning service has kept it stocked with supplies."

"Why do you not go in there?" Peyton asked.

"Because it's haunted by ghosts," Kyra replied, trying to be patient. She wanted his cooperation, but Peyton was treading on ground she wasn't ready to cover with him yet.

Peyton stared at Kyra for another thirty-five seconds before answering. "There is no scientific proof that ghosts exist. Your belief in their existence is illogical, Dr. Winters."

Kyra rolled her eyes and sighed at his very rational observation. "Yes. I tell myself that all the time. But when I go into that room, I still see a frightened woman tied helplessly to the bedposts while her husband did all sorts of horrible things to her."

"I see." Well, he didn't yet. . .but he sure as hell intended to find out. "Too bad you lack the ability to completely erase a sight like that from your memory. I guess that's one positive about being a cyborg."

Responding calmly to her explanation was very challenging when he wanted to have one of those outbursts she kept warning him about. He didn't allow himself to do so because he was afraid she would put him back into the cage if he did.

Kyra sighed and nodded. "Yes. I've often thought it would be nice to forget the whole thing completely. It's okay though. The woman managed to get over it by moving into this bedroom. A month later her husband moved out of the house and never bothered her again. That was years ago. Now she's mostly over it."

"The ghost—are you saying the frightened woman tied to the bedposts was you?"

"Yes, Captain Elliot. And I'm also saying I can't go back to that room to sleep. Any more questions before I get clean? I'm nearly too tired to bathe."

Peyton heard a clicking in his head and realized he was snapping his teeth together. "No. I have no more questions. I'll be here waiting for your return. I promise I will be wearing clothing of some sort."

Nodding at his agreement, Kyra slipped down the hall.

Peyton felt his anger rising. He looked around for something to bend in half, but there was nothing. He paced the width of the small room several more times until the feeling of wanting to kill someone receded to a manageable level. Finally he headed to the master bedroom in search of clothing. She had given him no other choice.

He glanced at the bed in the room, imagined Kyra tied to it for real, and vowed to destroy it first chance he got. Any decent man, cyborg or not, would have done the same. After directing his time management program to make a note about doing so, he went to the closet.

On one side were beautiful dresses and an assortment of feminine footwear. He slid a red high-heeled shoe from its storage space and held it in his hands. He couldn't imagine Kyra Winters—flat sandal wearing cyber scientist—walking around in such a thing. Putting it back, he moved his attention to the other side.

As Kyra had indicated, there was a variety of male clothing. Hoping to use some of the previous cyborg's clothes, instead of anything belonging to the dead man who had obviously abused Kyra, he ordered his cybernetic eyes to scan the cloth in a way he could determine which threads looked newest. Several pair of jogging shorts made the list. He held a pair up to his lower half and saw the fit would be a bit tight but manageable.

Peyton carried them into the master bathroom. His shower time was calculated for maximum efficiency because he wanted to be in bed and settled in before Kyra got there. He also wanted time to set his mood to a more calming level that would foster her trust and let her rest.

He was adjusting his pillow when Kyra finally returned. Reaching over, he flipped the covers back so she could climb in beside him. She did so hesitantly, sighing as she stretched out. Her stretching froze when he scooted next to her and pulled her tense body against his.

"I am wearing the clothing you requested. Please allow this minimal contact for warmth and relaxation. It will help you rest," he whispered, sweeping her damp hair back. "Now close your eyes, Doc. You are completely safe with me tonight. I won't exceed the boundary you've set."

His hands traveled over her shoulder and down her arm to her elbow, kneading the tension away. He saw the controller on her wrist and briefly thought about removing it. He'd cracked the code on his restraints about two hours ago. But he knew if she woke without it, his tired mad scientist would be greatly alarmed.

Kyra grunted her resistance to Peyton's strokes even as she spoke, but his hand rubbing her hip soon had sighs shuddering out of her. "Your massage may just be the best thing that's happened to me in years. I can see why all those women bought you, Peyton."

Peyton used one finger to gently tap her lips. "Flattery will only cause you problems you don't want. Sleep tonight, Dr. Winters. We'll resume our sarcasm swap in the morning."

Two minutes and seven seconds later, Kyra's even breathing told him she had indeed fallen asleep. He took it as a compliment after what she had revealed to him earlier. Tucking her body tighter against his, Peyton relaxed. He felt oddly content despite the hardness between his legs that would find no relief. He lay awake for another hour, cataloging his contentment, and trying to analyze why it felt so good. Finally he put his processor into quiet mode while his physical body followed Kyra's into sleep.

Chapter 10

Kyra woke abruptly when a large hand clamped itself tightly over her mouth. She reached up to grab at the restraining fingers only to hear Peyton making shushing sounds in her ear. Alarm skittered through her, but not about the potential intruders. Peyton's husky whispers were making her nipples pebble and chill bumps dance along her arms.

"There are two men in the house," Peyton reported. "One has a faint accent. They are actively looking for you because you weren't answering your handheld. I believe you now about being investigated."

Kyra relaxed and nodded, glad when Peyton's fingers finally left her mouth. "It's okay, Peyton. It's just my assistant, Nero. He's the only one with the house entry code. When he's stressed or excited, his New Delhi accent returns. Let me up and I'll go talk to him."

"I'm not sure it's safe. Their adrenalin levels are spiked and they reek of fear. It's so strong I'm not smelling you any longer," Peyton said, pulling her tighter.

"Captain Elliott—listen to me. I am safer with Nero than I am with you. Now let go of me so I can get out of bed," Kyra ordered.

When he finally did as she'd requested, Kyra rolled to the edge of the mattress and away from over six feet of warm, hard male. Regret had her huffing in mild protest as her feet hit the cold floor. Her aroused body was rebelling every way possible, but there was no going back to the warmth of Peyton curled around her, especially not with Nero prowling the house in concern.

Stomping to the bedroom door, Kyra yanked it open and stuck her head out. "Hey Nero—I just got up. Give me a minute and I'll meet you in the kitchen."

At Nero's mumbled okay, Kyra closed the door and headed to the chair where she had tossed her robe the night before. Belting it on over her t-shirt and sleep shorts, she turned to Peyton who was still watching her with a narrowed gaze.

"Some of your circuits must be malfunctioning this morning. I promise you there's no danger. It's Nero and probably his friend Brad. They must have stopped by on their way to work."

Peyton snorted. How had he ever thought this woman was evil? It must have been the lab coat. The naïve doctor obviously had no abilities to discern between friends and foes.

"Unless you want to admit you cyber scientists screwed up royally with me, my senses are shouting there damn well is cause for concern in this situation. Now I repeat—both men have elevated heart rates and I'm smelling high levels of adrenalin on them. That always means something is wrong, Dr. Winters."

Kyra shook her head and frowned. "No. You're still calibrating. Your sensory data is just now being understood by your human side. Stop trying to convince yourself there's a reason for unease." At his huffing and whispered swearing, she sighed. "Think of it this way—people under thirty-five have a way of turning everything in their life into something worthy of high drama. Have you seen what they consider entertainment? Violent vid games. Movies that have no redeeming purpose. Nero probably had some minor crisis at home this morning—something he dramatically decided couldn't wait until a reasonable hour to contact me."

"Since I see no matching signs of stress in you at the moment, I will defer to your judgment about those two men. However, my Cyber Husband programming is nagging me to enter full protection mode because the intruders are both anxious and unknown males to me."

Kyra stopped and pondered what Peyton might do if left alone, but she had to risk it. She needed to privately find out what had Nero in such a tizzy that he would use his key code to her house. He had done that exactly twice in twenty years and this was a third time.

"Look Captain Elliot—I can't have you going all full-blown cyborg on me in front of those men. Stay in this room until I see what they want. Run diagnostics again. Accessing the Cyber Husband chip should be completely voluntary by now so there's no reason for you to feel the need to follow any warnings it makes concerning me. *Now* what's wrong, Peyton? You're making a horrible face."

"I am?" Genuinely surprised, Peyton reached up and stroked his lightly bristled chin. His facial hair grew slower since he got the cybernetics installed, but he still had to shave a couple times a week. He felt the edges of his mouth forming a frown that matched Kyra's. "Something is off with those men. I don't know what it is, but I'll occupy myself with running diagnostics while you're gone. I'm also going to slip quietly across the hall to utilize the facilities."

"Fine. Do whatever you need to for yourself. Just don't come charging out to my kitchen, acting like a some jealous lover in front of Nero and Brad. I know that's the first suggestion in your husband programming to intimidate males you consider a threat. I swear to you those men out there are like younger brothers to me. Plus I don't want Nero more worried. He's already concerned you're going to hurt me and I don't know why he feels that way. He never worried about me being alone with Marshall or Alex."

Peyton snorted again, but louder this time. The woman wouldn't recognize an actual alpha male if she saw one. Her time had been spent with too many cerebral men. "Fine. I will remain here, but I will continue to listen for danger. If you have not returned by the time my diagnostics have finished, I will have no choice but to come looking for you. I will try to behave in an appropriate manner based on your directions instead of my inclinations."

"Thank you," Kyra said, relieved as she nodded and hurried out the door.

Peyton thought of how warm Kyra had been in his arms and how much he resented the men appearing when they did. This situation was not how he'd planned to wake her up this morning. He lay back down and closed his eyes to direct all his energy away from missing Kyra to his mental tasks.

***

When Kyra walked into the kitchen, both men let out audible gasps as they looked her up and down in her pajamas and robe.

"Did you two stop for java triple shots on your way here? Damn it, Nero. Peyton is aware of your stress and curious as hell about it. So calm down before we have a cyborg meltdown incident right here in the kitchen."

She watched them look at each other in stunned surprise. Before either spoke, they took several calming breaths. Sighing, Nero reached a hand out and gave her a porta-disk. He lowered his speech to a mere whisper.

"Here's the work you asked me to review, Kyra. Some of the findings are in a separate file. It's privacy level seven coded because I felt it was necessary. When you see what we discovered, you'll understand the precautions I took. I hate to say this, but you need to leave your house today. And you need to pack lightly—very, very lightly. Leave everything behind that you can stand to leave behind—and I mean *everything*."

Kyra closed her hand around the disk as her stomach sank with Nero's unspoken implications.

"Why? Do you think he. . .that. . ." She stopped the stammering question just before she said his name. She drew in a breath to rephrase her query, but Nero interrupted before she could speak again.

"We don't think, Kyra. *We know.*"

Kyra squeezed the disk even tighter. She knew if she freaked out about Nero's suspicions and got herself into a physical uproar, Peyton would for sure come running down the hall to pseudo-rescue her. As her brain searched frantically for a way to make sense of the situation, Alex and the shame he had never been able to shed popped into her head. Peyton had shown no signs of shame or remorse or any emotion resembling regret over his life at all. She had thought his constant anger was a more positive sign, but something could be suppressing those softer human emotions.

She had been willing—maybe even wanting—to excuse any lack of them as just being the type of male Peyton was. But now? Well now, she didn't know what to think. Nero was insinuating she'd slept snuggled up with a bad guy last night. Given more time, she might have figured out on her own whether or not Peyton was a walking, talking UCN spy. Evidently she didn't have the luxury of time anymore.

"Kyra? Are you okay?" Nero watched the play of emotions run across Kyra's face. He was suddenly sorry he'd had to share such bad news so soon. "To be fair, we've not had a chance to fully examine what information is being collected. We also don't know if the information is merely being stored or transmitted daily."

"If information is being collected, you can be sure it is for a purpose detrimental to me," Kyra said flatly. She spoke as calmly as she could, considering she wanted to scream.

Nero nodded once to confirm his similar understanding. "We will need access to your lab to find out for sure."

Conceding the wisdom of his request, Kyra nodded. Stepping back from Nero, she raised her voice and strove to sound as irritated with Nero as she could.

"Okay. Fine, Nero. You can use my lab for your gaming, but Peyton is showing signs of multiple malfunctions this morning. If his blips continue, I may need the lab back quickly. You can have an hour in there—*but just one.*"

Kyra watched Nero nod, then they both looked at Brad who was now the color of chalk. His gaze bounced warily to the kitchen doorway every few seconds. She rubbed Brad's arm briefly as she walked ahead of them down the hall. A very talented cyber scientist, Brad had been in the last group of young techs she'd trained before she left Norton. He'd been pulled away from her area after a few weeks and sent to work on one of Jackson's older projects. She didn't know Brad well, but he and Nero had become almost instant friends. It helped that Brad was a sympathizer for their cause so he well knew what was at stake with Peyton's restoration.

At the lab door, she coded it open and stepped aside to let both men enter. "You won't be able to get out without me. I'll check back in an hour."

Nero nodded. "Don't let us keep you from enjoying your morning with your new husband. I know you made the lab sound proof. I'm sure we won't hear you in the act of consummating."

Kyra knew Nero was teasing to create a cover for the sake of Peyton's enhanced hearing, but his words stung because sex with Peyton was never going to happen.

"Shut-up smartass. You know I haven't been able to bypass his violence settings yet. Thanks to Jackson I outgrew vanilla bedroom companions long ago. So until I fix Peyton 313, my new Cyber Husband and I are abstaining. Instead of sex, I'll be making us breakfast while you two are dorking around in my lab."

Nero gave Kyra a mildly chastising look as Brad ducked his head and scurried into the lab. He wasn't keen on embarrassing his reluctantly helpful friend who idolized Kyra, but to give her credit, the ruse was perfect for any recording that might be happening. He'd just have to fill Brad in later about why Kyra talked that way about Jackson.

Nero leaned into her and hugged. "Thanks for letting us use the lab. We won't need more than a hour—I promise."

***

Kyra waited until the door slid shut behind them before sighing loudly. She ordered the security to start its random cycle again. When she turned, Peyton was watching her intently with those golden eyes of his that softly glowed with his cycling cybernetic power. At first the unusual implants had disturbed her. Now she acknowledged they suited the rest of his intensely curious nature.

"Kids and their damn video games," she said sharply. "More power. It's always a search for more power. Were you ever a gamer, Peyton?"

He nodded while studying her face, not liking the rapid eye movements that kept Kyra's gaze from locking naturally to his. What had made her suddenly nervous about revealing her true thoughts to him? Had he done something to offend her?

"If I'm recalling my childhood correctly, I played military games until I was able to enter the actual service. Outside of that I preferred sports."

"Figures you would go into the Marines then," Kyra replied, walking past him. "Come to the kitchen. I'll make us some breakfast. They're allowed one hour in there and then I'm booting them out."

Peyton turned to follow her. "I noticed you lied to Nero about your sexual preferences. Do you do that with everyone in your life?"

Kyra glared at his question. "You don't know me well enough to draw that conclusion. But yes—what I said just now was meant to create a diversion. I prefer the men in my life to stay out of my business, even those I give a key code to my house for emergency use."

Peyton grinned. "Does that include me? When we were kissing, you seemed pretty interested in letting me into your *business*."

Kyra shrugged at Peyton's flirting, but smiled at his cleverness. "I see you've learned to use innuendo since yesterday. Maybe my fabrications with men and my kissing you were both just momentary lapses in good judgment prompted by my irrational human side."

Peyton grinned at her accelerated heartbeat as Kyra nervously attempted to divert his speculation. It didn't work, but he gave her a few points for trying. "You know Doc, for a scientist you sure use the word *maybe* a lot, especially when it comes to talking about yourself."

Kyra opened her mouth, then shut it again. It suddenly occurred to her that Peyton's keen observation of her habits and preferences might be part of the information he was collecting. "You have a good point, Captain Elliot. I'll try to be more precise in my descriptions going forward. Let's go to the kitchen. I can't think well when I'm hungry."

***

Later in her room Kyra collected a hundred-year-old titanium wrist portable from a dresser drawer. Upgrading the artifact to function with modern porta-disks had given her a hobby that filled the lonely hours after her divorce was final. Sure—by the time Jackson had left for real, she had been glad to see him gone. It was just the sudden silence in her once lively house that had taken considerable adjustment time. She had eventually learned to use it for something other than feeling sorry for herself.

The upgraded artifact had once been only a time keeping device. The expensive fusion crystal now running in it had been a crazy extravagance, but one she was glad she had made. The wrist unit provided a very discreet way for her to view Nero's research.

After checking that it worked, she slipped the wrist unit into the same pocket of her robe containing the disk, then gathered up the rest of her clothes. Having once again sent Peyton to the master bedroom and bath, she trekked into the guest bath across the hall. She turned on the exhaust fan and the shower to create cover noise. Sliding the disk Nero had given her into the wrist unit's reader, she muted the sound completely. Then she watched in disbelief as Peyton easily overrode her security to exit the electrically charged cage.

Quickly removing the disk from the unit, she put both into the pocket of the jeans she had hastily pulled on. Now she knew what Nero and Brad were doing in her lab. They were trying to alter the data Peyton's planted device might have already picked up. She was suddenly very grateful that her admiration of Tesla's Faraday cage shielding had prompted her to add similar shielding to the lab. If she was lucky, the shielding had prevented any broadcasting. If not, soon Norton would for sure know that she'd managed restoration on Peyton. Or at least she'd managed it to the degree she'd been aware of based on Peyton's standard cybernetics.

Obviously Nero's data extraction had raised other questions about his programming. For starters, how did Peyton crack her security codes? She had done that coding by herself. No one had those codes but her. But more importantly—was Peyton aware of what he'd done? Or was the secondary programming somehow running outside the knowledge of his primary processor?

Her suspicions went immediately to Nero who could be working against her while pretending to support her intentions of liberating the Cyber Soldiers. Thoughts that he might be the one betraying her threatened to explode her heart with more hurt than she could bear. If she ruled out Nero, the only other person who had even half the creator knowledge, then who other than him had the level of talent needed to wire in a secondary processor in a way that kept the primary one unaware? And if it had been successfully done to Peyton, what the hell had they done to the other cyborgs?

She believed Nero and Brad's theory. Peyton had to be double wired. That was the only explanation for his capabilities. But knowing who was responsible wasn't going to change anything. Even though the process was outlawed and illegal, she knew double-wiring had been done on several cyborgs as a test. The problem was that in all of the experiments, it had led to dueling processors, which led to mental meltdowns of the worst kind. One cyborg had gone uncontrollably berserk and destroyed a lab before they could shut him down. Mental instability combined with enhanced strength was just not a good combination.

Kyra chewed her lip. Should she do what Nero suggested and just disappear without taking Peyton along? Dressed in a tank top covered by an oversized sweater, she left the bathroom and headed down the hall, determined to figure it out in the next hour or two.

At the master bedroom door, she halted and gaped at the amount of destruction taking place in the room. "What the hell are you doing?" The irritated demand popped out of her mouth all on its own.

Peyton glanced Kyra's way, but didn't answer as he stacked the last piece of the four poster bed against one wall. "I found several references to ghostbusting in my long term data storage. I like the way that sounds as an explanation of my unauthorized actions with the bed."

Kyra swallowed, too stunned over what he was doing to argue. She had been meaning to get rid of the damn bed—and she would have—eventually. She just hadn't gotten around to it.

"Okay. Fine. Thank you for your empathy about my ghosts. There's room in the pod garage if you want to store the pieces out there until I can call to donate them. My ex took the pod when he left. I intended to buy an air jet, but find it's easier to rent when I have need."

Peyton nodded. "If you need me to see to the bed's complete removal, just let me know. By the way—it's been over an hour, Doc. Time to evict the gamers from your lab."

Kyra sighed. "Yes I know," she said quietly, trying not to reveal her true thoughts. "I was just on my way to do it. Are you going to able to see to all this—*ghostbusting*—by yourself?"

"Yes. I'm fine working alone. Can I remove the unnecessary men's clothing from the closet as well? I've collected the only pieces I can use. You said you wouldn't be buying another version of me. I believe that makes the ill-fitting clothes unnecessary to keep."

Kyra ran a hand through her hair. His conclusions were a calculation of data collected from their various discussions. The task would at least keep him occupied while she talked to Nero.

"Sure. I guess that would be okay too. Can I ask what motivated you to do my *ghostbusting* this morning?"

Peyton set his task aside and rose to walk to her. He watched her slowly look up into his face with a thousand questions in her gaze. He hoped they would find the time for him to answer them all. It was certainly a pleasant sensation to be hopeful. "It's my Cyber Husband training. I wouldn't want you to give me a bad rating in domestic tasks outside the bedroom."

Kyra snorted before she smiled. Peyton had the uncanny talent of being the only person she'd ever met with the power to continually amuse her. "Now you're mocking me, aren't you?"

He grinned at the twinkle in her gaze. "Yes. I believe I am, Doc. I'm discovering I have the same talent for humorous evasions as you do."

Motivated by the longing in his gut, Peyton reached out a hand to run his thumb gently over Kyra's bottom lip. She had been right about the PSI measurements. It was fairly easy to access the right pressure to use. Her slight quivering response was very appealing even against the reduced sensation of his cybernetic hand.

Kyra laughed at her instant physical reaction to Peyton's gentle stroking. Every woman who wasn't dead would be attracted to a man who could flirt as well as him. But never in her wildest dreams would she ever have thought *she* would like someone so physical. Peyton was military on both sides, not just his cyborg one. Everything would always be about conflict and its resolution. But then again, everything in her life was about that too at the moment.

She sighed under his gentle ministrations. "Thanks for getting rid of the bed for me. It was a dreaded task I just hadn't taken time to do."

Peyton lowered his hand without replying. But he did lean forward and replace his stroking thumb with his lips.

Feeling weakened by his gentle actions, Kyra didn't even try to step away when Peyton's head lowered. The kiss was light and friendly, as well as oddly reassuring. But it was just as powerful as the others they had shared. With his talented mouth sweeping across hers with focused precision, it was almost too hard a leap to accept Peyton might also be programmed to apprehend her. Knowing how Jackson had viewed the world, her sensual capitulation made a sick kind of sense. The kind of ease growing between her and Peyton could very well be what Norton's diabolic double-wiring bastards had been hoping would happen between them. They probably knew Peyton's kissing expertise had the capacity to make a normally intelligent cyber scientist forget her own damn name.

When Peyton finally let go of her mouth, she moved out of reach. "I'm going into the lab to talk to Nero. Don't leave the house. It's not safe yet," she ordered.

Peyton nodded. "No worries about that, Doc. I'm not going anywhere without you—I promise."

Kyra digested the various nuances of Peyton's too easy acceptance of her physical limits as she headed down the hall. But she didn't doubt for a single moment that he would keep his word.

Chapter 11

Nero walked to meet Kyra as she came through the lab door. "We securely wiped the device but no one should be able to tell without a forensic investigation. Brad's a genius at not leaving a technical footprint behind. We also put it in your electromagnetic containment drawer for a couple minutes just to be sure we killed the device's ability to record. It's dead and now back in its hiding place. And we left your cyborg mole's DNA on it so the UCN will think it was destroyed accidentally. Eventually he will check on it. You can count on that order being part of his special programming."

Kyra ran a hand over her hair. She needed a haircut, but hadn't had any personal time in weeks. "Thank you for destroying the bug—or whatever it is. I'm still trying to decide what to do about Peyton."

"*What to do?* There is only one decision here, Kyra. Your restored cyborg isn't really restored. He's double-wired," Nero protested.

Kyra nodded. "Yes. You've made that abundantly clear, Nero. But they had to copy over the creator code file to the slave processor to make them work together. There is no other programming choice that I'm aware of at this time. Chances are good, as an original creator, I have override access to the secondary processor."

Nero glared. "If that were true in this case, then why didn't both sides of him shut down when you did the initial restoration reboot?"

"Maybe they did. Maybe the secondary processor restarted when his consciousness returned. If the connection is wireless, Peyton could even now be getting new instructions for it while he's roaming my unshielded house. I can't know at this point, Nero. Whatever the case is, it doesn't change my goals for restoring him," Kyra declared.

"All those *maybes* could get you killed by a double-wired, rogue cyborg who may be programmed to forget how much he likes you," Nero argued.

Kyra released a slow breath, exasperated but unwilling to cut Peyton loose and risk his return to a full cyborg life. The first thing Norton would do is put the controller wiring back in him. Maybe her reaction to his friendly kiss was still affecting her, but the thought of Peyton suffering again made her own body ache in sympathy.

"I understand there are a number of variables we can't determine. Maybe Peyton only likes me because they're making him feel like he does. That potential reality hasn't eluded my thinking either. We could debate the *maybes* all day long without being any closer to knowing what the double-wiring is doing to him. It's been a failure in every cyborg I've seen it done to."

"If Captain Elliot was able to decode the containment cage security, I'm guessing his mobile restraints are deactivated as well. Check them and see, Kyra. Do it now," Nero ordered.

Hating to heed Nero's command, but knowing it was the sensible thing to do, Kyra walked over to her desk. She quickly accessed the console and typed in the test command as she put her wrist controller over the scanner. All security codes were reported as still in place and showed no signs of tampering so far. The only further testing she could do would involve hurting Peyton without cause. She just wasn't willing to do that to him when he was ghostbusting for her.

"I see nothing strange, Nero. If I test the links, Peyton's going to want to know why I thought I needed to protect myself."

Nero frowned. "Fine. But change the codes before you log out. You can do that without hurting him. Better yet—set them to randomly cycle. Knowing Peyton was sent to spy on you brings many things into question. It makes me wonder how many bio-tracking devices the UCN made Norton put in you."

Kyra swung her gaze from the console to Nero. Bio-tracers? That got her full attention.

"Could they have done that without me knowing?"

She saw Nero turn from glaring at her naïveté to look at his friend. "Scan her for bugs, Brad."

"If the app finds a bio-tracer, it's going to hurt like hell to kill it," Brad warned. "Maybe we should do it later—like much later—and out of Borg Man's hyper-sensitive hearing range."

"I helped Kyra build this lab. It's ninety-five point eight percent soundproof. He won't necessarily hear. Plus I'll keep Kyra from calling out. Just do it, Brad. We were going to have to kill all the bio-tracers when she ran anyway. Let's do it now to level her chances of escaping."

Kyra's face wrinkled in concern. "You genuinely think I'm being tracked by the UCN, don't you? Up to now. . .all I've had was a theory."

Nero walked to where Kyra stood staring at him. "What Brad uncovered on your surveillance recording convinced me I took your intuition about being investigated too lightly. I'm going to hold you now and put my hand over your mouth. But Kyra—finding a bio-tracer will just make your immediate departure more critical. Once the UCN figures out you've fallen off Norton's tracking radar, they'll waste no time coming after you. Of all people, you know how extreme they can be in their actions."

Kyra nodded and frowned. "Peyton said I was very strategic for a scientist. Maybe I was fooling myself. Given what we've learned, I'm surprised Norton didn't stop me before I worked on Marshall or Alex. If they're tracking me, they obviously suspect what I've been doing."

Nero put his arms around her and hugged. "No one has intervened yet because they are being strategic about not frightening the remaining cyborg creator into going underground. They wanted to know if you could succeed, which is what happened this time, Kyra. While not completely human, Captain Peyton Elliot is at least a cyborg who feels his emotions. If he hadn't been double-wired, I believe your restoration efforts would have worked one hundred percent."

"Thanks for at least saying that, Nero," Kyra said, her gaze fixed on the ceiling as she sought a solution for Peyton. She tried not to flinch when a man's hand covered her mouth for a second time that day.

What the hell was happening to her plans? And how did Nero know so much about what Norton was doing covertly to cyborgs? Hell—to its cyber scientists?

She watched Brad frown in resignation as he walked slowly toward her. He took a strange-looking scanner from his pocket that looked like the kind of portable hand-held used in medical facilities. After swiping through some screens, Brad ran the scanner over the front of her body covering every inch. Then coming closer to her, he turned the device to where she could see an outline of herself with three tiny, glowing red dots.

Brad shook his head. "I'm truly sorry, Dr. Winters. Looks like they have you tagged pretty good. Nero and I only had one each."

Her. The outline of the body on the screen was her. Kyra swallowed hard and nodded that she understood. She had three bio-tracers installed—which meant at some point Norton had inserted them without her even knowing they had done so.

Had they rendered her unconscious? How had they made her forget? Had Jackson had anything to do with it? To keep the unanswerable questions from driving her insane, she pulled Nero's fingers down so she could speak.

"Do whatever you have to do to make sure no one can track me," she ordered, feeling Nero's fingers immediately slide back up and tighten again after she finished.

Sighing heavily, Brad turned the device back toward him, keyed in a few commands, and then leaned the front edge down to shoot a red beam at each spot where a bio-tracer appeared on her. The pain was as bad as Brad had warned it would be, but she gave Nero no cause for alarm about her calling out. She bore the torture silently thinking of Marshall, Alex, and Peyton bearing their reboot pain as stoically as they had. Nothing done to her could ever compare to what those men had endured. But by the time the last bio-tracer was completely dead, she was breathing hard and feeling nauseous.

"The program to kill the bio-tracers uses similar technology as a light saber. Or if you're not familiar with that old movie reference, think of it as something similar to what cosmetologists use for cold laser body sculpting," Brad explained.

His teasing didn't ease much for her, but she knew Brad was trying to help. The younger man looked totally remorseful for having had to hurt her, but Kyra shook her head as Nero's fingers slid away from her lips. "Thank you for killing them, Brad."

When Brad nodded, Kyra tried her best to smile. It was hard with her stomach churning.

"You did great dealing with the pain, Dr. Winters. If you want, I can streamline your thighs to make them thinner. I did some cold laser lipo on my girlfriend's stomach. Not to brag or anything, but she looks seventeen again."

Kyra laughed weakly. "Thanks, but I don't think I can handle any more laser work today."

When Nero let her go, she grabbed the desk chair behind her to sit. Her legs were wobbly and she was feeling sick from the toxicity released when those things died.

She shook her head and laughed as she thought about Brad's offer to give her thinner thighs. Oh yes, having thin thighs would solve all her problems—if she wasn't a cyber scientist with a twenty million dollar price tag on her head.

"Do you think Peyton's body is bugged too?" She directed the question at Brad instead of Nero. She was surprised when the junior tech shook his head firmly.

"No way, Dr. Winters. Bio-tracers would be redundant in a double-wired cyborg. Among other things, the second processor works like a homing beacon. That's a normal part of being double-wired. Plus his cybernetics would neutralize the bio-tracers just as they were programmed to do with any sort of tracking device an enemy might install in him."

"I see. Can I ask how you know so much about double-wiring?" Kyra was starting to worry that she'd under-estimated others while over-estimating her own knowledge of what was going on.

She watched Brad's guilty gaze slide to Nero's before coming back to hers.

"I was hoping I never had to admit this to you, but I helped double-wire a cyborg once. Not your Borg Man though, Dr. Winters. It was another one. Actually, it was the woman who killed Dr. Channing. They were going to dispose of her, but decided to double-wire her instead. She was the first female too."

"I see. What kind of results did they get?" Kyra blinked and stared as she asked the question.

How much more had been going on at Norton that she hadn't known about? Her aversion to the behavior modification system had obviously taken her out of the 'need to know' loop.

She felt even more sorry now for the woman who had avenged her in a way she never would have had the nerve to do herself.

"I'm not judging you for what Norton made you do. Please tell me. I'd really like to know."

Brad shrugged and sighed. "There were some partial positives, but it seemed to cause that particular female cyborg to have more emotional bleed-thru episodes, like unexplained crying for no apparent reason. She also had a few really bad temper tantrums where she destroyed her containment cell furnishings. That's all I know about her. The woman was returned to the redefinition area for some extended down time. No one knows what they're planning to do with the cyborgs who are wired like that. She was in the lab where I was working on her when some military general came to evaluate her condition. He wasn't very complimentary about our efforts. He mentioned the others were all failures too in his opinion—except for one. Nero and I think the one success was your Borg Man—I mean—Captain Elliott."

"I see," Kyra said again, but she didn't. She didn't see at all. And now she couldn't talk to Peyton about the escalating situation either—unless she could figure out how to shut down the secondary wiring. "Something has to be done to stop this insanity. Someone has to stop Norton from trying to double-wire more cyborgs."

"Nothing more needs to be done by you, Kyra. Double-hell no," Nero insisted, his tone as adamant as he could make it. "I see where you're going in your thinking, but it's far too dangerous. Peyton Elliott could revert to some default set of codes and seriously hurt you—or worse."

Kyra nodded and bit her lip. What Nero said was true, but there was also a chance she could get the rest of his wiring disconnected. If an original creator couldn't accomplish stopping a double-wired cyborg—well that was knowledge the world needed as well, wasn't it? She turned a calm gaze to one of the few men who truly ever loved her.

"Yes. What you say is true, Nero. But a partially restored cyborg in hand is better than us trying to gain access to another fully wired cyborg later on. Norton doesn't want me dead. They want me working for them. They want me to continue helping them make organic robots out of the cyborgs. Well, I'm not going to do that and I won't let Peyton be used to force my hand."

There was silence in the lab as all three of them digested her declaration. Kyra lifted her chin and held Nero's gaze. "I have to try and finish what I started."

"I hate this, but I know it's a waste of breath to keep arguing. So what more can we do to help you with your insanity?" Nero asked.

"Nothing. You've bought me more time and made sure I can escape undetected if it comes to that. I need you two to leave soon because Peyton thinks I came to kick you out. I want it to look that way. I don't want to make him any more suspicious than he already is."

Nero put a hand out to stop Kyra when she tried to walk away. "What are you going to do about him, Kyra?

And about leaving? Do you even have a plan for what to do if your rogue Marine captain goes ape shit ballistic?"

Kyra reached out and took hold of Nero's arm. "No. I don't have all the answers yet. Now that we know the wrist and ankle restraints are still functioning, I'm not afraid of him losing control. So long as I retain the power to stop any attack he might make, I think I have to play this game until its end. If I win, Peyton wins—sort of. If I lose. . .? Well, let's just hope my luck is better than that."

Brad fished out a small round object from his pocket and held out his hand. "Here, Dr. Winters. This might come in handy if you have to make a run for it. It's my latest invention—a tiny portable sweeper. Not much power in it, but it will shield you for a short call if you need to contact us from somewhere outside your shielded lab."

Kyra took the small marble sized device. There was a tiny switch built into the side of it to turn it on. "Thank you, Brad. Thanks for all your help."

"It's my sincere pleasure to be on your rogue team," Brad said, nodding.

Kyra relaxed a little when she saw Brad grinning like the kid he mostly still was. It made his scary knowledge of cyborg double-wiring slightly fade from her mind.

"Rogue team? I guess that's as good a word as any to describe us. Brad, are you ever going to call me Kyra? You technically don't work for me anymore."

"I figure I can do that when you're a hundred years old and I'm a lot older than I am now. Until then, I'd like to keep things mostly professional between us. That way if anything happens later on—like you decide you want a younger man to keep your bed warm—well then we'd have somewhere less professional to go with our relationship."

Kyra laughed at Brad's outrageously flirty comment, and then laughed more when Nero smacked Brad hard on the back of his head.

"Dude, stop hitting on Kyra. Stick to Gloria," Nero ordered.

"Gloria?" Kyra repeated the name, smiling warmly at Brad who looked sheepish at the mention of another woman in his life.

Brad sighed and answered reluctantly. "Gloria is every man's dream woman. Nero here is just jealous because I have a girlfriend and he doesn't."

Snorting, Kyra reached out to rub the tightness between Nero's shoulder blades. "Well, Nero here could have lots of girlfriends if he wanted. He's selective about women, which is a rare quality in a man."

"Oh yeah, sure. If you don't mind sleeping alone all the time," Brad said, shrugging his shoulders.

Smiling at the simple male logic, Kyra opened the lab door as she listened to Nero haranguing Brad over his skirt chasing. She secretly thought Nero should do more of his own, but had long ago learned to keep opinions of that nature to herself.

"Out. Both of you heroes," Kyra ordered, stopping just beyond the lab door. She saw Peyton quickly disappear from the hallway into the kitchen. Had he been eavesdropping through the lab door?

After exiting, Kyra ordered lab security to cycle entry codes, then she walked the men to the front door of her home. Nero surprised her by hugging her fiercely again. He also glared once in the direction of the kitchen before reluctantly leaving.

Kyra waved as they both climbed into Nero's sleek air jet. Then she closed the door and headed to see what her double-wired cyborg spy was up to in her kitchen.

Her mouth dropped open when she found Peyton using her stainless steel teakettle to boil water. "You didn't have to use my artifact. The water dispenser has a built-in heater."

"Your stress level has been elevated almost since the moment we woke up. I thought you might need a little something normal to help you reach a state of calm again."

Peyton kept his back to Kyra hoping the non-aggressive action would help her lower her guard with him again. He was trying not to come across as commanding and controlling. Without using the Cyber

Husband chip's recommendations, he was finding his aggressiveness hard to monitor on his own.

"While you were in the lab with your friends, I investigated the teakettle and realized you actually use it instead of the water dispenser. It wasn't hard to figure out how it worked. I'm assuming that efficiency is not the goal of using this antiquated device."

Kyra smiled as she walked to the table and sat. "No. Using the teakettle is not efficient, but it offers a lesson in patience to wait for the water to heat in it. Did you get the bed and clothes moved to the pod storage area?"

"Yes to both. Now are you going to tell me what's really wrong? Or are you going to keep trying to convince the giant cyborg you don't fear that you're intimidated over something those two skinny young men said or did?"

Kyra studied Peyton's back, which was still turned to her. There was no getting around his extraordinary perception where she was concerned. To lie to him or not was her choice to make at the moment, but she suddenly wished with everything in her that those broad shoulders of his could share some of her mental burden. Her wishful thinking made her sigh. It was impossible to keep her emotional distance from a man who had obviously memorized how she took her tea after watching her make it only once.

"Sorry if I seem a little weird today, Peyton. I've never had a man make me tea in my own kitchen before. I think I could get used to having a real Cyber Husband who did such things. I'm almost sorry now that I'm going to have to cut you loose one day."

The teakettle's whistling signal finally sounded, and she saw Peyton snap off the heat source in response. She watched him pour boiling water carefully over the powered tea. Then he stirred it with the spoon the same number of times she did before removing it from the cup to add honey. His careful consideration of all details involving her ritual was just a matter of excellent memory programming. She couldn't let herself forget that no matter how charmed she was by his thoughtfulness.

But it still suited her to believe that Peyton's intuition about Nero and Brad destroying her calm was part of the real man within.

When Peyton set the tea in front of her, he smiled when she sighed over the steaming cup of liquid.

"I think I got it right. I'm finding I have to make notes about things like this now. I have a sense that the human part of me keeps arguing about what's important and not important enough to have to recall. I should have recorded your actions when I observed you making tea earlier."

"Thank you. I'm sure it's fine." Closing her eyes, Kyra lifted her cup to her nose and sniffed. The smell of minty green tea never failed to soothe. "If I'm not very calm today, it's because I still have many things I need to tell you. Nero and Brad added to my mental stress with their interruption this morning."

Peyton watched Kyra sip the tea he had made. It gave him a sense of satisfaction. While not as great as the pleasure he'd felt removing her old bed from the house, it was still pleasing to see her relax even a little. As she sipped, her gaze kept moving around the kitchen to rest on some spot in the space here and there. Kyra seemed more lost in her thoughts than usual and that was saying a lot for the restless scientist he was coming to know. Too bad her brain wasn't as readily accessible to him as his was to her.

"Sharing data with me would be a lot easier if you were a cyborg too, Doc. I could tune myself to the frequency of your thoughts."

Kyra had heard such links were created for military reasons, but she had not been part of that work. "Your military programming was done outside the scope of the codes that keep your cybernetics running and functional. That protocol functions on top of what I developed. What's it like to be 'tuned' into other cyborgs?"

Peyton thought for a moment about how to describe it. "It's a hierarchy based on rank. No one above captain was cybernetically combat modified to the best of my knowledge. After my field promotion, I had the highest rank among my group of Marines. My communication capabilities extend to all Cyber Soldiers, but my officer programming focuses most specifically on talking to *my* Marines. Basically, being tuned into each other means once I'm on the same frequency as they are, I can issue orders wirelessly, which they have to follow. When we used that during the war, the trick was to find a com channel the enemy wasn't monitoring. With just over two hundred options, I'm proud to say our government managed to creatively cycle through those better than anyone else."

Kyra sipped and narrowed her gaze, her mind working quickly. She had been wondering how they could possibly collect other cyborgs discreetly. It would be great if Peyton could literally call them to him. "Can you tell if that military protocol is still enabled?"

Peyton nodded. "Yes. It is a chip based functionality and my diagnostics show that all military chips are still active. Some of mine do seem to be in some sort of sleep mode at the moment. I've actually been trying to run diagnostics on the protocol chip directly, but something seems to be preventing the level two check from happening. I noted the anomaly on the report I sent you. Didn't you see that?"

"No. What report?" Kyra asked, surprised by the information.

"Each time a diagnostic report finishes, I'm having it sent to your portable. I created a wireless connection that allows me to send, but not receive from your unit," Peyton said, intrigued by her eyebrow lift. "Is that a problem? You seem to use your portable far more than your handheld devices."

"No—no problem. How did you get around the password?" Kyra watched Peyton's eyes for any sign that he was running some sort of decryption software but could find no fluctuations in his eye movements or any other facial tics.

"I figured a cyber scientist wouldn't ask such a basic question. No password is needed for one-way communications, Dr. Winters. You have your portable set to receive all incoming communications without prior approval. I assume you have that setting so your incoming email isn't restricted in any way."

"That's right. I do. The level of spam communication I get as a result is daunting, but I'm always afraid I'll miss something if I change it. Were you ever an IT Tech?"

Peyton shook his head. "No. Any knowledge I seem to need is just there in my help files. I access them when I have a question. They seem to be running at a hundred percent efficiency. I don't know how current the data is though because I don't have access to the last date my uplinks were flashed for upgrade. The Cyber Husband report indicates I'm as up to date as I can be made to be."

The answer to her dilemma popped into her mind much easier than she could have ever predicted. Peyton's last upgrade was probably when his secondary processor was installed. Since the upgrade information was being hidden from his primary processor, she wondered if the secondary processor's very existence was being kept from Peyton's conscious mind. If the secondary processor only activated during his down time—like when he was sleeping—Peyton might never think of the episodes as anything more than very active dreams, if he remembered them at all.

Thinking Peyton might actually be clueless about his double-wiring made her feel better, but it brought up additional ethical considerations.

Should she tell him about the situation straight out while he was awake?

Was she risking possible apprehension if her revelation set off a code launch?

Or should she try to get Peyton back into the lab where she could attempt to use the creator code again to shut him down? Checking his upgrades definitely gave her a damn good reason to look for the secondary processor.

Kyra leaned across the table. "If you want, I can make sure you're upgraded. That will help you with your assimilation and may even be the source of your blips. Maintenance information should be instantly accessible to your processor at all times. It's strange that you can't recall the last date you were upgraded. Those facts are generally stored in the processor's routine backup files."

Peyton frowned. "Does fixing the blip require me going back into the chair?"

"Yes—unfortunately. Shutting you down is still the only way I can safely work on you. I didn't leave myself that option with Marshall and Alex. If I had, they might still be alive."

Peyton didn't like the situation his reformed mad scientist was describing, but he hated the idea that there were still cyber blocks on his memories more. "Okay. I'll let you take another whack at fixing me. Are you planning to record the session?"

Kyra nodded, unwilling to lie about that fact. It was bad enough that she was not revealing the extent of what she intended to do to him. "Yes I am intending to record what I do and find. I warned you I would be doing so for everything we did to you.

Peyton nodded back. "Yes, I remember. I'm mentioning it because I want to see the recording afterward. I have a right to know what's going on with my head."

Kyra nodded again, totally in agreement, and happy he had stated it that way. "Yes you do have that right. In fact, I have several recordings to share with you. I've just been waiting for the right time. Your request tells me you're feeling ownership of your body again."

"Good. Then let's do this, Doc. The sooner we get it over with, the better as far as I'm concerned." Peyton stood when Kyra did. He had to hustle to prevent her from leaving. "Wait. I need one more thing from you before I get into that damn chair again."

He put a hand under her chin and lifted her face to his. "In case I don't come out of this next round of cyber tinkering as good as we'd both like me to, I just wanted you to know it was damn difficult to let you out of bed this morning. The urge to keep you there was not prompted by anything stored in the Cyber Husband chip either. It was the result of your toned ass squirming against me all night and giving me erection after erection I couldn't use. If those guys hadn't shown up this morning, this day would have started very differently. I was intending to seduce you. . .and not bragging or anything. . .but I damn well would have succeeded."

Before her brain could get over the shock about how sure he sounded, Kyra felt herself lifted to her toes. His mouth on hers was gentle, but his fingers gripped her hips firmly as he pulled her flush against the front of him. She would probably have bruises from that fierce grip later, but it was hard to care when Peyton's tongue was dipping in and out of her mouth in a rhythm that made her want to let other parts of him do the same thing.

Kyra found herself suddenly wishing they were in another time and place where his seduction could have just happened naturally between them. By the time her mouth was finally free, her heart was hammering against her shirt. "You make me want things, Peyton Elliot. I don't know whether to thank you or hate you for it. My life is complicated enough already. The attraction between us makes it worse."

Peyton pulled her close and rested his chin on top of her head. "You make me want things too, Doc. And I'm ninety-nine point ninety-nine percent sure that's the human side of me feeling it instead of the cyborg. I can't say a hundred percent yet, but I see that as a real possibility with you."

Kyra pulled away, but slid her hand down to his. She used their linked fingers to tug him along. It was the sweetest moment she could remember having with another person in a very long time. "You're a hell of a man, Peyton Elliott. If you survive this, I may just let you show me heaven after all."

Peyton grinned as they headed to the lab. "I just ordered my brain to make a note of that comment and date it. This is yet another time I wish I had been recording you, but I'd rather you not be worried about talking to me."

Kyra turned and leaned her head against his arm. "I don't know why any woman ever sent you back. You're pretty terrific out of bed as well as in it."

"Flattery again, Doc? Well right back at you. I don't remember who I was with any of those other women, but I like the man I'm becoming with you," Peyton said softly.

She pulled away and patted his arm. "I hope that remains true, Captain Elliot. I hope that remains true."

Kyra coded them into the lab as she chastised herself for allowing such an intimate moment between them without telling Peyton everything.

Chapter 12

Kyra fastened the band around Peyton's chest first. Then she moved to his wrists. "I'm leaving both sets of restraints in place. By the way, I changed the mobile restraint codes when I was in the lab this morning."

"I know. I have a military chip that runs an unlock decryption program on every security device it encounters. It was wise of you to start cycling the restraint codes. By the time my chip breaks one, you've got another running. My processor would have to work very fast now to beat your system."

Kyra paused, then resumed her task. "Really? Can your decryption program *ever* beat the cycle?"

"Why, Doc? Do you want me to try to break out of your kinky restraints? What kind of games are we playing here?" Peyton asked, winking at her.

"No. Of course I don't want you to break the restraints. That would make it harder for me to trust you." Kyra shook her head at her hypocrisy, but was unable to think of a suitable light response to his teasing.

When she knelt between his legs, she heard Peyton groaning like he was in great pain. Her head popped up instantly between his knees. "What's wrong? Are the chair bands too tight?"

Peyton laughed at her concerned questions and the innocence in her gaze. "The bands aren't too tight, but my pants are with you down there between my legs. Geez woman. Weren't you married once?"

"Not to a man as easy to arouse as you seem to be." Kyra snickered as she used Peyton's knees to push herself back up to standing. "Don't worry, Captain. In a couple of minutes, sex with me will be the last thing on your mind."

Peyton snorted and shook his head. "You might be surprised, Doc. I noticed your ass was nice when I first met you, and I've been thinking about having sex with you nearly every conscious moment since. If nothing you've said and done so far hasn't kept my dick from saluting you, I don't think you're going to change whatever is left of my mind no matter what kind of dinking you do with it today."

Kyra patted Peyton's knee before putting some distance between them. All she wanted to do was crawl into his lap and make them both forget what was going on. "I don't dink, Captain Elliott. I fix. Remember that. Just focus on that thought while I shut you down."

Peyton settled himself more comfortably in the chair, not wanting her to know how bad he hated what was about to happen. "Don't forget your promise about heaven, Dr. Winters. Every soldier in the field dreams about returning to a warm body and a woman's welcoming arms. Just so you know, I'm going to be dreaming about you while I'm under this time."

Kyra's resolution faltered. Her heartbeat thudded hard against her shirt. "Don't put me on a pedestal, Peyton. I don't deserve it."

Peyton sighed at the sadness in her response. "You just had to ruin my harmless fantasy, didn't you? I know what you are, Doc. You're an evil cyber scientist and I'm your monster. Now let's get this additional dinking shit over with before I lose the rest of my carefully constructed illusions. And by the way—you definitely talk too damn much."

Kyra's hand fisted on her hip. "I beg your pardon. Those are some pretty ballsy insults coming from a man strapped to a medical chair."

"You heard me, Doc. I'm not taking it back. I may have a few blips in my communication these days, but I damn well don't stutter about what's important," Peyton said, grinning when Kyra glared harder. "Shit woman, you're really cute when you're pissed. Let me loose so I can kiss you for real."

"No. Now I know why I always avoided military men. You just *love* conflict, don't you?" Kyra exclaimed.

"Yep. Eat it for breakfast," Peyton declared, closing his eyes. "Do whatever you intend to do and get it over with, okay?"

Finding it impossible to stay offended, Kyra sighed and finished her restraint checks. "If cyborgs dream while they're shut down, I hope you have only good ones."

"Personally, I hope I have x-rated ones of you. See you on the flip side," Peyton declared, closing his eyes. He heard her chanting another series of the creator codes and decided to record them for further study. Of course if they were voice activated as he suspected, he'd need Kyra's exact intonation to make it work. He knew a recording wouldn't even get it right because she had found a way to make sure it always had to be her in person.

When a full minute passed with nothing happening to him, Peyton opened one eye to see Kyra frowning. "Seriously. No more fooling around, Doc. I'm ready when you are."

"Shut up and let me think. It's not working," Kyra said in surprise, walking around in a circle as she thought. "I don't understand. The secondary processor seems to be ignoring the creator code. How can that be possible?"

Peyton opened the other eye so he could glare with both of them. "The hell you say. What secondary processor?"

Kyra tilted her head until her gaze was on the ceiling. The blank whiteness helped her think. Peyton's angry comments did not.

"I was hoping I wouldn't have to tell you all these details until I had resolved the problem, but yes—you apparently have two sets of cybernetic wiring. Experiments in double wiring were originally done only on cybernetic units whose personalities failed to cooperate with their primary processor. To date, double wiring has never been proven to work correctly or even well. It is not routine."

"What the hell are you talking about now? Are you saying I'm more of a freak than even you can understand?"

"I'm not sure what I'm saying. I can't think over your swearing," Kyra declared, swinging her gaze to his.

She paced around his chair and thought aloud so Peyton would shut up and listen.

"A standard artificial intelligence processor can run some functions from a second set of code, but in cyborgs the commands collide between processors causing a human mental melt-down eventually. You can quiet the human side from expressing itself, but you can't get the body to completely turn it off. Mental confusion always results because the second processor has to run a duplicate set of creator codes to work."

"And? So. . ?" Peyton demanded, wanting her to explain what the hell was going on.

"So I don't know why your secondary processor isn't responding to me. It has to be running some version of the creator code or it wouldn't be functional. All I can think to do is to find the secondary panel and attempt a manual shut-down."

"*Manual?* Like in more brain surgery?"

Kyra dropped her gaze from Peyton's glare to study a spot on the floor. "Yes. I guess that's what I'm saying. If you refuse, I have no choice but to leave you strapped in my chair to face your fate alone. You've been following your secondary processor's commands whether you realize it consciously or not."

Peyton shook his head. "That's a crock of shit, Doc. I've done no such thing."

Kyra walked to the chair and lifted her wrist until her antique unit was in front of Peyton's face. Retrieving the disk from her pocket, she loaded it then swiped the screen to play the file Nero and Brad had provided. Peyton's jaw got tighter the more he watched, but he didn't respond with his usual amount of anger. She was more alarmed that he seemed to want to deny what he saw even though it was a very human reaction.

When the security camera clip finished, Kyra lowered her wrist and walked to where the bug was stored under her desk. Retrieving it with the end of her sleeve so she wouldn't put her prints on it, she lifted the device to let Peyton see.

"Not bullshit—*fact*," Kyra said stiffly. She replaced the device carefully and backed away to retrace her steps to his side. "Since you're not responding to the creator commands, I have to try and disconnect the secondary processor manually. *Now may I proceed*?"

"Fucking shit, yes. Just do what the hell you have to. I'm tried of being everyone's science experiment," Peyton declared.

He closed his eyes as Kyra gently turned his head. He felt her tentative fingers exploring his scalp until they paused on a tiny knot. They grazed it lightly just before he felt her depress it. He couldn't help calling out as a huge bolt of lightning shot through his head.

"Damn it. The door was rigged to protect the access panel." Kyra's fingers flew as fast as possible when the secondary access panel finally opened. The secondary wiring had not been elegantly done. Judging by the agony on Peyton's face, the pain it was sending through him was at excruciating levels—the kind used to shut down the human mind and re-program it to obey cyber commands. Without the controller wiring, they had to be using his own cybernetics to cause the pain.

"Fight it all you can, Peyton. I'm hurrying. I swear I'm hurrying. Whoever did this was a hack. It's hard to know what will happen if I disconnect anything."

She used one finger to trace the circuitry and thought she had found the slave processor chip when every muscle in Peyton's body clenched. He let out an ungodly sound of distress and started spontaneously reciting numerical codes.

Her finger hovered. Should she pull the processor or not? Did she really have a choice?

Before she could make a final decision, Peyton's whole body seemed to electrify. Self-preservation sent her stumbling back to avoid being fried by the current suddenly running through the chair. He evidently had more prosthetic enhancements than either of them had known about because everything metal in his body sent current surging against the chair restraints.

She could do nothing but watch and see if his torment would end before Peyton broke free. First the chest restraint popped, followed by the one on each wrist. The only restraints left on his upper body were the mobile ones.

Peyton turned his head to her. His eyes were flashing and rolling like something out of a video game. His face was contorted with whatever was happening to him.

"By special apprehension order number 407738 authorized by the United Coalition of Nations, Cyber Unit Peyton 313 is hereby directed as a reactivated military soldier to capture Dr. Kyra Winters by any means necessary. Any resistance to apprehension will be answered with the appropriate force necessary to achieve her retention. To avoid bodily harm, Dr. Winters is ordered to proceed with Cyber Unit Peyton 313 to the nearest UCN location to be officially charged for crimes against the UCN."

Kyra backed up steadily as Peyton reached down and broke the electrically weakened chair restraints still holding his ankles. Now there was nothing to prevent him coming after her except the mobile restraints. She glanced at her wrist controller but again her hesitation in acting was her undoing. By the time she raised her gaze to see where he was, Peyton was already standing in front of her.

He repeated his orders to apprehend her as he reached out to grab one of her wrists. When she instinctively protected the one with the mobile restraints controller, he gripped the other in a tight hold she found she couldn't break. She vaguely realized his pressure sensor was not functioning correctly when she heard a little pop coming from under his fingers. Kyra called out as pain radiated up her arm to her elbow and was mildly surprised when Peyton instantly released her.

She clutched her wounded hand to her chest as she stepped out of his reach. "I think you broke my wrist, Peyton. Are you still in there at all? Don't let them do this to you. I set you free so this couldn't happen again."

For one moment, Kyra saw his face smooth out and his eyes slow to move back and forth across her and the lab. Peyton looked first at her, then at the room, and finally at the wrist she still clutched to her chest. She knew she'd lost him though when he resumed citing his orders to capture her.

"No. I can't let you deliver me to them just because I care what happens to you," Kyra said firmly.

As she spoke, she inched away from Peyton, moving toward the door. She could never outrun a cyborg, but the mobile wrist restraints just might be able to incapacitate Peyton enough to give her time to escape. If that happened, she wanted to be as close as possible to the lab's only exit.

"*Stop walking,*" Peyton ordered. "*Continued resistance will result in the use of more force. I have consulted my data banks. You are identified as Dr. Kyra Winters. You must proceed with me to the nearest UCN location for processing.*"

Kyra shook her head. "Sorry, Captain Elliott. But I'm not going with you today."

She watched Peyton take two steps in her direction before she managed to use one numb finger to swipe at the controller on her good wrist. Current shot through Peyton's body, sending him to his knees. Kyra almost peed herself in relief when it worked. But when he started to climb to his feet again, she shook her head and sobbed for what she had to do.

"*No. No. No.* I'm sorry, Peyton. I'm so sorry. I have no choice but to do this. Death would be a better fate for you than the things Norton will do once they get you back."

Wincing, Kyra used a knuckle on her injured hand to run the restraint power adjustment to maximum. Then she yelled out in frustration as she swiped at the send command. It was not what she wanted to do to a man who she had only wanted to save from this fate. Damn Jackson and Norton for making her take these measures.

The maximum voltage the wrist unit could convey to his mobile restraints surged through Peyton and sent him to the floor again. This time he hadn't even called out as he fell.

Groaning with the knowledge that she might have mortally wounded or even killed him, Kyra looked at the lab's door and planned to make a run for it. She could escape now. She knew she could. If his cyborg body was capable of healing itself, this was probably the one and only chance she was going to get to do so.

Her gaze went to Peyton's twitching body still prone on the floor. Her mind flashed back to his kiss—the one he'd given her earlier without asking first. Peyton wasn't a bad guy—he was one of the good guys. But at the moment, he was some scientist's tool—some scientist like her—another Frankenstein doctor trying to create the perfect monster.

"You're stupid for not running. Stupid. Stupid. Stupid," Kyra chanted as she ran to kneel by Peyton's head.

Using her unbroken left hand, she rolled Peyton's face until she found the secondary access panel just above his ear. Wishing her right hand was still functional, it took several attempts with her uncoordinated left to pull all the chips she could from the compartment. She left the wiring, but finally yanked out and threw the secondary processor across the room.

Just as she was standing up to run, Peyton raised his head and looked at her in complete confusion. His tortured gaze rooted her feet where she stood. "Peyton? Are you still with me?"

In answer, he swept out with his arm, taking her down to the hard concrete floor in one swipe. Kyra heard another crack just before the world went dark.

Chapter 13

"Dr. Winters, I know it's hard but it's time to wake up again."

"No. Leave me...alone." Kyra heard the commanding female voice, but didn't want to answer. If she had died and gone to hell, she'd just as soon not know about it yet.

"Just wake for one minute and then you can sleep again," the stern voice ordered.

Kyra opened one eye. The light made her squint. A pretty woman in her early thirties met her gaze behind black framed glasses. "Am I in hell?"

The woman sighed at her question and looked around. "Pretty close I think. This is some sort of off-the-grid bunker slash lab out in the middle of East Bejesus, Nowhere. It might as well be hell. Feels like hell as far as I'm concerned."

Kyra tried to smile at the woman's sarcasm. She raised her right hand to her head, alarmed when she saw it was in a cast. "What happened to my hand?"

The woman pulled up a chair. "You have a broken wrist, Dr. Winters. There's a healing band applied under the cast. The break should mend in a few more days. What do you remember?"

Kyra lowered her hurt hand back to the bed. "My head hurts too badly to think right now."

"I know. Your head is bandaged too. As best as I can determine, you have a moderate to severe concussion.

There's also a pretty nasty gash on the back of your skull. I taped it shut and wrapped wound gauze around it. Stitches weren't possible at the time. I'm glad you're finally awake. We were all starting to wonder if you were in a coma."

Kyra turned her head slowly against the pillow. The movement made her feel dizzy, but at least her vision was starting to clear. "How did I get here?"

"Nero—ultimately. I mean he's the reason this place exists, but a big cyborg dude carried you in here. I must say that I'm really curious about his story. Borg Man spends his days in the com room doing research but comes around every hour to check on your condition. This is the first time you've been completely awake in five days. He doesn't seem to sleep much because he spends his nights with you sitting in a chair."

"Do you know what happened to put me in this condition?" As much as taking in information hurt, Kyra found she still wanted answers about how much the woman knew.

"Well, I have no idea how you fell. No one told me and I didn't ask. With Nero, I've learned you're better off not asking questions and just doing what he says. I'm technically on 'vacation' here while I'm taking care of you. His cover stories only work if you follow protocol."

"Nero? What's Nero got to do with this?"

This time when her head throbbed, Kyra lifted her left hand instead of her right. She felt her face and then ran a hand up to her forehead. Sure enough there was a gauze bandage wrapped tight. She remembered Peyton squeezing her wrist too hard. She remembered pulling all the chips from the second compartment in his head. She remembered looking down at him. . .his arm sweeping out. . .and suddenly full memories of her fall to her lab floor returned. Reliving them was painful. Her attention was harshly pulled back to the present when the woman started talking again.

"Nero isn't here just now, but I'm sure he'll check in shortly. I don't know who's been more worried about you—him, Brad, or Borg Man."

The list of those concerned didn't surprise her. They were the only ones who knew what was really going on. "Head hurts bad. Can I have some water and maybe some pain medicine?" Kyra asked.

The woman stood and nodded. "Sure. My name is Ella. I'll just slip out to the commissary and bring you something back. Now that you're awake we can remove the IV and the take-care-of-your-business tubes. Welcome back to the land of the living, Dr. Winters."

"Thanks," Kyra said, closing her eyes. It eased the insistent throb in her head to be in the dark.

After she heard Ella's footsteps receding, she opened her eyes again and met Peyton's intense gaze with shock. Her survival reflex kicked in, making her scream, but the sound came out as an unimpressive croak while she thrashed around the bed trying to escape. Extreme pain shooting through her head with every movement made her want to throw up. She felt gentle, but insistent hands pressing her down firmly into the mattress.

"Kyra—stop. It's okay. I'm not going to hurt you. . .ever again. . .I swear. Nero and Brad checked what you did to me and it seems to have worked. They don't think I'm going into psycho soldier mode ever again now that the secondary processor is gone."

"I'll believe that after I've tested you myself. We'll get to it soon, if my head doesn't explode off my shoulders first," Kyra said.

Peyton looked at the busted up woman in the bed who dared to challenge him even after he'd attacked and hurt her. Her audacity when she was afraid was a huge turn-on for him. Too bad the last thing Kyra Winters needed at the moment was some perpetually horny guy lusting for her. She was now officially a UCN fugitive and that had to be dealt with first.

"Okay, Doc. You can check the mostly empty holes in my head if you must, but if I'm going back in the chair, it's going to cost you big this time," Peyton teased.

He sat down in the seat Ella had vacated and crossed his arms to stare at her.

Kyra snorted at his bossy tone. "Will it cost more than a broken wrist and a severe concussion? You're an expensive Cyber Husband to maintain, Captain Elliott. And extorting money from a UCN criminal is a plan doomed to failure."

Peyton snorted back. "What I want isn't money, so you might think the cost is worse. I want one whole night with you to do anything I want—with the caveat that it won't be any of the sick shit your ex did to you. The truth is I think about sex with you nearly every second I breathe, and I'm tired of not acting on those urges. You're going to enjoy your time with me. I promise."

"I don't see how your constant physical arousal is my problem. And you don't know anything about what Jackson did to me. I never told you about my life with him," Kyra said, ignoring his other comments. She wasn't up to dealing with his attraction to her. Maybe in his mind nothing unusual had happened, but she was still trying to reconcile the fact that he'd been programmed with orders to capture her.

"I don't have to know the details to know what happened made you afraid of sex. If you can still talk to me after I hurt you the way I did, what's left to come between us? Not your bastard ex's behavior, that's for damn sure. Hell, Kyra. Technically, I'm still your Cyber Husband of record. I want to be with you and I know you want me too. Why do you have to argue about this?"

"I don't know, Peyton. I got along wonderfully with my other two Cyber Husbands who tried to kill me. It didn't work out so well for them in the end though, so you may want to think twice about messing with me. Then again, you're the only Cyber Husband who managed to knock my head against the lab floor," Kyra complained as she closed her eyes again.

Peyton sighed and nodded. "Okay. I deserve that sarcasm. But for the record, you know that psycho cyborg bastard you fought in your lab wasn't the real me. I was caught in one of Dante's seven levels of hell while someone used my brain and body to accost you. Nothing that happened was my choice. And now I totally understand why you had to take such extreme measures with me and the first two cyborgs you tried to reverse engineer."

Kyra grunted at his concession and his defense of his own situation. Yet all of it was true. "Of course I know you didn't attack me on purpose. Why do you think I didn't run away while you were down?"

"I think you didn't run because you trusted your judgment about me, which turned out to be damn right," Peyton declared.

Needing to act, he moved from the chair to slide into the bed until he was lying next to her.

"What in hell are you doing?" Kyra demanded, wincing as her head exploded over and over.

"Apologizing better," Peyton said calmly, kissing the top of Kyra's bandaged head.

"No need. Your first apology was accepted. Now move your big ass out this tiny bed, Captain Elliott. There's barely room for my ass in here."

"You're right about that, Doc. We'll have to bump asses better later. Just ignore that erection growing between us. I can't seem to stop it from happening when I get this close to you. It goes away eventually."

"Will you please move your horny, pervy ass back to the chair?"

Kyra winced as Peyton turned her toward him instead of answering. But she closed her eyes in relief moments after when she felt his light massage on her injured arm. The problem was the front of her rubbed the front of him with every stroke he made. Was he intentionally trying to drive her insane?

"When I breached the second processor compartment's security, you became one mean SOB, Captain Elliott. I hope I never make you that upset with me again."

Peyton let out a ragged breath as he pulled his ballsy savior closer. His strong emotional attachment to a woman who could shut his brain down whenever she wanted was baffling, but he was still recovering from his ongoing panic. This moment of holding her in his arms again almost didn't get to happen. He had been programmed to use as much force as necessary to apprehend the remaining cyborg creator. Nero had analyzed the code on the chips Kyra had pulled from him and they had discussed the ramifications of what her apprehension orders meant. The UCN would rather see Kyra Winters dead than working to free any other cyborgs.

He lifted Kyra's injured hand to his mouth and kissed her fingers. "You had every reason to run and yet you didn't. All the words of gratitude in my data banks are inadequate, so all I can say is thanks for being brave enough to come back. Tripping you with that arm swipe was just an accident—I swear. When I looked up and saw you standing over me, my arm just seemed to move on its own. Next thing I knew, you were knocked out cold on the floor with me. Luckily for both of us you had Nero on your handheld's rapid call."

"I had no choice but to hurt you. Using the mobile restraints was the only way I could stop you. How did you get us out of the lab?" Kyra asked, the question muffled by his shirt.

Peyton paused his stroking. He knew he had no choice but to tell her the truth. He'd had a lot of those to deal with in the five days and three point seven hours she'd been unconscious.

"Nero discovered I'd been upgraded with an enormous information repository. Without even knowing it, I've been recording you every time you entered and left the lab. Once the second processor was gone, I got access to all the hidden info I'd been collecting. It was painful but all I had to do was cycle through the information containing access codes to eventually hit the end of the loop. Good thing too—it allowed me to let Nero in to help us. I wasn't in much better condition than you were when he finally got there."

Kyra made a strangled sound in her throat. "So the bug you planted in the lab was just for show? Damn it. How much data did you record?"

"Literally everything that has happened since we've been together, with the exception of your original reboot. The recording feature only shut down at night after you were asleep. I have to admit the information has been useful because I've been able to revisit everything that happened before I went nuts this last time. That second set of wiring functioned like a shit list of important things I had forgotten to do. The list was insistent even after you pulled the plug on the secondary processor. We have to talk about that pain stuff they do to get a cyborg's full attention. Last time I checked, we don't even treat war prisoners that roughly. I'm sure it would have been twice as bad if you hadn't already removed the controller wiring. They literally electrified my prosthetics and used the current to shock the rest of me."

Even though it hurt, Kyra pushed out of Peyton's arms and rolled to her back to stare at the ceiling again. "I never understood what it was like for a person to live as a cyborg until I started trying to reverse the process. It wasn't that I was apathetic. I just didn't think about how much the code was using pain as a means of controlling your mind. The pain was meant to keep you from harming yourself, not to be used as a way to harm you."

Peyton leaned over her. The remorse contorting Kyra's face demanded soothing. Sure she wasn't without blame, but she wasn't like the ones still trying to use him to kill her either. His face was lowering toward hers when he heard someone clearing their throat nearby.

"Hey Borg Man. What'cha think you're doing with my patient? Dr. Winters is not in good enough condition yet to be fooling around with you."

"Hello Ella," Peyton said, feeling a grin start when his face great hot with embarrassment. He hadn't even kissed Kyra. He rubbed his jaw and reluctantly climbed out of her bed.

"Thank you," Kyra said with genuine relief, ignoring the fact that she also instantly missed Peyton's warmth. Her head throbbed like a heartbeat as she pushed and pulled herself up to a semi-sitting position. She reached for the cup of ice water on the tray her caregiver held down to her. She took several sips before sighing in contentment. "I've been trying to get Peyton to leave me alone. He hasn't been listening well. Tell Nero that Captain Elliott's hearing needs to be checked."

Ella laughed as she slid the tray onto the stand next to the bed. "Borg Man's just happy you're finally awake."

Kyra let fly a disbelieving grunt against the rim of the cup as she sipped. "You obviously don't know the hell I've put the man through. He hates my guts."

Beside the bed she heard Peyton softly swearing. She grinned at the idea that he might be offended. His reaction was extremely promising—for a variety of reasons.

"Stop complaining and do something productive, Captain Elliott. Find a giant blank porta-disk—or seven—and copy that massive data bank you profess to have been amassing. Bring me back the disks and a handheld I can review it on."

"No. No reviewing data yet. You need more rest first," Peyton commanded in return.

Though it hurt, Kyra turned her bandaged head to look at him. "Don't make me get out of this bed and chase you down to get what I want from you. I'm still recovering from our last fight. Chasing you down would only piss me off further."

Knowing Kyra meant her threat made his pants even more damn tight. Peyton smiled at his own frustration as his gaze went from woman to woman. "Did you hear that Ella? You're my witness. Doc is flirting with me."

Ella giggled at their exchange. "Gee. . .and you're not even wearing your *Cyborgs Do It Better* t-shirt. Way to go, Borg Man."

Peyton laughed loudly and put a hand over his stomach to feel his muscles contract. He had little recollection of having spontaneously laughed much in his life—like ever. The most he had was a vague memory of doing it with his fiancée in some kind of beach setting. Those memories were at least a decade old. He sighed when he realized Kyra was looking at him with a kind of hopeful fear. "What's up, Doc? Did my laughter scare you?"

Kyra painfully shook her head. "No. A sense of humor is the most mysterious of all cognitive behaviors, but it's also a very basic one that can't really be controlled. Congratulations, Captain Elliott. I do believe you're mostly human again at last."

Peyton didn't let himself care about his audience as he rose and bent over the bed to kiss Kyra's startled mouth. He gripped her chin after to make sure she listened to him.

"I'll never be able to say this enough, but thank you for coming back to save me. Most people would have run like hell. Only a good guy stays in the fight. Remember that."

His voice turned gruff as he straightened. He didn't want to leave her, but they couldn't really talk about much that mattered in front of Ella.

"Guess I'll go see what I can do about getting you a data dump."

***

"I'm just curious about how involved you are with him physically because Ella said she saw him kiss you in a no-nonsense man-woman way," Nero said bluntly.

Kyra shook her head, but didn't bother looking away from her screen. She queued up the next file and made sure it began where the last one ended.

"What Peyton is feeling for me is just a whole lot of gratitude. From his perspective, he's my patient and I saved his life. It's a clear case of the Florence Nightingale effect. I'm quite sure his infatuation with me will pass in time."

Since Kyra wasn't meeting his eyes, Nero stared at her back. "Where did the cyborg sleep last night? It wasn't in his assigned room, Kyra. I know because I looked for him there when I arrived."

"Stop baiting me with information you already have. You know damn well he was with me. Peyton feels responsible for my injuries, and frankly his remorse is a good sign, Nero. Besides, the medical room is cold. He takes up a lot of room in the bed, but sharing his body heat is better than an extra blanket," Kyra said. She stopped her task and swung a glance at Nero, taking in his frown. "Relax—will you? Nothing sexual is going on between us. And what is your problem anyway? You're the one who rescued both of us."

Nero sighed and nodded. "At the time it happened, I had no choice. Captain Elliott seemed truly fixed and we needed to confirm it, didn't we? I have to look at him as our first completely restored cyborg, but that doesn't mean I have to like him trying to have an intimate relationship with you. His presence here is merely a matter of science."

"Will you simmer down? I was convinced of that fact long before you went all paternal protector on me. Look—I'm twenty years older than you and not nearly as susceptible to a hot ass. Yes—I like the man in general. No—I'm not indulging in carnal relations with him. Give me some credit for being able to deflect his obsession with me until it passes on its own."

Kyra turned her face back to the monitor. Behind her, she heard Nero sighing.

"Forgive me, Kyra. There's no scientific reason for you not to indulge with Captain Elliott if that's what you feel the need to do. The man is still very much a cyborg, but we all believe the restoration was completely successful. Brad said Peyton's EEG scans are clear of all rogue processor interference now. His mind seems to be his own as far as we can tell."

Kyra stopped reading to nod. "Good. I've been very careful with Peyton so far. He's trusts the bond between us and I have to honor that, regardless of what else does or does not happen. That's great news about the EEG scans. I'm about two-thirds through reviewing the data Peyton recorded. Outside of the discussion he and I had about my personal life with Jackson, there's not much else in the recording that bothers me."

"How can you say that? He recorded all your access codes to the lab," Nero exclaimed, listing the issue that bothered him the most.

Kyra shrugged. "True. But the UCN has devices to bypass almost any security anyway. I still don't know what happened to the device Peyton used to escape his cage. He said he doesn't remember either. Did you see it when you and Brad found the planted device under my desk?"

Nero shook his head. "No. Brad found the UCN bug almost as soon as we entered. Our time involved dealing with that."

Kyra nodded. "So when are you going to tell me how you managed to create this secret scientist lair?" She swiveled in her chair to again face the man who kept surprising her lately.

Nero rose to pace. "I know you better than that, Kyra. You joke to cover your anger that I kept this from you. But if I hadn't created it, you'd have no place to hide right now. Think about it—your apprehension would make anyone rich enough to never have to work again. You're going to have to hide from the UCN and their hired goons for the rest of your natural life unless something drastically changes. They could easily send more military cyborgs after you. This site will not be very helpful against them if that happens."

Kyra got up and walked to stand close enough to look up into Nero's worried gaze. "My goals haven't changed just because I was successful in restoring Peyton. Yes, I can free other cyborgs as well *if* we can figure out how to get to them. But if Plan A doesn't work out, my Plan B is still to take down Norton Industries. I'm not going to lie to you no matter how hard it is for you to keep hearing me say it. I cannot afford to lose your respect, but I'm more determined now than ever."

Nero reached out and jerked Kyra into his arms for a hug. "Peyton is right about how hard-headed you are. Can you not see any other way?"

Kyra sighed as she returned his hug. "Easy, Nero. You're bringing back the headaches squeezing me so tight. And don't make me cry. You know I hate that."

"A woman's mind should not be so totally analytical. Crying is an effective way to release emotional pain. Instead of weeping alone, you need to learn to do it in someone's arms, Kyra."

Kyra laughed as she pulled away. "It's way too late for me to change the kind of woman I turned out to be. I'm mostly stoic—if you don't count my sarcasm as emotion. The crying I do over the cyborgs is prompted by extreme guilt and shame. It's just the physical expression of my repentance—nothing more."

Nero huffed, but didn't argue. He knew it would do no good. Instead he told her the only news that would distract her from contemplating her own death. "Peyton has an idea about how to collect the other cyborgs. If successful, it will require us to have several holding cages to constrain them. We've already moved the one from your personal lab to here. Several others are under construction."

"What's his idea?" Kyra asked.

Nero shook his head as he walked back to his station. "Ask Captain Elliott to explain it. It should make great pillow talk between the two of you tonight."

Kyra grinned at Nero's sarcasm as she went back to sit in front of the desk com. "You're confusing me. Do you want me to play bedroom nice with Peyton or not?"

Nero flapped his arms and let them hit his sides. "I don't know what to think or want. I've never been around a cyborg who acts like he does. It's like he's only human when the subject of discussion is you. The rest of the time, he's in full cyborg mode. He's making more military strategies than I'm comfortable with him doing. And yes—it makes me nervous that someone like him likes *you* so much. He's not your type."

"Hmm. . ." Kyra said, pondering Peyton's military strategizing. "Maybe the resumption of his military thinking means Peyton has established more control over his cybernetics. That's good progress I think. One of his last normal memories is of his conversion. After that, he has only total recall of the war. It was like he just came home from fighting the day I replaced his primary processor."

"Hmm. . ." Nero mocked, "maybe we don't know whether it's the man or the machine who is in charge of his actions right now though. Despite his restoration, Captain Elliott is still dangerous. You seem to keep forgetting that the whole world fearing the capabilities of cyborgs is a large part of why there are no more wars. Peyton's prosthetics are not just replacement arms and legs. They're robotic weapons, Kyra."

"I have not forgotten that, Nero. But robots with AI processors are nothing but machines. They have no conscience and no morals outside their programming. Peyton is not a machine. He's a redefined human with technologically advanced prosthetics, which he got for the benefit of the world. I have full confidence that he will use them for good now just like he did originally. We can't be the only two humans alive capable of thinking that way."

After making her declaration, Kyra found herself defending Peyton to a white-coated back. Nero had returned his attention to his own work, refusing to debate the subject further. Shaking her head, Kyra gave up and returned to her work as well, but what Nero said had her mind pondering much more than just Peyton's collected data.

It wasn't unusual for cyborgs to be routinely redefined by having their chips and processors wiped clean or replaced with newly coded ones. But Peyton's processor wasn't like any other. His wasn't orchestrating every tiny decision of his entire life anymore. Though she hadn't shared the details with Nero yet, Peyton's processor was yet another prototype, not the one he knew she had been working on. She had completely removed all programming that required pain as a behavior modifier, even the safety protocols. With the secondary processor now gone, Peyton was further liberated.

Free from the ability of other cyber scientists to ever harm him again, Peyton was literally the first cyborg with full access to all of his humanity. A living testament to being both man and machine, Peyton's cyborg existence was now a whole new twist on redefinition.

Only time would reveal what he would choose to do with his unique life. But wasn't that the case with all non-cyborgs as well? Wasn't she still redefining her own?

Kyra picked up headphones to listen privately to the parts of the recordings with conversations between her and Peyton. She rolled her eyes when she caught herself sniffling through some of them. She hadn't been exaggerating when she told Peyton she was the most optimistic person alive on the planet. That statement was especially true when it came to him.

Chapter 14

"If I'm tired, it's because I worked all day. I have a small headache, but other than that I'm fine. There's no reason for you to watch over me while I sleep."

Kyra looked at the sparseness of Peyton's sleeping area. There was nothing in it but a chair, a desk, and a bed, which was at least larger than most of the others. Nero had been thoughtful enough to provide Peyton with something big enough accommodate his size. She supposed it was better than the two of them sharing her single bed in the medical area.

Earlier in the day she had secretly visited his room and others. While all rooms were dormitory in appearance, most of the surprising number of people using them had found ways to make them their own. Whether it was some personal item tossed on a bedside table, or an article of clothing flung across the bed itself, their sleeping areas were already reflecting their identities. Peyton's bed looked like no one had ever slept in it.

"I guess you will never get your personal things now, though I doubt Norton was really planning to ship them to you anyway," Kyra said sadly.

"I have reached similar conclusions. Fortunately, my personal needs are small. I'm sorry to report your house was raided shortly after Nero retrieved us, and is now being watched closely. I wanted to retrieve your personal items, but it's become unsafe to do so by myself. Perhaps at some point in the future we can collect them."

Kyra shrugged. "The only items worth anything to me came from Nero. So long as he's doing okay, I can live without the material things I've collected. I'm not very sentimental about possessions."

"You seem fond of some. What about your water boiling device?" Peyton asked.

Kyra snorted, amused at his recollection. "My teakettle? Yes, I'll miss that I guess, but only because it's my favorite ritual. Making tea is my substitute for smoking. After the world ban on e-cigs as well as real ones, I had to give up that vice and look for another way to calm my nerves. Tea making was the best thing I tried and relatively healthy. It was a win-win solution. The teakettle made the ritual last a little longer and be a little more fun."

Peyton tried to imagine Kyra smoking e-cigs. He couldn't bring a visual forward. She just didn't look the type. "I don't see you smoking, but I do see you wearing those red high heels in the master bedroom closet. Will you miss those?"

Kyra laughed. "No. And I can't believe you looked at my old shoes."

"I merely noted the pattern difference in what was in that shared closet versus what I saw you wearing daily. I admit to finding the variation intriguing and wondered why you owned those shoes," Peyton reported.

She walked to the edge of the bed and sat. "That study is not worth the expenditure of your brain power, Peyton. Let's pull your Cyber Husband chip tomorrow. You're still too focused on me. I can fix that instantly for you."

Peyton grinned and shook his head. "No thanks, Doc. I wish to keep my remaining chips, including the Cyber Husband one."

Kyra laughed for real. "Why? You don't have to do anything for me or any other woman. Getting back your free will is the whole point of the restoration. You don't have to learn anything more about what I need. You can just be focused on your own needs now."

"Nero is right. You redirect conversations when you don't want to answer questions."

"No I don't. What question?" Kyra demanded.

"I am choosing of my own volition to learn more about you. Now in what circumstances did you wear those red high heels?" Peyton demanded back.

Kyra dropped her chin to stare at the floor. "If you must know, I wore them for the same reason all women wear those torture devices. They made me look tall and thin and my husband liked seeing me in them. Sometimes I enjoyed the illusion of being taller, but Jackson's approval didn't bring me much pleasure in the long run. Can we please talk about something more interesting than my old shoes?"

Peyton walked to the door of his room to close and lock it. It was more to keep Kyra confined in the room with him than to keep anyone out. Then he went to the bed and sat down next to her.

"Dr. Winters, you are exhibiting multiple trauma symptoms from whatever it was your ex-husband did to you. I know because I was fully trained to deal with that in the Marines who served with me. You're never going to be able to liberate yourself from the lingering pain of those events until you can bring yourself to tell someone what happened."

Kyra stared at her hands. "No thank you, Peyton. I appreciate your good intentions in asking—but no. I don't want to talk about it. It happened many years ago. Jackson is dead and I don't even know who the other men were. I was blindfolded the whole time."

Peyton stared at Kyra's bent head, ordering himself to focus on her body language instead of her words. Also, he couldn't risk getting angry over her past and destroying the bed beneath them. That wouldn't help either. He had already made his personal decision about sleeping with her, but it was obvious Kyra hadn't come to a similar conclusion about him yet.

"Are your bad memories of your ex-husband keeping you from being intimate with me?"

Kyra stood and walked away from the temptation of the man and his softly spoken question. "Not really. It's just that I believe your desire for me is being motivated by your Cyber Husband chip. The more normal reaction in our situation is for you to continue to hate my guts. Trust me on this one, Peyton. I pulled the Cyber Husband chip from Marshall, but I left the one in Alex for a couple months before pulling it. So I know the difference removing it makes. I should never have left the chip in you either, but I did it because I needed your cooperation. In many ways, you're still programmed to be my husband. That's why you're so focused on being intimate with me."

Peyton shrugged. "Doc—I know this is going to be hard for you to believe—but I don't care what's causing me to want you."

"But it's not right for you to feel that way—that's—it's—*illogical*," Kyra protested, throwing her hands up in the air.

Peyton stood and walked to her until he could stare down into her face. "No one knows better than you do that logic will forever be my default setting. I have studied how I was programmed to be nice to the other women that bought me. That was handled as a set of protocols, which called a series of insistent commands I could not resist carrying out without experiencing pain. While you left the basic information about you in place, I'm aware you removed all pain motivation to follow the commands. At this point the Cyber Husband chip is no more than a help file specifically about Kyra Winter's likes and dislikes, which were based on the application you filled out. The chip isn't forcing me to do a damn thing where you're concerned."

Kyra laughed harshly. "I filled out that information about the same time you got stabbed in the heart. It wasn't very long after Jackson had left for good. I don't even recall where my head was at the time I answered those damn questions. I doubt I answered with much sincerity."

"Which is why I plan to amend the file as we go along. I want to keep it current—I want to learn more about you," Peyton said.

Kyra shook her head firmly. "There's no need. Don't you get that? Why don't you go focus on finding your fiancée? Once you tell her what happened, she might even want to be with you again. Anything is possible for you now, Peyton. The two of you could hide from the UCN.

There are plenty of global providences that don't condone cybernetic enslavement."

"There is no chance of my old fiancée wanting to resume our relationship. She's married to an artist. They live in Maryland and are raising two children. Seeing a visual of her did not even activate any memories that were worth pursuing, nor did it cause me to have the arousal I consistently have when you're nearby. I have concluded my fiancée merely represented that woman back home all military men at war dream about while they're in the field. Thoughts of someone like her can keep a man sane, but those relationships have a low success rate of outlasting the service period anyway. I like you for reasons I'm still investigating. And I want you."

"But I *ruined* your life, Peyton. I gave the UCN a power over you they should never have had. How can you not hate me for what am I and what I've done?"

Peyton used Kyra's tortured question as a reason to touch her face. Her gaze was full of a kind of pain much worse than any he'd experienced from internally battling his cybernetics. He knew there was never going to be an off-switch thrown on her deep regret for not acting sooner. Kyra Winters, reformed cyber scientist, was going to hold herself accountable for every cyborg's suffering until the day she died.

"Maybe you haven't always been a good person. But from what I've seen, you have bigger balls than any man I've ever known, and I've known some hell-raisers. And no—I don't really understand why I feel this way about you. All I know is that I want to comfort you in moments like this. . .and I want to do a whole lot more with you as soon as it seems right for both of us. When I saw you unconscious on the lab floor, the little voice you woke up inside my head chose that time to announce to the rest of me that fucking you was never going to be enough. How's that for balls-to-the-wall honesty?"

His mouth descended to hers gently. Kyra's tears ran between their lips as they kissed. But he didn't let her weeping stop him from sweeping his tongue into her mouth when it opened under his. Little by little he pulled

Kyra into his arms until finally he lifted her and carried her to the bed.

***

Two sets of eyes were glued to the monitoring console as they watched the couple. Their twin grunts of surprise when Peyton lifted Kyra into his arms was the only disruption of silence in the room.

"Okay. I've seen more than enough. There's no stopping her from liking him," Nero declared.

Brad smacked his forehead and held a hand out to point to the screen. "*Dude*—Borg Man made her cry and now they're going to get it on. What are you going to do about the way he's manipulating her emotions?"

Nero shook his head. He didn't necessarily like Kyra's growing relationship to Peyton Elliott, but something in the way the man had talked to Kyra had him reconsidering his concerns. Just from what little she had revealed in conversation, Nero now realized what Jackson had done to Kyra was far worse than anything he'd ever imagined because it hadn't been consensual. If the sexually abusive bastard had still been alive, he probably would have found a way to have killed Jackson Channing himself.

"Nothing, Brad. We're doing nothing about Kyra and Captain Elliott. Let them do what they want. Being with him will probably be good for her. At least he's trained to treat her well," Nero finally said.

He turned off the camera feed and removed their room from those being monitored for the evening. He also deleted the recording that had started the moment Kyra and Peyton had entered the room. Whatever happened would remain between the two of them—and only them.

"Dude—how can do that? Dr. Winters is brilliant. She deserves someone a lot better than Borg Man."

Nero nodded. "Yes, Brad. She does deserve someone better. But it's not raining men she likes, and you heard what Jackson did to her. This is between her and Captain Elliott. We're moving on and letting nature take its course."

"I still don't like it. Borg Man might be restored, but that doesn't make him less creepy or scary."

"We have to adjust to him. We're about to get more like him. Is Gloria here yet?" Nero asked, trying to distract Brad, who was still grumbling.

His friend had always had a giant crush on Kyra, but competing with someone like Peyton Elliott was a waste of his friend's time. Kyra and the cyborg were bonded through her saving him, and for other reasons Nero couldn't fathom. He and Brad needed to set aside their concerns and let Kyra live her own life. It should be easy for Brad to put his attention on the mysterious Gloria—the woman his friend continuously bragged about being so perfect.

Brad sighed in defeat as he glared at Nero. "Yes. Actually, I brought Gloria with me this time. She's in my room. I'd introduce you two, but something's wrong with her throat. She can't talk right now. Maybe later, Dude."

"Fine. If you two last, we'll get to introductions eventually. Go enjoy her company, Brad. I need time alone to think anyway. We'll talk again tomorrow," Nero ordered.

Brad shrugged. "You don't have to tell me twice, Bro. *Hasta la vista.*"

Once the observation room was completely silent, Nero drummed his fingers on the monitoring console as he brooded. Something wasn't right. Every instinct inside him was screaming, and the insistent demand for knowledge was never, ever wrong. But he and Brad both had run every check on Peyton they could. Nothing alarming had shown up.

Rising, he decided to distract himself by checking on the progress of the cages. Counting Kyra's, three were finished and ready. Two others were more than half done. By this time tomorrow, they would have holding cells wired into the main security links and ready for five cyborgs.

Giving up on finding any answers just sitting, Nero strode out of the monitoring room.

***

Kyra woke to darkness, cold and alone. Her eyes were crusty with dried tears and hard to keep open. Rubbing them clean, memories started coming back to her. Peyton had kissed her passionately and carried her to bed. But instead of seducing her, he had simply held her while she had cried herself to sleep.

And damn the sympathetic man. . .she had almost told him about Jackson watching other men have sex with her. Knowing she had agreed to such a thing was bad enough. Rehashing her stupidity in thinking it would save her marriage was simply not something she *ever* planned to do. That horrible mistake was over. . .and done. . .and out of her mind as far as she could put it. Jackson was also dead. As far as she was concerned, that was the official end of her sexual stupidity story.

Kyra rolled from her back to her side, wondering where Peyton had gone. Then she saw him sitting in the solitary chair in the room. He sat still as a statue, hands spread on his knees, but his eyes were tracking back and forth in the darkness. She could tell they were humming with quiet power—cybernetic power. He was physically resting, but he was also performing some cybernetic function. Multi-tasking was exactly what she had programmed all cyborgs to do.

She swallowed the epiphany so it wouldn't find verbal expression. Peyton was still a cyborg—just as Nero had insisted. But that wasn't all he was. Peyton Elliott was much more than the sum of his cybernetic parts and functions. Each passing day he exhibited more of the best of all human emotions. His actions demonstrated compassion, thoughtfulness, even the understanding of verbal nuances.

And Peyton was right about her past having damaged her, but wrong about the present manifestation of its effects. Jackson's abuse had traumatized her, but that one night of bad judgment was nothing compared to the horror of living with the rest of her mistakes. Every day she clung to the hope that what she and Jackson had done to soldiers like Peyton had not truly taken their humanity away. She had meant everything she had said about that. Giving Peyton back his free will was as close to an act of redemption as she was ever going to get.

Choosing to trust whatever cybernetic tasks Peyton was doing was okay and not a threat to anyone, Kyra rose quietly and went to use the adjoining bathroom. She washed her face and all traces of her meltdown away as best she could. The woman in the mirror over the sink looked old and tired. But thankfully, the woman did not look frightened.

"We shall call that lack of fear—*progress*," Kyra whispered to her reflection. Then she turned and walked back to the bed.

Climbing in between the covers, Kyra squirmed as she tried to get comfortable again. Without Peyton's body heat, the single covering on the bed didn't help much. They were in a remote facility Nero had built in the remaining wilds of rural Montana. Its solar heating system didn't keep the place very warm, but it kept them off all energy grids, which guaranteed she stayed temporarily lost from UCN radar. As her teeth chattered, she reminded herself that discomfort was a small price to pay for her continued freedom.

"I can see you shivering under the covers, Kyra. Are you cold?" Peyton asked.

Kyra sighed. "Yes, but I don't want to interrupt what you are doing. You look...busy."

"I couldn't sleep so I decided to use the time to run maintenance again. I was investigating my occasional *blips*, as you call them. Sometimes it's a thought I can't bring forward. Sometimes it's a short-lived, but numbing indecision about how best to act. You warned me those situations were going to happen, but I'm trying to reshuffle my data storage until information access is instant and mentally comfortable. My mind never stops thinking. Even asleep, processes keep running. I am getting better at disconnecting from them though."

Kyra nodded against her pillow. "I don't think I can change your human-cyborg dynamic without completely removing all the cybernetics from your body. Your current body dynamic is as good as I can make it for you. I will keep trying to improve it for as long as I live."

Peyton fought the urge to shrug. Absolute stillness made the processes run fastest and he could better study them while they did. "I wasn't complaining, Doc—not really. It was more like mentioning a fact. My current situation is better than my life has been for years. I'm sure about that now."

"Is it?" Kyra whispered the question and then waited for an answer.

Peyton ordered his processor to stop and mark where to pick up next time. He walked to the bed and slid in beside Kyra. "Yes, Doc. It's not perfect, and still not what Cyber Soldiers were promised, but it is better. I gave that a lot of thought during the days you were unconscious."

"Do you think other cyborgs will be able to think the same way about it?"

Kyra knew it was her fear speaking, but she still wanted to hear what Peyton thought. If they went forward with more restorations, she fully expected to find other cyborgs who would react like Marshall and Alex. They would not be grateful. They would be resentful. Some might even try to kill her. At the very least, they would hate her for what she had not done until now—even if Peyton miraculously didn't.

"Each will have to make their own decision in the matter," Peyton said. "Isn't that your ultimate goal?"

Kyra nodded. Peyton always offered rational logic about irrational things, and the man had a memory that was inspiring. "Yes. That is the goal, but that doesn't make my responsibility for their pain any easier to accept. I never intended to invent a way to enslave people, but that's what my prosthetics code turned out to be."

"Well, let's look at your actions from another perspective. If you hadn't had your change of heart and done what you did for me, despite all the challenges, I would still be in the Cyber Husband program without any freedom at all. Would you rather some other wife was lying beside me, keeping warm right now?" Peyton asked.

The question about how they came to be together caught her off-guard, but her surprised reaction was the real shocker. Kyra reached out while shaking her head and Peyton wasted no time pulling her on top of him. Her mouth was on his before she could give herself anymore time to analyze why she didn't want any other woman doing it.

"I really like the way you kiss me. I don't want to kiss any other woman, Doc. How about you try believing that for a while?" Peyton whispered between breaths.

Kyra's groan of surrender was as much for herself as it was for him. Her hand slid to the front of the pants he was still wearing. She stroked the evidence of his desire and looked for fear inside herself. Maybe enough time had finally gone by because she felt absolutely none. Or maybe it was just that Peyton was not like any other man.

"You're wearing too many clothes for this to be done efficiently, Captain Elliott. I suggest you remove them as quickly as possible if you want this to happen."

Kyra found herself promptly deposited back on her pillow while Peyton removed all his clothes. She swallowed hard because her throat was tight with nervous anticipation. It wasn't that she was afraid of sex with Peyton. She was more afraid she wouldn't be able to respond enough to enjoy what was happening between them.

"Okay, I'm naked. Now your turn," Peyton ordered, assisting by pulling her shirt over her head. But he left her shorts on while he pulled her naked chest against his because he couldn't wait any longer for some real skin contact. He hadn't even noticed the absence of a bra under her shirt earlier. It wasn't like him to miss such details. It was probably one more blip he needed to study, but he'd worry about it later—much later.

He held her soft breasts flattened against his hard muscles and then remembered that Kyra still had a weak wrist. The break had partially healed, but he didn't want to hurt her again by having her lean on her bad arm. He released her and rolled until he was partially over her. Her hands came up instantly to explore his shoulders. It made him feel even bigger than he knew he was.

"Were you built like this before the enhancements?" Kyra asked.

His non-cybernetic hand swept across her soft stomach and felt it ripple under his touch. "I was military lean, but stronger than I looked. It amazes me still that I don't have to work out to stay this way. I've concluded the cybernetic pulses affect my muscles like exercise."

"Actually, that's true. Your intelligence far surpasses what your records indicated was possible for you. I'm glad you know so much about what's happening. I'm doubly glad you got there on your own. It means all cyber scientists were wrong about cybernetics being able to control a human mind completely. I'm sincerely and ecstatically happy about that," Kyra whispered.

"Back to talking science again, Doc? Let me see if I can distract your mind with something more interesting." He fastened his mouth to hers while he slipped a hand inside her sleep pants. Finding a trim set of curls, he brushed knuckles through them as Kyra moaned and shifted restlessly.

Careful not to tear the material of the meager clothing available to them, he swept the shorts off her hips until they slid to her knees. Moving the clothing farther down her legs would require stopping and he had no plans to do that. Instead, he moved the hand not propping him up to cup a breast. He must have gotten the pressure right because Kyra moaned again and kicked her shorts off the rest of the way.

Peyton lifted his head. "Tell me if I do anything that worries you. I'm trained to be patient and not rush a woman, but my urges for you keep overriding my programming."

Kyra lifted a hand to his face. "I tried dating after I lost Alex. I even got to this point with a man once, but I ended up not being able to go through with it. I don't think I'm going to have that problem with you. What I feel for you amazes me."

Peyton chuckled under her hand, which had gone exploring again. This time it was on his stomach and inching lower. He smiled in the dark. "Don't even think about this not happening. Those restraints were torture, but that pain is nothing compared to my concern about not getting inside you."

"Why do you think you feel that way about me? I'm trying to understand it and I can't," Kyra said, her hand stopping.

Peyton gently took her hand and moved it lower until he could show her. "Because you make me feel like this. Given our history, the arousal I get around you is totally illogical. Yet it is also very real. Maybe it's just one of those emotional outbursts you said I might experience while I adjust. Since this particular part of me does feel close to bursting, I assume you were right to warn me about such things."

Kyra closed her eyes and snickered at Peyton's joke. When she stopped laughing, she pushed his hand to the side so she could grip his erection the way she wanted. She stroked and felt him lean into her hand. Her heart beat hard and for a moment it fluttered in mild alarm. She pushed away the panic and opened her eyes to see Peyton's interested gaze on her face.

"Please don't look so alarmed, Doc. I find you very pleasing to stare at for long periods of time," he said.

For some reason, his compliment struck her as incredibly funny. "I'm sorry I'm laughing, but you're supposed to say you find me beautiful, Peyton."

Peyton grinned as he rolled on top of her. Her grip released him, which let him settle his erection in the crease of her thighs. "I was trained to tell women they're beautiful, but what does that ever mean? I was trying to offer you a more sincere compliment. That was the closest truth I could share with you. Would you rather I said you were beautiful? Because you are."

His revelation had her melting under him. It also sent more tears streaming down her face. Kyra shook her head and let her legs fall apart until Peyton's hips fell between them. "No. And I'm sorry I ruined your moment of honest sharing. I'm glad you find me pleasing to stare at for long periods of time. I don't think I've ever heard a nicer compliment."

Peyton eased up and forward, his body asking if it was time. Kyra spread her legs farther in answer. In his excitement his mouth came down hard on hers, harder than he intended as he began to slide inside. Her body was hot, wet, and so appealing. Her hips arching up changed the angle and allowed him to burrow deeper. Lights flashed through his brain at the extreme pleasure. It even hurt a little, but not as much as stopping would have.

The rhythm of their lovemaking happened organically. He moved in and out of Kyra's writhing body, feeling awe the whole time. Something more was happening than he recalled ever experiencing in the act. Maybe it was new synapses firing. Maybe it was just that he was inside Kyra Winters.

When he was so close that he feared he would disappoint her, Kyra's body suddenly tightened around his with an urgent grip that held him captive and at the same time sent him reeling in release with her. He moved against Kyra as much as her body allowed, rocking away the orgasm that had taken over both of them. Lights flashed through his mind again as his body did what was natural.

When the lights cleared away, his thinking was laser sharp and clear for the first time in days.

He kissed Kyra in gratitude, and tried to kiss her tears away, but there were too many. Kyra had wept all through her release and continued to weep afterward. He'd had that happen before with other women, but it had never bothered him the way it did with her. He wanted to know why she wept over pleasure, but didn't want asking to ruin her enjoyment. Her arms were still tight around him when he felt her heartbeat finally calm.

"Thank you," he whispered. "I feel much better now."

Kyra laughed, her face hidden against a rock hard shoulder. "Thank you back. I feel much better now too."

When he lost the last of his erect state, Peyton slid from Kyra and rolled them to their sides. "I didn't worry about having unprotected sex with you because I can't give you children. The heat from my cybernetics keeps me sterile. The heat also keeps me disease free. In the military, I thought both of those would be good. Now. . .well with such a long life ahead of me, it might have been nice to have a family. . .even if I followed the suggested limit of one child per adult."

Kyra swallowed back her groan of dismay. Okay. Cyborg sterility was just one more thing she would have to work on fixing. She mentally added it to her already long list before she spoke. "Well at least it crossed your mind. Protection didn't even occur to me. I confess I wasn't thinking of anything at all except what we were doing."

"Good," Peyton declared, letting the smile take over his face. "That's all I wanted for our first time."

Kyra snorted at his assumption. "First time? You think this is going to happen again?"

Peyton bent his head and playfully bit a nipple until it sprang to attention against his tongue.

"Maybe," he whispered, licking the pebbled tip.

Kyra knew he was making fun of her using that word, but she couldn't find it in her to care as much as she should have. All she wanted was for Peyton's mouth to close firmly around the nipple he was torturing. She glared at him for making her want him again.

"Maybe it won't," she warned. She put her still healing hand over her aroused nipple to protect it from his talented mouth.

Peyton's laughter as he pulled her hand off her breast had her struggling, but that ceased the moment his mouth did the very thing she had wanted so badly. A couple minutes later, they were both breathing hard again. But after he stopped, it was another shock to her when Peyton's fingers pried hers away from gripping the bed covers. They stared at each other in the dark, each absorbing what their renewed arousal meant.

"I think there is a ninety-nine point nine percent chance of it happening again," Peyton declared softly. "But just so you know, there's a hundred percent chance of it lasting a hell of a lot longer next time, Doc."

Kyra groaned softly as she pulled his hand up to cover the breast he had tortured. "I'll run the percentages myself later to check, but maybe you're right," she admitted, closing her eyes in pleasure at what his fingers were doing.

Chapter 15

Kyra eyed the restraining cages with trepidation. She and Nero had constructed the one in her lab before she'd bought Marshall. At Norton they were part of every lab. For her, the cage had been a necessary piece of equipment for one specific purpose, not something she'd ever planned on having to use again and again. She found it alarming to see five cages spaced out around the large room. These were deliberate too—and planned—*and* they had the same purpose as the one she'd built.

She drew in a ragged breath and let it out. Her gaze went back to Nero, who was looking at the cages with satisfaction. She wanted to say something to discourage him from feeling that way, but that wasn't fair. He had saved her and given her sanctuary. She owed him loyalty not criticism.

"Why five cages?" she asked instead.

Nero shrugged. "Because I didn't have money for six. We'll just have to capture a few cyborgs at a time."

"And just how are we going to do that?" Kyra demanded.

Nero barked out a laugh and shook his head. "What did you and Peyton talk about last night? I guess I know what you *didn't* talk about. I hope you enjoyed each other's company at least."

Shaking her head, Kyra turned away. She didn't want Nero's censure. She had enough of her own worry about what she had let happen between her and Peyton.

"We didn't discuss abducting other cyborgs. Sorry if I just didn't have it in me to discuss the impending cyborg revolution while I was falling asleep."

Kyra turned away and started back toward the door.

Nero huffed out a frustrated breath. "Kyra—wait. I'm sorry. I'm tense and taking it out on you. I barely got the rest of my money into safe accounts before the UCN tapped my records. They're probably watching to see if I give any of my money to you. I had to buy my dream game system just to throw them off the trail."

Kyra bit her lip and raised her face to the ceiling. There were never any answers there, but she kept hoping. "Your involvement in this crazy scheme is on my head as much as anything else. I just hope like hell I'm right about all this."

Nero walked over and turned her to face him. "I'm sorry I made you doubt yourself. You're right about this and you always have been. Humans should not be made into cybernetic slaves. If we let that happen without attempting to disrupt it, eventually no one on earth is going to be safe. We need to free those we think will work together in the best of ways to help us stop that future from happening."

Kyra closed her eyes and nodded. "I know. I just. . .God, Nero. Watching Peyton struggle to adapt is difficult. I see even more clearly now that there were many other ways we could have ended the world wars. We didn't have to treat our soldiers so cruelly. I changed his life forever when I developed the creator code, and now I will never be able to completely undo all the damage."

Nero nodded. Kyra's enormous compassion was one of the reasons he liked her so much. It was probably also the reason she had slept with Peyton Elliott. But whatever came of Kyra and Peyton's relationship, in the end Kyra would be the one standing alone when she faced the wrath of the other cyborgs she freed. Only an original creator could go near a rebooted cyborg without fearing death. They might try to hurt her, but Kyra had codes that would keep them from killing her. That failsafe had been built into the programming all along. But he didn't envy Kyra having to endure each individual awakening to the horrible truth of what she had helped do to them.

"Look at me, Kyra," Nero ordered. When she did, he held her gaze. "What's between you and Peyton Elliott is your business. Just promise me you'll be careful. I feel like there's a traitor to our cause nearby, but I haven't been able to figure out who it is. Peyton is the most likely suspect. There is still so much we don't know about his military programming and we haven't had the time to be sure he's as fixed as he thinks he is."

Kyra nodded. She trusted Nero's instincts. He had given her many reasons over the years to do so. "Okay. I'll keep watching for anything unusual, but cybernetic anomalies are becoming a daily occurrence for Peyton. On the plus side, he seems more and more human each passing moment."

"I'm well aware of his changes," Nero said, dropping his hands from her arms. "Peyton has a plan for how to draw the other cyborgs out, and I think he's right about how it could work. Since you're the key to it working, you really need to talk to him about it yourself. I suggest you do so as quickly as possible."

Kyra nodded. But it was hard to ignore the ball of dread growing in her mid-section.

***

She tracked Peyton down and found him reading. His explanation about learning how to build a pulse cannon had her running an agitated hand over her freshly cut, shorter hair. Peyton explained the pulse cannon was needed to capture those cyborgs who refused to come with him willingly. He had no qualms about using it because it rendered them completely unconscious. He informed her being unconscious was a lot better fate than being tortured with controller pain as the processor fried.

Kyra nodded, the ball of dread expanding as she did so. "How close do you have to be to the others to activate the military protocol code?"

"One and a half klicks—almost a mile. I can't believe measurements never standardized after the wars were over. How can there possibly be peace among people who still can't agree on basic math?" Peyton demanded.

"A mile. . . that's good. That's fairly close proximity, and yet still safely out of range of the actual target. I can see many reasons why the military chose that distance for their purposes."

Kyra's mind drifted off after hearing the answer she had been seeking. Ignoring the rest of Peyton's commentary was pretty much standard practice for her now, even though doing so never seemed to slow him down from expressing his random thoughts. Each day found him getting more in touch with his opinions and what she considered to be his feelings.

"That's a strange look, Doc. Don't tell me a cyber scientist never thought about standardizing basic measurements?"

Kyra shook her head. And nine times out of ten, no matter how hard she tried not to engage in off-topic conversations, Peyton pulled her right back into them. The man loved to talk.

"Everyone has had that thought, but it's not something I can change, Peyton. Learning all measuring systems in use on the planet has served me best. Code language is different though. Leveling isn't merely logical. It's a necessity. So your conclusion only applies to clothing sizes, food preparation, distance, and weight. I can't explain why no one has cared."

Peyton grunted at Kyra's intellectual reply. The woman's mind was every bit as logical as any cyborg's and just as prone to ignoring nuances. "Well all I can say is God forbid we do anything simply for the sake of logic."

Kyra wrinkled her face at his statement. She was having trouble keeping up with his thinking today. "Are you using the term 'God' for emphasis of your point or are you now pondering the existence of an actual deity?"

It irritated her when Peyton ducked his head. She could see his shoulders shaking. His sense of humor was developing in ways she couldn't fathom, and she often didn't get what he thought was so funny. Maybe it was because a lot of what he laughed at seemed to be something she did or said.

"I didn't ask the 'God' question for your amusement. I was being serious."

His silent grin and arched eyebrow made her roll her eyes and throw her hands up.

"Never mind. Forget I asked. So once you build your pulse cannon, what's next? My guess is that we need to target which cyborgs to go after."

"Already did that. I'm targeting men who I know will pretty much feel the same way I do about this situation. If we recover those five, we'll have the kind of cyborg apprehension group you and Nero have been dreaming about. I've already located them. They're living in relatively the same area in Virginia. From the looks of things, the most dangerous cyborgs were kept fairly close to Norton's headquarters. If the creator code and cannon both work, we should be able to collect all five in a single day—one way or the other."

Kyra bit her bottom lip as she thought about it. "Don't you think it will look suspicious when five Cyber Husbands just up and disappear?"

Peyton shrugged. "No more strange than my disappearance. The UCN will step up their search efforts, but they're also going to do their homework. It won't take them long to figure out I'm putting my favorite fire team back together. That's four of the five. The other one I'm rescuing is my best sergeant. They'll panic when they see who's gone missing. . .and they should. They know what we can do together."

"What do you mean?" Kyra asked, her gaze riveted on Peyton's tight jaw.

"These men were enhanced in a way that served all of us. We were trained to work efficiently as a group. As captain, I shouldn't have had to do much fighting, but during the war, we all did what needed to be done. I fought alongside them more often than anyone knew. I never found anything the six of us couldn't manage to accomplish. And that's what the UCN is going to be most worried about."

Kyra sighed. "Should we be worried about what the UCN will do in retaliation?"

Peyton shrugged again. "Only until the guys are restored. Then you won't have to worry so much. Nero won't either. We'll take over handling apprehensions, security, provisions, and safety. All you two will have to do is keep fixing the cyborgs we bring to you."

Kyra shook her head. "This is not what I planned to do to fix the cyborg situation. I confess I had more terroristic methods running through my mind."

Peyton got up and walked to her. He lifted Kyra's chin with a finger to make sure he made eye contact. "Listen to me well, Dr. Winters, because we are *never* having this discussion again. Your martyrdom can never accomplish as much as your continued work can if you have the courage to fix other cyborgs the way you fixed me. All your fears about their reactions are more than possible—they're probable. So accept that because you're going to have to deal with them being pissed at you. But if you truly want to stop what you set into motion when you helped make us machines, then restoring them is your best option."

Kyra nodded reluctantly against his fingers. "Okay. I get it. This is mostly my problem to set right, and it's not fair to try and pass the responsibility along to Nero and other scientists."

Her reward for her right answer was Peyton's mouth branding hers with a sample of the desire that always danced between them.

Chapter 16

Kyra had suspected Nero was wealthy, but she was learning he spent his money on far more than just gaming and bad dates. The air jet she sat in was top of the line and being piloted by its owner. Peyton sat across from her, checking the pulse cannon for the hundredth time. If she didn't know better, she'd have called Peyton's repetitive actions a mental problem.

But she also realized she was faring no better. She kept swiping her hand across the short blonde spikes of hair that represented her new look. With the eye shades, subdued earrings, and black clothing, she looked like a wealthy heiress, gone slumming. She hadn't recognized herself in the mirror. If she was lucky, no one else would recognize her either.

Peyton was wearing black also, but he looked like some woman's wet dream come to life. As if privy to her thoughts, and she still wasn't sure he wasn't, Peyton's head lifted to grin at her.

"Nervous, Doc?"

Kyra laughed. "Why do you ask? I'm not the one checking my weapon every two seconds."

"With as much gel as you put in your hair this morning, I think I'd call those spikes of yours weapons. I'm almost afraid to touch you now."

"Good," Kyra declared.

Peyton grinned. He had touched her all he had wanted to last night. In fact, he'd had her pleading for release before he'd let either of them get there.

"I didn't say I *was* afraid—I said *almost*. I said it the way you as a scientist say *maybe* all the time. Guesstimating is a nuance I learned from you. I would have thought you would recognize it."

"The word is *estimating*—not *guesstimating*," Kyra corrected, frowning at his blips.

"Right. And thanks for correcting me on my joke." Peyton shook his head over her statement, but ended up smiling at the low level fury in her sharp gaze on his. "Better stop glaring at me, Doc. Having you ever heard that the definition of insanity is to keep doing what doesn't work? Unless you want me to find a place we can take advantage of your glare's side effect."

"No. I thought it was another blip. That's all," she hissed softly. She hoped Nero hadn't heard their argument and Peyton's threat over the jet's drone.

Peyton smiled at her irritation. He enjoyed it way too much, but today he was using it to keep her mind occupied until it was time to act. "So when I go all cyborg on you again, are you going to freak?"

Kyra shook her head. "No. Of course not. Why would I do that?"

Peyton leaned forward and felt his clothing straining against his taut body. "Because we've both been happy to forget that I'm not all human. I've even hidden my routine maintenance from you so we wouldn't have to talk about my cyborg functions. But today you're about to see the other part of what I am again, and now I'm concerned about what you will think. Maybe I should have forced us to face this before we got on the plane to get the others. It was irrational of me to avoid it."

"Yes, maybe you should have," Kyra said, purposely mocking him.

Peyton shook his head and leaned back. "I'm still coming to terms with some things, but I'm nearly one hundred percent certain I can be a full cyborg when I need to be one. I just want you to know I'm also the human man that made you scream in pleasure last night. Don't forget that."

Kyra shook her head, frustrated when no hair swished around her face. "Shh. . .stop talking about last night. I don't want to talk about it. I don't want Nero hearing about it. Let's just do what we have to do."

Peyton nodded tightly. "Fine. You're just going to have to deal with whatever you see."

"Dealing is not a problem. Dealing is my specialty," Kyra declared.

But when Nero landed the air jet in a parking lot in the middle of Arlington, the anxiety in her stomach lurched up into her chest.

"Kyra, stop worrying. Too much of that will have you making foolish decisions. You need to have as much faith in what we're doing today as you did in buying me," Peyton ordered.

But all Kyra could do was nod as a black dressed Nero motioned it was time to leave the plane.

***

Kingston West lifted his head from his gardening task. There was an annoying signal buzzing through his cybernetics like a fly buzzing around a ripe peach. When an old military activation code starting running through his mind, King answered it by activating his maintenance program to see what was the matter. The military code instantly shut it down and commenced running again. That let him know it was for real.

"Kingston? Have you finished with the tomatoes?"

King turned to look at his latest wife. She was at least sixty years older than him, which was probably why they hadn't had sex—not even once. Instead of a full relationship, Annalisa used him for tasks around her house. "I think I have a cybernetic malfunction that needs to be addressed. Perhaps I require upgrading."

He watched Annalisa touch her face in alarm. She liked to act like an old school Southern belle, complete with fake fainting spells.

"Oh dear. I'll check your records, but I'm fairly sure they said you could go several years more without needing any updates. Are you able to keep working?"

"I am receiving a military communication that is overriding all other functionality."

King looked at the tomatoes. They would be ready for picking in two more weeks. He had estimated the ripening time for each individual fruit. But he suddenly knew he would not be around to see his estimates become reality.

When location coordinates came through, King laid down his tools and pulled off his gloves. "I have to leave. I am being called back to active duty."

"Oh dear. Are you sure about this, Kingston?"

He nodded. "Yes. When I arrive at the destination of my coordinates, I will ask that you be notified. I apologize for distressing you. Wait. . .the code is coming in clearer now. It is overriding my Cyber Husband programming. Code 57896—yes. That's definitely a military recall. Are you familiar with subsection 10.9 of our contract?"

Annalisa took out her handheld and looked it up. "Oh yes—I see it now. There is a call back clause in that part of the contract. This is highly inconvenient, but it says you will either be returned or another will be sent in your place. I guess you have to go, Kingston. Do try to let me know what's going on. I have really enjoyed our time together."

"I will do what I can," King said. His feet were already moving toward the front gate. As he walked, his arm started tingling. When he went to scratch it, he found a panel had opened up just above his wrist. He looked down at it in surprise at what it contained. He was trying to figure it out when he heard a voice in his head.

Don't touch the contents of the panel. Just come as quickly as you can to the coordinates.

He closed the panel cover and lowered his arm, instantly obeying the commanding voice. Picking up speed, King hurried at a rapid clip to an alley that ran between two buildings. Inside the alley, he found three people wearing black. Two were fully human. The one who was a cyborg like him removed his eye shades and stared at him with glowing golden orbs. He searched his memory trying to find a match for the man's face.

"Hello Kingston. Do you remember who I am yet?" Peyton asked, grinning at his friend.

King raised a hand to his head. It was hurting something fierce. "You look. . .vaguely. . .familiar." His eyes darted around as he tried to recall the man's name. Thinking about it made his headache worse.

"Kyra, do your magic. You're going to want to deactivate King *before* he figures it out," Peyton ordered.

"I can't use the creator code out here in public. Someone might overhear it," she said.

Peyton sighed and lifted the cannon. He fired once, but King only wobbled. He fired a second time and King stumbled forward to take a wild swing that fell way short.

"What are you doing to me?" King asked. "Who the hell are you?"

"I'm your captain and we're rescuing you, Numbnuts. I know it doesn't feel like it at the moment, but that's what's happening," Peyton said sharply.

Hating to do what was necessary, he stepped a bit closer and lifted the cannon again. He fired one last shot at close range straight into King's chest. The nearly indestructible cyborg went down hard, something that never would have happened if King had been in touch with all his faculties. If he actually went back to being his old self later, Peyton knew King would make him pay for shooting him with the pulse cannon.

"I thought you said it was only going to take one cannon shot to bring them down," Kyra exclaimed.

Peyton shrugged. "That should be true for all the others. I wasn't completely sure the cannon was going to work at all on King. His prosthetics absorb most pulse blasts and use them to create a electro-magnetic shield against other weapons. That's one of his unique enhancements."

As they walked forward, Peyton passed the cannon to a reluctant Nero to hold. He bent to lift the now unconscious King over his shoulder. "You've become a heavy SOB in a decade, Kingston West. Your wives must have made you do all the cooking."

They walked to a large white carrier pod. Opening the double back doors, Kyra climbed in and motioned for Peyton to lay the unconscious man at her feet.

Peyton did it, but reluctantly. "You can't ride back here with him, Kyra. It's too dangerous."

"I'm safer with him than you would be, plus I have to put the restraints on while he's unconscious. What's the chances of those even working on this guy?" Kyra ordered herself not to be afraid of the unconscious giant who was even bigger than the cyborg she was used to.

Peyton thought for a moment. "Dial the power on the controller all the way up and don't be afraid to use it. King's not going to be a good patient if he thinks he's in danger. But the good news is he's going to be the hardest one we have to deal with today. That's why I wanted to pick him up first."

"Oh good," Kyra said, wincing as she clipped the restraints around giant wrists. They almost didn't fit and she hoped they wouldn't have to be used. She placed a cybernetic scrambling device over his head and inserted a signal broadcaster into each ear. If it worked like she hoped, Kingston 691 wouldn't wake up until he was strapped to her operating chair.

They repeated the military recall process and collected two other large cyborgs before it was decided they had to return with the first three because five would never fit into Nero's air jet. Kyra noticed that Peyton seemed to get more satisfied with every cyborg they procured. His satisfaction almost seemed like happiness.

She adjusted her speak-through and tapped it to broadcast to the men who were driving their transport vehicle. "Care to share why you're so pleased with this whole collection process, Captain?"

In the front seat, Peyton smiled at Kyra's irritation. By now her voice nuances were all recorded and logged in the file he kept updating on her.

"I was just thinking about how much the guys were going to owe me for rescuing their asses. And after that I was thinking about what kind of favor I would collect from each of them because of their gratitude."

He glanced sideways at Nero to see if the younger man found his bragging funny, but Nero seemed intent on nothing but navigating the carrier pod.

Peyton shook his head. "Are you worried my motives are a little *too human*, Dr. Winters?"

Kyra considered the question. "Not really," she answered.

Peyton grinned at the mild comment from the queen of understatement. He heard a sizzle in his earpiece. "Problems, Doc?"

"Eric 754 keeps trying to wake up."

Peyton nodded and grinned even though Kyra couldn't see him. "Not surprising. Eric has the capacity to reboot himself—over and over and over. We once knocked him out twenty-five times just to see if he had a limit. His face got severely damaged before we found out for sure."

Peyton heard Kyra swearing and then a cyborg grunting. After that there was silence.

"Doc? Sounds like you have even more problems. You sure you're okay back there?"

"Can you please go back through the acquisition list and make some notations about any enhancements that might make future apprehensions a challenge? It would be far more useful to choose their restraints based on that rather than your willy-nilly guesstimating."

"Maybe I could do that," Peyton said firmly, wincing a little when Kyra swore at him. He laughed in her ear and earned another round of blistering commentary about his lack of sensitivity and his poor sense of humor.

Beside him he saw Nero whip off his speak-through and glare at him. "Lose yours too."

"Can't fight with you right now, Doc. Nero and I need to talk privately for a moment. Hang in there. Buzz if the guys give you too much trouble."

Peyton slowly removed his speak-through and stared at Nero. "Got a problem?"

"Yes," Nero answered sharply. "I want you to stop fucking with Kyra. And I mean that every way possible. You don't deserve her compassion and she doesn't deserve your shit. She barely stays one mental step away from walking into Norton Industries and ending them along with her own life. I have worked for years to give Kyra a purpose to keep on living. I will see all cyborgs permanently deactivated and carved into parts before I'll let any of you hurt her. That goes double for you, Captain Elliott."

Peyton scratched his nose even though it didn't itch. His awareness of the unnecessary action made the ends of his mouth turn upward. More and more he was discovering his body just wanted to react without conscious thought. More and more he was learning to let it. At times he was close to being giddy with the amount of emotion he was feeling. In the center of his return to his humanity was a woman he should hate but instead felt everything for except that emotion.

"I wasn't fucking with Kyra—not really. Keeping her pissed at me makes her brave, and it keeps her from being nervous about what we're doing. She has to let go of her perpetual guilt trip and start getting motivated in a healthier way. As for our physical relationship, I'm her husband and it's none of your damn business what we do with each other when we're alone."

He watched Nero pound the drive console. "Do you really know what you're saying? You're a freed cyborg. You have no obligations to her at all. She's your creator."

"Yes I do know that. I also know we're exactly point three six five klicks from the air jet and I know it without checking any instrument. I'm absolutely still cyborg when it comes to noticing details. You're way more nervous than Kyra is about what we're doing, and you didn't eat this morning because your stomach is making noises like two dogs growling at each other. Now calm down, Nero. I know what I'm doing. I may have been a lousy Cyber Husband to my other ten wives, but my relationship to Kyra is one I intend to work on for a good long time. I like her and she's going to need at least one cyborg always on her side because I guarantee you, the UCN is going to send other cyborgs to kill her just like they sent me. They don't want her to succeed in restoring us."

Nero huffed out a breath. "You're right."

Peyton shrugged. "Yes. I know I'm right. Unless we get the upper hand quickly, we're all in danger. The UCN still has hundreds of soldiers like me. There are only a few of us capable of activating the military recall program, but you have to know I'm not the only one."

"Yes. I know that. So does Kyra," Nero reported.

"Then don't make me worry about you as well. You've got to hold your shit together and keep focused on what it's going to take to release as many as we can. Once I have my team restored, we're going to look for the others like me. If we can restore the leaders before they get modified to prevent it, we might be able to get this revolution done more quickly."

Nero nodded. "Okay. Just. . .just stop giving Kyra shit in front of me. She's practically my mother. I don't handle it well."

Peyton fought not to laugh. "Okay. I'm sorry. I'll keep your sensibilities in mind when I give Kyra shit in the future."

When the speak-through started flashing, both Nero and Peyton snatched theirs up. Peyton got his working first. "What's up, Doc?"

"Peyton, how many times do I have to tell you—that joke is not funny to me. The idea of a talking rabbit does not even make sense. Now a chimpanzee doing sign language or a dolphin with a translator makes at least a little sense. But a rabbit? I don't think so. Twentieth century people were strange. I'm glad my parents never let me watch cartoons as a child."

Peyton laughed at her tirade. He looked over then to see Nero smirking as he rolled his eyes. "We'll have to upgrade your cartoon education as soon as we can, Doc. Right now I think Nero here needs some driving lessons. Next time, he rides in the back and you can drive."

"Me? Why? I hate driving. Why can't you drive?" Kyra demanded.

Peyton smiled at the irritation in her question. She was most likely upset because she didn't understand why he would say something so out of character for the military control freak he was discovering inside himself. As he recovered more of his past, and blended it with his present, he kept messing up her stereotypes. He was thoroughly enjoying her surprise when it happened.

"Being cyborg, my driving precision would be too much for you and Nero to handle. I have a tendency to go hard and fast which tends to make those riding with me ill before we arrive at our destination. I make a better passenger than driver, unless I'm operating a military drone or chopper."

"I certainly believe the hard and fast part. I've seen enough evidence of those traits to be convinced," Kyra answered.

Peyton grinned broadly as Nero smacked the drive console in frustration. "Wow. Are you flirting with me, Doc? Remember your pseudo-scientist son—brother—or whatever he is up here is still on our com channel. Better save the innuendo for later. He's starting to blush."

"I was *not* flirting with you, Peyton. I was merely making an observation based on data I collected from our tests and. . .oh never mind. Sometimes I don't know why I bother trying to talk to you. Ninety percent of the time it leads to an argument. Don't ever call me irrational again," Kyra declared.

Peyton heard another zap and another grunt. He winced as he thought about Eric being on the receiving end of Kyra's impatience with his teasing. "I see the air jet up ahead. I'll take over zapping Eric on the flight home."

"Thank you. That's very thoughtful of you, Peyton. The signal devices aren't working on him like they are the others. I can't get him to shut down. That's going to be tricky when I try to restore him. I think I'm going to see if I have access to their original conversion records. Jackson wired the first hundred while I worked on the code. Your team has some unique prosthetics I don't think were ever replicated again. They were probably too costly."

"I never saw other cyborgs with them either. So I think you're probably right," Peyton agreed.

The carrier pod stopped and Nero immediately hopped out. Peyton shook his head and climbed out too. He was thinking it was going to be a very long day regardless of how much actual time was passing.

Chapter 17

Kyra wiped her eyes on her sleeve as she continued to ignore the man standing against the wall of the lab. And it wasn't easy. Peyton was watching everything she did as she rewired the cyborg strapped to the chair. She hadn't bothered to set a recording up. Peyton's eyes hadn't looked away in the four and a half hours she'd spent working on Master Sergeant Kingston West. She'd just use the data Peyton was collecting.

King 691's controller wiring had been more extensive than Peyton's, but with the sophisticated scanner Nero provided in the lab, removing it had taken a mere thirty minutes. Being able to see the path left nothing to worry about. The rest of the work—well, the rest was making delicate choices about which chips to leave in the unusual man and which to replace with more benign versions that could be overwritten at his discretion.

The other glitch was that she'd also had to alter the code on Master Sergeant West's new processor to more carefully handle his unique prosthetics. That had meant stopping in the second hour and taking the time to update the file she was using. But what it meant for the cyborg was that he would eventually be able to decide for himself when his enhancements were activated. At the moment, she left them shut down for everyone's safety.

Startled by what she'd seen, she had even revoked Peyton's military control of the man's enhancements.

Though in retrospect, she could only hope it was the right action to take, since she couldn't consult the military person who helped make Kingston 691 into a weapon. Personally she hoped Master Sergeant West would never again have to activate his enhancements. Since she wasn't an expert in explosion devices, removing them completely was out of the question. She had refused Brad's help with the restoration precisely so he wouldn't alarm Nero with her discoveries on their very first captive.

"It surprises me you've watched this whole time and haven't asked me a single question," Kyra said finally. Her voice was husky for not having talked much while she worked.

"Well, I do have one question, but I didn't want to distract you while you were fixing King," Peyton said.

Kyra glanced once last time in the cybernetics compartment. Then she slid the processor into position before using an electron knife to turn it on. Kingston West's body flinched with the power surge, but his eyes remained closed.

"Now the hardest work begins," Kyra declared.

Then she walked to a chair and dropped her exhausted body into it.

"What's harder than what you just did?" Peyton asked, truly surprised at her statement. Kyra had never stopped once she'd started and hadn't taken a single break. She had every right to be exhausted.

Kyra tiredly met Peyton's curious gaze, wishing she had his sustainable energy. "The hardest part is waiting to see what Sergeant West will be like when he wakes up."

Peyton pondered her statement as he rolled an extra chair over and put it next to hers. He sat beside her, still dealing with his awe about what she had done. "Can I ask my question now?"

Kyra snorted. "My mind is mush, and I thought you just did. I thought I answered it too."

Peyton shook his head. "No. That was just regular conversation. I have a serious question that's been on my mind since you started working on King."

"Sure. Ask. But I doubt you're going to get an intelligent answer out of me. My brain is fried right now.

Being that careful takes a lot of energy. Mine doesn't last as long as yours, no matter how many booster pills I take."

Peyton lifted one of her hands and linked her fingers with his. "I just wanted to know if you cried the whole time you worked on me too. I don't think you had a dry moment while working on King."

Kyra tried to pull away, but he wouldn't let her go. "Maybe I cried a little," she said finally, not really wanting to admit the truth.

Peyton snorted at the understatement. "I already saw the recording of you fixing me, so I knew the answer. I just wanted to hear you admit it, and I want to hear why it happens."

"You know why it happens." Kyra swung her free hand toward the operating chair and the man strapped into it. "Your friend's condition is my fault and not just the restoration. If it wasn't for me, that man might not be in that chair."

"Why is it your fault?" Peyton asked, letting her hand go. "I read your file. You created code that allowed prosthetic arms to be calibrated with a person's brain. Did your discovery have to be used to create a killer's cybernetic arm? My records don't show that as part of your invention."

Kyra shook her head. "Well. . .no. Of course not."

"So let's agree that cybernetic abuse—such as wartime application to weapon prosthetics —is not an innate part of the technology. If there is evil, don't you think it is in the people who want cyborgs to make them money, bring them power, or win wars?"

Kyra lifted her gaze to his. "Is that some kind of cyborg philosophy you're developing?"

Peyton snickered at her sarcasm. Him laughing at her was as unkind as what she said. And he didn't need any sensitivity chip lighting up to warn him to be nice, even though his immediately did just that. He could ignore such things now without fear of painful consequences. Kyra had made that possible. But he paid attention to those warnings because he found it helpful with her. His cyber scientist was a lot more sensitive than she realized.

"Yes. Philosophy is my new hobby," Peyton said dryly. "And I'm sorry for laughing at your comment. Mostly I just wanted to offer you another perspective. You need to stop feeling guilty and become the heroic person you want to be."

Kyra gave him the look she reserved for her younger techs. "You're just saying nice supportive things so I'll keep having sex with you."

"Maybe," Peyton admitted. He registered her free hand smacking his arm and chose to interpret it as only mild frustration with his teasing.

"How long are you going to keep verbally torturing me with that word that I do not use as often as you say I do?" Kyra demanded.

"Doc—you need to face the facts. You're just not the evil science bitch you think you are. Last time I checked, the bad guys don't usually cry over their victims. Only the good guys ever cry, and they do it even more when no one is around."

"You don't cry," Kyra said.

Peyton laughed. "That's because I have cybernetic eyes. Plus I'm male. My first response to most trauma is to beat on something until the situation improves."

Kyra glared, but her exhaustion made it too weak to make a dent in Peyton's rapidly growing ego. "Can you not see that is the exact reason people are scared of cyborgs?"

"Well they should be. Just like they should be scared of people with guns and invisible biological weapons that can wipe out an entire population. Fear is a reasonable reaction to beings who are more powerful than you are. But if I wasn't a good guy I would never have gone into the military in the first place. I wanted to save people, not hurt them. All the people I hurt were bad."

Kyra dropped her gaze, stared at the floor, and sighed. "You're right. You're absolutely right. I'm just tired and thinking irrationally."

Peyton laughed softly. Leaning over he scooped Kyra up and tucked her into his lap while she yelped.

"Stop. I'm working. What do you think you're doing?" Kyra demanded.

He reached up and tucked her head under his chin. "I'm holding you. Holding a woman who is tired and frustrated is the fastest way to restore her energy. The affection activates her hormonal responses and gets endorphins flowing. After a sufficient amount of time—which varies by female—she will start to smile and level out."

Kyra snorted against his shoulder, but had to admit Peyton holding her was helping her feel better. "If you keep this up, I don't think I'm ever going to remove your Cyber Husband chip."

He hugged her closer and kissed her forehead. He was already getting hard. The woman did that do him every time he touched her.

"Dr. Winters—we've already had this discussion. I don't want you to remove it. But even if you did remove it, or it got accidentally zapped, I would be fine. I've been routinely backing up the data on it to my long term storage. All that information about you is too important to me to lose."

Kyra laughed. "Sometimes I think you're learning to be a much better human than I could be no matter how long I live. I hope that tendency exists in all cyborgs. We did a psychological profile on the soldiers we were converting, but those don't account for what they endured during the war and the last decade."

"I can only vouch for the motivations of the five we have rescued so far," Peyton said, kissing her forehead again.

A groan from the chair had her sliding from his lap and hustling over.

"Yep. This is just like the old days. King made a point to interrupt every conversation I ever had with a woman. It was his fault that I almost never got laid. Sometimes I'd even see him with the woman later. If he tries that shit with you, I'm going to kick his cyborg ass. I don't care how much bigger than me he is."

Kyra checked the restraints and then checked his vitals. "Wear steel-toed boots so you don't break your toes. What's a prosthetic ass look like? I can definitely see this giant having one."

"It was figure of speech, Doc."

"I know. I was making a joke, Peyton." She looked up at his chuckle and smiled. "I like you, Captain Elliott. I like your sense of humor and your ethics. You make me be a better person when I'm around you. That's a serious comment on my part."

Peyton crossed his arms and grinned. "Nice to hear. Are you flirting with me, Doc?"

Kyra nodded, but didn't look back. She didn't want to see his satisfaction when she admitted it. "Yes. Yes, I am definitely flirting with you this time."

"Good," Peyton declared. "And it's about damn time you admitted it."

There was silence as they watched the man in the chair open his eyes.

"Master Sergeant West?" Kyra asked.

"Yes. That's me," King said. "Did I hear Captain Elliott just now or was that just some nightmare I was having?"

Kyra smiled into his worried gaze. "My answer depends on how freaked out you're going to be when I say yes."

King's laughter made his head hurt. "You're pretty funny for a medic, Doc. You're pretty cute too."

"You make one move on this woman and I will kick your ass to hell and back, King."

"Oh God—I knew it." King squirmed in the chair, finally realizing he was strapped down. "What the hell is going on, Captain?"

Peyton clapped a hand on his shoulder. "Hell is a good word for it. Just know you're safe for the moment and Doc here is fixing you up. Going to get a little rocky before it gets better, but eventually it's going to be better than it's been for a long damn time, King. Trust me on that one."

"*Semper Fi*," King whispered.

"*Oorah*," Peyton answered.

Shortly after, he heard Kyra uttering the shut-down codes in King's ear.

Kyra reached out and gently removed Peyton's hand from the man's shoulder. "Master Sergeant West can go back to his cage now. I'm going to leave him recuperating from the modifications until we've gotten this far with the others. There's no use telling the horror story more than once. We'll wake them and tell them all at the same time."

Peyton nodded. "Can I carry him?"

"He's a bigger man than you are. A transport chair would be easier," Kyra offered.

Peyton shook his head. "No thanks. If King's anything like I was, he'll get this memory back later. I want him to know that I cared enough to make sure he got treated respectfully."

Kyra swallowed, fighting tears. "Okay. Whatever you want to do is fine with me. Bring back the next guy you want me to work on. I'm going to get some food and take a booster. I have at least one more restoration in me today."

She watched Peyton gently pull the giant out of the chair and lift him over one shoulder. Then he walked out of the lab, pretending that he wasn't straining under the man's greater weight.

She blinked hard and didn't let the tears trickle down her face until Peyton was completely out of sight. Regardless of her discussion with Peyton, at the moment she didn't feel much like a good guy at all.

Chapter 18

Nero knocked on Brad's locked room door impatiently. "Brad? I know you're in there. Open up."

The door slid silently open. As he walked in, a very attractive brunette was climbing off Brad's lap. She was straightening her skirt as Brad was zipping up his pants. As cited, the infamous Gloria was very hot and frankly seemed pretty far outside his friend's dating league.

"Sorry to interrupt," Nero said flatly, but he wasn't. Brad was in goof-off mode, which meant nothing the man committed to was getting done. "I waited all morning, but you never showed up. Kyra hasn't taken a break yet. She's down to fixing the last one and is trying to get him done today. I thought you were going to help her with the physical restorations."

"Dude—I offered. Dr. Winters said she would call me if she needed my help. I was so bored watching from the observatory that I came back to my room for some actual entertainment. You have that top of the line game system in the lounge, but no access outside. What the hey? This is the longest I've been away from my gaming in years," Brad exclaimed.

"You know why we can't have outside access wide enough for gaming. I open a data pipe only for what's necessary and it's hard enough to keep that secure. Don't be such a whiner about everything, Brad. If you want to do something productive, Kyra asked me to get the schematics of each soldier's enhancements. Your system access at Norton Industries has been wider than mine since you helped double-wire that woman."

Brad held up a finger. "Wait—hold that thought." His gaze shifted to his companion. "Gloria, scram. Nero and I need to talk some business. Go fix your hair. . .or do something else girlie."

Nero watched Brad stare at the brunette for almost a full minute. Her eyes finally blinked a few times, then she gave a disgusted grunt as she left.

Nero directed his gaze at the ceiling as she disappeared. "You never pick the intellectual winners, Brad."

Brad snorted. "I know. But what Gloria lacks in intelligence, she makes up for in many other pleasant ways. It's a decent exchange, Dude. You'll just have to take my word on it."

"Whatever," Nero said, bringing his attention back. "Are you going to help me or not?"

"Sure," Brad said, running a hand over his hair. "Sorry I've been slacking. I've just been. . .I don't know. Apprehensive, I guess. Kind of nervous about Borg Man having full run of the place. Aren't you worried about Kyra removing all the cyborgs' controllers? Frankly that scares the shit out of me. What happens if one goes nuts on us? How would we stop him?"

Nero snorted. "Why would one go nuts? Peyton seems to have adapted well enough. None of the others have been double-wired so far. I think we're in the clear with this set."

"Captain Elliott was a prototype—same with the others you collected. The last couple hundred that were done—well, they probably won't be so nice."

"What makes you say that?" Nero asked, surprised at Brad's comments.

Brad frowned and shrugged. "Let's say I have a hunch, but what do I know?"

Nero frowned back and clapped a hand on Brad's shoulder. "Tell me about it. I've had a weird feeling for days but nothing bad has happened yet. I think it's just this whole rescue venture is riskier in reality than we could anticipate back when it was just an idea."

"You know how much I love Dr. Winters, but Dude—her relationship with Borg Man has me spooked. Why doesn't she look for a real man? I've been right here—waiting for her to get a clue. I'd even give up Gloria for her."

Nero shook his head as Brad laughed at his own joke. He let go of Brad and turned toward the door. Brad's crush on Kyra had its usefulness, but it also creeped him out at times.

"Their relationship worries me some too, but nothing I say makes any difference to Kyra. She's following her own instincts where Captain Elliott is concerned. Maybe it's because he's her first successful restoration."

Brad shook his head. "I'm suddenly getting a bad feeling about this whole situation, but let's get her the info she wants. It's probably a good idea for us to know what we're up against anyway."

Nero nodded. "Their assimilations will be done tonight. But if they react anything like Peyton did when she brings them out of it, I'm going to be replacing all the furniture in the cages when they wake up."

Brad frowned and nodded again as he followed Nero out the door.

***

Peyton set Eric down gently on the cot. His restoration has been the hardest. Eric had kept fighting his way out of the shut-down and Kyra hadn't been able to stop him. Even with his cybernetic processor pulled, he kept waking up alarmed and in great pain. In the end, Kyra had given him anesthesia to put his human side under. Doing so had been worrisome to her, but it had allowed her to finish the restoration work on him.

Now all five were back in their respective cages outfitted with mobile restraints in anticipation of their release. Kyra cybernetically suspended those who were done while she fixed all the others. Each man would occasionally wake and use the restroom, but other than attending to basic body needs, each slept as she had ordered. It actually worried him that Kyra retained the ability to force even her restored cyborgs into such a controlled situation, but she assured him it was a necessary precaution. Doing a complete search of his memories and maintenance records, Peyton concluded Kyra hadn't misused that power with him. But it was still a bit alarming when she had removed all other controls.

"Eric's body is already recovering. I don't know what is going on with his prosthetics, but he's recovering approximately five times as fast as the others. I can't wait to see his schematics. As much as my ex-husband was a dipshit, he was also a brilliant medical engineer. His college application was rejected by MIT. I never understood that. We met at Yale when we tied for a science award. His was for the first prosthetic that could be wirelessly connected to a person's brain. Mine was for a code chip that corrected common mental illnesses, such as schizophrenia and bi-polar conditions. The programming on my chip could re-route failing synapses. It allowed a person to be functional in normal society without altering their brain chemistry with drugs."

Peyton shook his head. It sounded to him like they had both been brilliant. He could imagine a youthful Kyra heading out to save the world with her codes and chips. He could also imagine she had chosen her ex-husband for having similar motivations.

"It sounds like you both were good guys back then. What happened to Dr. Channing? What changed him?"

Kyra looked around the room, silently observing the sleeping men. When she thought of the brilliant and idealistic scientist that she met and married, it shocked her soul to admit that Jackson was also the instigator of what the men in the cages had been subjected to.

"I don't know what happened, but over the years I did ignore some problem indicators. For example, I bought those red shoes in my closet because Jackson liked me to dress in a way that made me look sexy and dumb. When we went out to dinner with people, including UCN chancellors and other global dignitaries, Jackson would never let me talk much. You see, when I talked, it didn't take long for those we were with to realize I was just as smart as he was. Looking back on those events now, I find it amazing that I was able to play the quiet wife for fifteen years. I can only rationalize it by saying Jackson was a fun distraction for me initially—not outstanding, mind you—but fun. It was only during the last five years we were together that he became the man I grew to hate."

"Any idea what prompted the personality switch?" Peyton asked.

Kyra thought of their last months together. Jackson had gotten depressed, then turned morose. Finally, he had asked for the sexual favor she'd reluctantly agreed to because he had sworn it would prompt a return to his old, more jovial self. Not only had that never happened, his sexual demands after the incident had gotten worse—much, much worse. Since she never emotionally recovered from the incident, their marital sex life afterward became non-existent. She had moved into the guest bedroom to give herself the space she needed to heal. Refusing everything else Jackson wanted became automatic for her. Eventually, he turned to other women and stopped asking.

"There was a point where Jackson was trying to get funding for several ventures, one of them being the Cyber Wife program. It wasn't happening fast enough and he became severely depressed. I remember him complaining that the dignitaries at the UCN lacked vision. When I asked about what—he would talk in terms of a higher definition of mankind than had ever been possible before," Kyra said quietly. "Maybe he was going mad and I was in denial about it. I've asked myself many times if I should have made him get some therapy. He wouldn't have done so voluntarily of course, but the UCN contract for our continued support of the Cyber Soldiers was contingent upon the two of us passing a mental health exam every year."

"Did you always pass yours?" Peyton asked.

"Well—yes. You don't have to sound so skeptical."

Peyton smiled at her tone. "I'm not surprised you passed, Kyra. I'm just wondering now if Jackson always passed his."

Kyra snorted. She had never thought to check. Maybe she would look into it. "I could probably find out. After his death, I gained the right to look at all Jackson's medical and work records."

"Knowing might answer some questions for you—maybe explain some things," Peyton suggested. "Do you think I would pass the exam?"

"If you could keep your wiseass sense of humor under wraps long enough to answer the questions seriously," Kyra said.

"Well don't hold back, honey. Tell me what you really think," Peyton declared, making her laugh.

"Sorry for the automatic sarcasm. Yes, Peyton. I think you could pass with flying colors, even the creative questions that require consulting your philosophy. I don't know what you were like before you became a cyborg, but you're just fine now from what I've seen."

Peyton motioned with his head towards the cages. "What are their chances of passing a mental health exam, Doc?"

Kyra sighed as she looked around. "I wish I could tell from the work I did, but there are no factors indicating anything about their mental states once freed of the constant codes. Every one of them has prototype cybernetics that I never even knew existed until the last few days. Until they wake up and have their individual reactions, your guess is as good as mine."

***

Brad connected the fifth storage disk to his portable. "Nero—Dude. This is the last one. I didn't bother getting Borg Man's. I'm assuming she already has his."

"She does," Nero said, not lifting his head from his task. "I retrieved Peyton's myself."

Brad tilted his head and raised his eyebrows. "You did? When was that?"

Nero snorted as at Brad's surprise. "Hey, I do research sometimes. I looked him up and downloaded the info after we discovered he was double-wired. We never found that device he used to open the cage. I wanted to see just how many hidden compartments he had in his body—outside the normal ones. The answer turned out to be two and both are in his head."

"The bypass remote is probably still in the lab somewhere. Maybe he hid it in the cage. No one would look there."

"No. I checked. Nothing was in the cage. He'd demolished the bed at some point and bent it back into shape. Kyra says Peyton has a pisser of a temper when he's mad. I don't doubt it after what I saw."

Brad frowned. "That's all the more reason to be concerned about him running around loose, isn't it?"

Nero lifted his head, this time in concern. "That's the fourth or fifth time you've said something to that effect. Are you having second doubts about what we're doing here? Because if you are—it's a bit late to voice them, Dr. Smith. We've got five more cyborgs waking up soon. It's likely some of them are going to be angry about what's happened to them. It would be unnatural for a rational, feeling human being to just say 'no problem' to learning the UCN has had them working as man-hos for a decade now. Don't you think they have a right to be a bit pissed?"

"Yeah. Sure. I guess I would be too," Brad agreed, nodding.

Nero nodded back. "Of course you would. Leave the disks when you're done and get some rest. I'm sure the perfect *Gloria* is getting lonely without you."

"Jealous much, Bro?" Brad asked, grinning as he pulled the fifth disk from his portable.

"Not of your luck with women," Nero said, grinning back. "But I'd love for my brain to work like yours does. Next to Kyra, you're the smartest human being I've ever met. Even Jackson Channing wasn't as smart as you."

Brad sighed in happiness. "Thanks, Dude. Now if I could just find something to do for a living that wasn't dog-ass boring, I'd be a happy, happy man."

"Well you'd probably get more job opportunities if you sounded as smart as you actually are. Want some advice? Take some language lessons," Nero chided.

Brad carried the five disks over and sprinkled them on Nero's virtual console. He laughed when his friend scrambled to catch them so their shadows wouldn't activate the keys.

Nero growled. "Brad, you sorry piece of shit. Those disks better not have broken or you'll be repeating your boring-ass research again tomorrow."

"Can't hear you, Bro. Got to go see *Glor—Glor—Gloria*. She is *glor-glor-glorious*. And mine. All mine," Brad sang.

Nero chuckled at his friend's silliness and shook his head as Brad walked out.

***

Kyra protested being dragged down the hall, but it wasn't doing her any good. "Peyton, stop. I don't want to be away from the cage room. They're all going to wake up soon. Nothing is stopping it from happening now. I don't want them any more frightened than they're already going to be once they start remembering the past."

Peyton locked the door behind them after practically throwing Kyra inside. "At initial waking, each man remembered me and serving. They even remembered my name. That means they're still soldiers. I left intel in the cage for each of them that will move them into acceptance. Let's let that happen as organically as possible before you start apologizing for your part in their situation. They went to sleep fighting a war and are waking up in the middle of a prison camp. The sooner they understand the reality of their situation—the more cooperative they will become."

"Intel? What intel?"

Peyton sighed. "Their Cyber Husband history. Their military records. A smattering of current events to convince them time had passed. . .and something else."

"What something else?" Kyra demanded.

Peyton tilted his head until he met her gaze. "I also gave them the restoration folder Nero copied from your portable to his—including the holographic message you made. Nero found it when you were still unconscious. It didn't take much to figure out I was the password."

"I suppose it was logical for Nero to review everything on my portable. That doesn't mean I'm ready to discuss it yet. I made that recording for personal reasons. . .wait." Kyra stared at the bed, instincts sizzling.

Something was wrong. "Peyton? Did you go through my briefcase looking for something?"

"No. Why would you ask that?" Peyton swung his head. His eyes scanned the room and his hand shot out to stop Kyra from walking forward to check her things. There was a lingering heat signature indicating the person hadn't been gone long. Someone had come into their room shortly before they got there. "I brought the briefcase back when you were in the cage room because I thought it might contain personal items. What exactly was in it?"

"Just equipment. My portable was in it because I used it in the lab, but now it's in the cage room. The handheld I modified myself should be in there too. You saw the porta-disks Nero brought. I also had the little sweeper Brad gave me. You might not have noticed it because it was the size of a marble."

Convinced the reason for the search had to do with the contents of the bag, Peyton walked to the bed and dumped the remaining items out on the cover. Everything she had mentioned was there on the bed—except the small item she had called a sweeper.

"Sweepers weren't around a decade ago. What are they?" Peyton demanded.

Kyra put a hand on her head to help her think. "Okay. Let's see if I can explain. The sweeper creates a scrambled communications field about three feet wide in diameter that briefly allows one com channel to be used for a short, but truly private conversation that can't be recorded. Sweepers are expensive to make and require a lot of stored power. They were ineffective as a commercial product, but do still serve a function for governmental use. Brad was one of the premier creators of them when he was in grad school. I think he may own a significant portion of the patent or something. His work on sweepers is why Norton hired him as a tech. He gave the little sweeper to me so I could call Nero if I got into trouble dealing with you. Brad has always had a little crush on me. The sweeper was his way of making sure I stayed safe."

Peyton glared. "Well somebody is probably trying to use his little love gift to call out of here. Who knew about the sweeper other than you and Brad?"

"Nero was there when he gave it to me. But they're common now in the sense that most people would recognize one if they saw it, even one as small as the one he gave me."

Kyra didn't like the determined look on Peyton's face. "What are you going to do?"

"I'm going to wake up my men and then we're going to see if the sweeper has been used."

Kyra put her hand on his arm. "No—wait. Rushing the wake-up process is not a good idea. Let me do a quick search for the com field and see if I can find any traces. It would show up on any basic scanner. That's why the technology was not very successful commercially. It actually aided espionage. It only works if no one is looking for its use."

Peyton knew Kyra was practically weaving from her exhaustion. If he started shit about the missing sweeper tonight, neither of them was going to rest. Tomorrow they would have enough to deal with. "Do the scan and then we'll make a decision," he said, finally agreeing.

Kyra walked over to her handheld, smiling as she lifted it from the bed. "You'll be happy to hear that Brad's not the only resident tech genius here. I upgraded this handheld myself. I was bored after Jackson moved out and it gave me something to do with my time. It's been so useful that I'm considering converting another. I can do as much with this little antique device as Nero can with his new top-of-the-line portable. The best part is that my power source is a prototype crystal that I bought for a small fortune, but one day it will be less than a dollar. So the future application of my device will be inexpensive as well as a huge power saver."

"Sounds like your handheld could make you some serious money," Peyton said, trying to make conversation while they waited on the scan to complete.

"Of course it could, but I have never needed more money. Okay—we're clear. There are no traces of sweeper signal use within the facility. If you want, I can set the scan program to notify us if anything gets detected while we're resting."

"Yes. Do that," he ordered.

Peyton checked the bed and the bathroom thoroughly before he finally looked at her again.

"Time to sleep, Doc. Tomorrow we have to alert everyone who's helping. No one is safe if we've got a traitor."

Kyra nodded as she climbed into bed fully dressed and passed out.

Chapter 19

They fought about whether or not they were purposely avoiding the cage room, even though they had checked the monitors. As expected, they witnessed a myriad of reactions ranging from outright anger to stoic staring off into space. Peyton insisted they tell Nero about the missing sweeper first. Brad happened to be with him, so they got to tell both men at once.

"This is going to be one of those days that totally suck," Kyra said, when they were out of earshot. Behind them Brad and Nero were still arguing about who could possibly have taken the sweeper.

Peyton nodded as they walked. "The only two people who knew about it, other than you, were equally alarmed that it was missing. They exuded nearly the same adrenalin levels. If one of them took the device, it's not obvious. Their mutual yelling fest about it makes me think it was neither of them."

Then suddenly the inevitable couldn't be avoided any more as they stopped outside the cage room. Kyra bit her lip and realized she was breathing hard.

"You don't have to go in. I can face them without you," he offered.

"No. I can't avoid their condemnation forever—no more than I could avoid yours," Kyra answered, swallowing hard.

"Okay then. Let's do this." Peyton touched the panel beside the door and it slid open smoothly. Inside, five sullen, angry men stared at them from behind bars.

"What the hell is going on, Captain?" King demanded.

Peyton stepped forward. "I know. This whole situation is FUBAR'd. At least you didn't destroy your bed like I did while I came to terms with it."

Kyra cleared her throat. "Your anger is normal, Master Sergeant West. And you'll be able to control it and all your other emotions soon. Your mind is already busy making it possible. I removed all sources of programming pain from what's left of your cybernetics."

King snorted at the doctor's scientific explanation and turned away before he let loose a stream of cursing guaranteed to turn the air blue. "Science can never explain how the world we saved conspired against us."

Not knowing what to say back to the man's rational, calm statement, Kyra simply turned away. In doing so, she met the heated glares of the others with as much courage as she could exhibit while Peyton went on talking.

"Your confinement is a necessary, but temporary precaution. I spent time in a cage a few weeks ago and now I'm out. If you've taken the time to look at the intel I provided, you're as up to speed as I am. Individual concerns will be addressed, but at the moment we have bigger problems. The UCN and its agents are trying to stop Dr. Winters from freeing more cyborgs like us. Her life is now in danger because she's worked out the restoration process most of the world still believes is impossible. I was her first success. You five are the next ones because I will not accept less than your full recuperation."

King hit the bars of his cage rattling them with the force of his anger. "Are you telling us every Cyber Soldier was turned into a slave?"

Peyton nodded. "Yes. A cyborg remains unaware of their captive situations until Dr. Winters frees them. I don't know how yet, but I plan to change that for all cyborgs. To do it, I'm going to need your help—*all* of your help."

"What happened to our families. . .our *real* families? How could they just go along with this shit and let us be sold to the highest bidder?"

Kyra looked at Lance Corporal Marcus Kells and lifted her chin to answer his question.

"Like you were deceived about the restoration, your families were deceived into thinking that cyborgs were nothing more than war-time killing machines. Some families demanded proof. When that happened, you were programmed to act in ways that validated what the military wanted your family to think."

Marcus glared at her. "So you're telling me my children think their father is nothing more than a robotic killing machine?"

Kyra shook her head. "No. . .not. . .necessarily. I can't actually say what they think. Hopefully someday you can find that information out for yourself. But today is not that day. Today you get to decide how you're going to handle what was done to you. You can get too mad to help and that would prove them right. Or you can let the agony of your captivity eat away at your gut until you see your own death as some kind of answer. That's what two cyborgs did before Peyton, who got mad and destroyed his bed. Please choose what motivates you to survive this and take back control of your fate. Anger seems a more healthy reaction, but just remember we're in hiding from the world and beds aren't exactly falling from the sky here."

She saw Marcus turn away from her lecture to stare blankly off into space. She made a mental note to keep an eye on him.

"When do we get out of the cage?"

Kyra turned to look at Corporal Eric Anderson. "In approximately three days you'll be released. Your emotions are returning and it takes a bit of time to process them all. On the third day, you'll be mentally tested. If you pass, you'll be let out of the cage. Two weeks after that, if all goes well, your mobile restraints will be removed."

"You mean these fancy bracelets?" Eric asked, holding up his wrists to look at them in disgust. "We used these on POWs we captured. Now I'm wearing a set. This is a bucket load of shit, Doc."

Kyra nodded. "Yes it is. Worse—if I have to activate it for one of you, all of you will feel the impact. I regret this extreme action but there are humans helping here that have to be protected. Despite Captain Elliott's relative success, restoration is still an indeterminate process."

Eric snorted. "Hey now, Doc. What kind of word is 'indeterminate'? Didn't Captain Elliott tell you we were the good guys?"

Kyra's lip trembled, but she refused to cry. Another charming cyborg. They seemed to get to her most. "Yes. Captain Elliott did tell me that, and I believe him, Corporal. I wish I had a better way to handle the situation, but this is all I know to do at this time."

Peyton's hand clamping hard on her shoulder instantly stopped the tears that had started flowing. "That's enough explaining, Kyra. They're okay with precautions because nothing bad is going to happen. Right, Marines?"

Kyra counted their nodding heads—everyone nodded but Marcus. She started to say something to get his attention, but the door sliding open behind her stopped the words from reaching her mouth. She watched Peyton turn and move lightning fast toward whoever entered, but a pulse cannon blast to his chest sent him flying past her.

"*No!*" Kyra yelled as Peyton landed in a heap on the floor. She looked at Brad in shock before running to Peyton's side.

"Relax. Borg Man is going to be fine, Dr. Winters. Up close like this, I can see how someone his size would be fun in the sack for you, but don't tell me you actually care about what happens to him? He's a cyborg. He's never going to love anyone who helped make him the freak of nature he is."

Brad's words fell on her, heavy as stones. But she couldn't let them break her. Kyra brushed a hand over Peyton's head and turned his face gently until his still open, cybernetic eyes were facing in Brad's direction. She hoped Peyton's recording mechanism worked while he was unconscious because she wanted a record of what happened, even if it was just recording her death. Her body would never be able to handle a pulse cannon blast the way a cyborg's could.

She rose slowly from the floor and stepped toward Brad so she could better face him. "Where's Nero?"

"Last time I saw Nero, he was taking a well deserved nap while I turned off all room monitoring so you and I could talk in private. He's very peaceful right now. I doubt he's even going to remember the little chat he and I had about the missing sweeper. I still think he took it to study it, but I couldn't drag the truth out of him no matter what I pumped into him. Drugs these days are so amazing in what they can do. And they work great on people who are still all human."

Kyra stopped when she was a few feet away from him. "I don't understand, Brad. I thought you were going to help us free the cyborgs. And I thought you were Nero's friend."

Brad swung the hand with the pulse cannon still in it. "Free more of them? I don't think so. All soldier models should be incinerated. They're not safe to be around and we don't need them anymore. We only need the *idea* of them. There are way better uses for cybernetics—like my new girlfriend here."

Her gaze followed Brad's head inclining in the woman's direction.

"Dr. Winters, meet Gloria. She's doesn't talk because I don't let women give me too much shit. She does everything I say now, don't you, Gloria? If I were a bragging sort of guy, I would say she is my most important achievement so far."

"Did you pass your last mental exam, Brad?" Kyra glanced at the woman by his side who was staring blankly ahead.

"Now that's not nice—not nice at all, Dr. Winters. I can't believe you're insulting me after I did you such a big honking favor."

"What big favor?" Kyra demanded.

Brad smiled. "We'll get to that before your mechanical boy toy wakes up. First, we need to find that sweeper I gave you. Losing it was pretty careless for a woman with a twenty million dollar bounty on her head. I say no one is going to turn you in to the UCN unless it's me. You're the smartest person alive on this planet—well, next to me, that is. I have other plans for you, Dr. Winters, and you can rest assured I will treat you a lot better than Jackson Channing ever did. He didn't deserve to breathe the air you breathed, which is why he doesn't get to breath air anymore."

"What. . .what plans do you have for me?" Kyra stammered.

She was amazed the question came out at all because she was numb inside. Brad had obviously sacrificed his sanity to act out some kind of power trip. Nero was drugged and Peyton was unconscious. All other potential rescuers hated her guts at the moment because she had them locked in cages. If Peyton had been awake, he would have said the current situation was further FUBAR'd and he would have been absolutely right.

Grinning, Brad pointed the pulse cannon at King. He shot a pulse through the bars of the cage and they both watched the giant go down hard, flipping the bed over as he fell.

"Stop it, Brad. There's no need to harm any of these men. They can't get out of the cages to hurt anyone."

Kyra stepped in front of King's cage so Brad couldn't shoot a second time without hitting her. Something told her that would be a last resort for him. It was her fault King's cybernetic shields weren't activated. It had taken three bursts to bring him down when they had been working.

"You don't have to do anything more to hurt anyone. Just tell me what you want, Brad. You have my full attention," Kyra ordered.

"Good. Can I call you Kyra now? How long have we known each other? It's been oh. . .what? Seven or eight years now I think. But in all the time that's passed, I never forgot a single moment of what being with you was like. It was nice of Jackson to invite me to his Kyra sex party, but even nicer that the two Chancellors let me go first."

Kyra put a hand to her gut. She wanted to throw up—right after she screamed. Her head was shaking no and she couldn't seem to prevent that from happening. "You. . .you were one of the men Jackson brought to me?"

Brad smiled. "Well don't get all mushy on me. . .Kyra."

Her head wouldn't stop shaking. "I was blindfolded. There was only supposed to be one of you. . .not. . .not three. I didn't know who and didn't want to know. After you finished. . .it was supposed to stop. But Jackson wouldn't let it stop. He let the others do anything they wanted. They did things I never agreed to doing."

"I know. I stuck around and watched. It was so not cool of him—which is why I programmed his Cyber Wife to kill him. Now she sits and stares out a window all day long, waiting on me to come get her and undo her wiring like I promised. But I haven't had time to take care of that little piece of unfinished business. It's been nothing but busy, busy, busy since you bought Borg Man."

Kyra's gaze slid from Brad's to Peyton who still hadn't moved.

"Now tell me the truth, was the man really worth the eight mil you spent to sleep with him? Come on—don't you think that's a bit much to spend on a ho? Gloria here. . .now she was free. I just picked her up at a campus coffee shop and smuggled her right into a waiting chair at Norton. Voila. . .custom hot lady friend in twelve easy steps. I even made my own creator file for her. Aren't you proud of me? No one has done that except you and Jackson. He and I had a cozy chat about what was in it one day. He talked better on the drugs than Nero did."

Kyra stared at the woman next to Brad now, stared in horror at what the younger scientist had done. What if there were other scientists in the world like Brad who were cloning the creator code? She couldn't allow that to happen. She couldn't.

"She's. . .she's absolutely incredible, Brad. And you. . .creating your own creator file. . .well, that's amazing too. Nero always said you were the smartest person he ever met next to me. All my life, Jackson never wanted anyone to know how smart I was. I'm flattered you at least recognize my talent."

Brad laughed. "I hate to talk bad about the dead, but Jackson Channing was a total ass. Your intelligence is why you and I are the perfect match for a power couple. Now use that amazing mind and imagine a whole world full of *Glorias*—or Hell—*Bens*—we can make Bens too. Can you imagine what people would pay for a custom companion who did anything and everything they wanted?"

"Isn't that what the Cyber Husbands and Wives already are for their spouses?" Kyra asked, hoping the questions would keep Brad talking until Peyton came around.

"See? That's what I mean. You never miss the important details. Yes—the constant code program already does that partially, but as you see Gloria is much safer. She was never a soldier and doesn't have any of those nasty, dangerous prosthetics that could cause a world crisis if used wrong. Gloria is just a normal woman with some really great new features. The controller wiring makes her behave and follow her custom programming without any flaws. I even figured out how to keep her from talking. Pretty amazing, isn't it?"

"What about the hormonal surges that causes blips in women?" Kyra asked.

Brad laughed and smiled. "And there's that great mind at work again. You always know what questions to ask. The answer is. . .I don't know. So far, I haven't seen any indication of problems. Of course I did promise to turn her voice back on if she behaved, so maybe the secret is that I motivated the human side of her through providing hope," Brad said, considering the answer.

Kyra looked at the woman. Something was not right. The woman was not responding to her visual assessment of her. It's like she was ignoring her on purpose.

"May I look at Gloria up close?"

Brad fairly beamed at the request.

"Rockin' A. Check her out."

At his nod of encouragement, Kyra walked closer. She inspected the woman he called Gloria while the woman's gaze stayed fixed on some focal point across the room. Kyra lifted one of the woman's hands and found her fingers slightly curled. As she straightened them under hers, a tiny round object rolled into her palm. Her eyes widened as the woman's eyes flared. Kyra squeezed her fingers and put her hand with the object into her coat pocket. It looked like Jackson wasn't the only one who underestimated the power of the human mind to overcome cybernetic programming.

Knowledge and the hope it carried straightened her spine as she turned her most serious stare back on Brad. He was standing in front of the cage belonging to Marcus who still wasn't looking at her or the others. But what she was thinking at least gave them all a chance.

She walked slowly toward Brad but stopped short of getting too close yet. "I confess I'm. . .well, I'm impressed. . .no, make that *intrigued*. I want to know more about how you made Gloria. But first. . .you're right, I owe you thanks."

Brad smiled. "For bringing you the opportunity of a lifetime? My pleasure, Kyra."

Kyra shook her head. "No. For that too maybe, but mostly for getting Jackson permanently out of my life. If you stayed, then you knew you were the only decent man he brought to me that evening. The others. . .I still can't bring myself to talk about what they did to me. It made me hate being touched for a very long time."

Brad lowered the gun until it pointed to the floor. "I'm sorry you married such a shitty man. And you're welcome. Jackson's brain was like totally gone by the time he bit the big one. You were the bribe he used on the Chancellors to get his funding. They didn't test him anymore and they approved the Cyber Wife program, all because of the Kyra sex party. I never thought that was fair. That should have been your program and your funding. You're the one who earned it."

Kyra swallowed and ordered herself not to throw up at hearing she was again responsible for even more cyborg misuse.

"Can I. . .can I hug you? I just realized I've never even hugged you in all the time we've known each other." While Brad stared, she walked just a little closer, but stopped short and looked at the floor again. "I'm nervous. .

.this is not easy for me. You scare me a little with that pulse cannon in your hand."

When he reached out and grabbed the front of her jacket to pull her the rest of the way to him, Kyra used all her strength to push Brad hard against the bars of the cage. The gun fell just as she yelled, "Marcus, quick! Grab him!"

Hands reaching through the bars wrapped themselves around Brad's arms like a vice.

"Thank you," Kyra said, nearly breathless with fear as she pushed off Brad. She was shaking as she ran to the console and hit the open command on all the cages. "As far as I'm concerned, you all passed your mental tests. I have a new definition of crazy now."

"But Kyra. . .how could you do this to me? I thought we were finally. . .you know. . . *bonding*," Brad declared.

His genuine confusion made Kyra come back to stand in front of him again. Eric appeared at her side, but it didn't deter her.

"Maybe you could argue that I agreed to being with you that night, but now I know you could have stopped those other two men from doing what they did to me. Jackson could have as well. But both of you did nothing. I can only imagine what you've done to poor—*Gloria*—or whatever her real name is. But you know what Brad? You're wrong about cyborgs. The human side of them will always find a way to make itself known. I tried to tell Jackson. He never believed me. Just look what your creation gave me when you introduced us."

Kyra held out her hand with the sweeper gleaming in her palm. Then curling it back into her palm again, she swung her closed fist and punched Brad as hard as she could until his head spun. So much adrenalin was pumping through her at the action, she didn't feel anything but a tiny sting on her knuckles.

Looking stunned over her violence, Brad's gaze swung to the woman still standing on the other side of the room. He opened his mouth, but Kyra put the hand she hadn't used to punch him over it. She raised her other in a fist again where Brad could see it.

"Oh no you don't, you sneaky bastard. If you say anything, anything at all, I'm going to rip off your testicles and let Gloria do whatever she wants with them. Eric, there's some wide tape in that desk drawer under the console. Get it so we can make sure this guy doesn't utter another syllable."

"Damn Doc. You can be one scary science bitch when you want. I hope you never get pissed at me," Eric declared, scrambling to do what she asked.

Kyra snorted at his teasing. "Punching Brad is nothing. You have no idea how scary I can be. There's a good reason Peyton called me Dr. Frankenstein." She probably shouldn't have admitted such a thing in front of her newly freed captives, but in her anger, the truth had slipped out. Her mind was already planning what to do with Brad and it wasn't going to bother her a bit.

Still riding her adrenalin rush from punching Brad, Kyra let her gaze bounce around the room. All the cyborgs were watching her closely but their smirking scrutiny didn't faze her resolve. She was finally clear about what needed to be done and Peyton was right. Blowing up Norton wasn't the answer. With crazies like Brad running loose in the world, the cyborgs definitely needed her to stay alive.

Her hand was shaking hard by the time Eric made it back with the tape. Out of the corner of her eye, Kyra saw King climbing slowly to his feet. Now if only Peyton would come around.

"Master Sergeant West, when you've recovered, will you carry Peyton to our room? I can't stand seeing him on the floor."

King stumbled out of the cage, staring in wonder at the unbelievable scene. "What the hell happened here? Did I miss everything?"

"Yeah, but we're used to that," Eric said, slapping a third piece of tape over evil Brad's mouth.

Calmer now that Brad couldn't speak, Kyra walked into the cage where Marcus still had a death grip on Brad through the bars. She put a shaking hand on one arm. "It's okay, Marcus. We're safe now. Thanks to you—we're all finally safe."

Marcus let go of Brad as suddenly as he had latched onto him. The shocker was when he burrowed into Kyra's arms instead. Pretty soon, her sobbing was as loud as his as she rocked them both in her arms.

"I'm sorry. I'm so sorry you had to go through this. We'll find your family when we can. Peyton will help. That man can do anything. I know because he talked me into loving him."

Marcus nodded against her shoulder before letting her go. "Thanks for hugging me, Doc. Crying is a bitch of a reaction. Now my head hurts like a mofo. Got any aspirin?"

Kyra laughed and nodded. "Yes, but it won't cure your despair. Nero has food and maybe even some beer in this place. I'm a tea woman myself, but I'll see you guys have what you need to feel more appreciated. Now let's get you all out of here. Eric's right. Only bad guys belong in cages."

She grabbed his hand and pulled Marcus out with her. There were two more men standing around Peyton now. One he'd called Vincent. The other he'd called Steve. All five were looking at her, waiting no doubt for orders. She wished their captain would wake up and take over that work. She had stuff she needed to do.

"Let's get Peyton to his room. Then I have to check on Nero to see how badly Brad drugged him. I suggest we put Dr. Smith here in Marcus's cage. Tie him to the bars until we can decide what to do about him."

She watched as Vincent and Steve dragged Brad into the cage while he thrashed and squealed under the tape over his mouth, but it didn't stop them from securing him to the bars with more of the tape Eric had fetched.

"What about her—evil Brad's woman?" Eric asked, pointing across the room.

Kyra sniffled, but refused to let the tears fall as she walked to the woman named Gloria. Her body was quickly running out of the chemicals that had kept her upright and functioning for her showdown with the obviously insane Dr. Smith. Eric and Marcus followed closely behind her.

"Can you understand what I'm saying?" she asked. At Gloria's nod, Kyra nodded back. "Good. I will have to study your wiring to see what can be done about reversing Brad's handiwork."

Kyra started to walk away, but thought of another question. She turned back. "Can you act on your own volition and make independent decisions so long as Brad is kept from speaking to you?"

She saw panic flare in the woman's eyes. Kyra took that to mean the woman had no clue what was going on with her situation. Sighing, she rubbed the woman's arm. "Don't be alarmed. We'll deal with whatever happens. Just try to act in normal ways. Okay? Just try. . ."

"It's okay, Doc. I'll watch her for you." Marcus interrupted, wiping his eyes on his sleeve. "I'll also make sure she doesn't break the bad guy out."

Kyra turned to look at Brad, now secured to the side of the cage. His squealing had ceased, but he still seemed stupefied about how he had lost control of the situation. Ironically, Brad's revelation about her abusers had given her a sick kind of leverage at the UCN. And because of it, she now had a potential means of resolving her mistakes on a much larger scale.

King started to lift Peyton from the floor, but before she could blink Peyton was on his feet and King was flying across the room to land hard against a wall. His massive body left an impressive dent behind as he fell to the floor. When he bounced up almost instantly, there was full-out fury in the giant's glare, directed at Peyton. Kyra winced and prayed the lab wasn't about to be torn apart.

"What the fucking hell, Captain? Is this beat-the-shit-out-of-King week or something?"

Peyton's wild roaming gaze finally focused, and he held out a hand. "Kyra? Are you okay? Did Brad hurt you?"

Kyra shook her head as she headed straight for the safety of Peyton's arms. She hugged him as tight as she could and then backed away to talk to him. "I'm fine. We're all fine. Marcus saved us."

"No, I didn't," Marcus denied. "You did. You fed the man's crazy until he cracked."

Kyra winced at the description of her chat with Brad. "Peyton, I need you to check something. Were you recording what happened or did the pulse cannon interfere?"

Peyton went still as he checked. "Yes. I have a record. And a visual for most of it. You were smart to turn my head."

"Good. Don't review it yet. I don't want you coming back to beat up Brad. I have other plans for him. We're going to make another little movie, better than our last one. In fact, this one will be a live performance. Care to help me with my evil plans, Captain Elliott?"

"Will it involve you crawling into my lap and kissing me again?" Peyton asked, listening to the snickers of his men. God, it was good to hear them laughing. He had missed them.

"No. This movie is not going to be a love story. This movie is going to be a horror flick for the UCN. And you may not like me much afterward because some of it is going to be real as well," Kyra said.

Peyton shrugged. "It's okay, Doc. I'm really good at dealing with all kinds of scary shit."

He walked over to arm hug King. "Sorry. I was in survival mode."

King snorted. "Lucky for you I'm feeling mellow today."

Kyra sighed and bit her lip as they left the cage room and walked down the hall. She wanted to laugh hysterically when her mind finally registered just how badly she needed to pee.

***

Several hours after the Brad crisis had passed, Kyra stood weeping in the industrial shower attached to the room she had been sharing with Peyton. The day's events were mostly behind them. Whatever drugs Brad had given him, Nero was fine now, but truly hadn't remembered anything. He had watched Peyton's recording of Brad's attack on her with a coldness she'd never seen him exhibit. Afterward he had kissed her cheek and hugged her tightly before heading off to talk with the newly freed cyborgs.

But Nero's disillusionment with a man he'd thought was his best friend was only part of the reason she was weeping. Who knew how many other Brads were out there, building on her original technology to make custom cyber slaves? Stopping that sort of greed for power was going to be a never-ending battle. Her head hurt just thinking about it.

Her body hurt too, but for a thousand other reasons.

And she wondered how many more hits her heart could take before it just exploded inside her chest. She was so caught up in her misery she didn't hear Peyton slip into the shower with her.

"You've got to find a better reaction to catching the bad guys than crying. I mean I know you're a girl and all, but hell Doc. . .this weeping shit has to stop. If anyone should be upset, I should be. You would have been killed if Brad had turned that weapon I built on you, and I would never have known it even happened. We need to develop some kind of pulse-cannon-proof vest for you to wear."

Peyton turned Kyra around and pulled her flush against his body. Her wet, soapy arms slipping around his middle were sexily erotic and just about the most sensual experience they had shared to date. He backed her up a step, until the water sluiced between them and washed the soap off her. He ran his hands over her short spiked hair and got instantly hard. . .well, in six point five seconds anyway. But measuring the time it took said nothing about the mystery of how the intelligent cyber scientist's every touch and word made it happen. There was just something fundamentally sexy about the woman in his arms.

He shifted when one of Kyra's talented hands left his back and slid between them with no hesitation at all. Peyton gave himself a minute to enjoy what she was doing before breaking the intimacy with words that badly needed to be said.

"Is that the same hand you used to punch Brad?"

He was disappointed when her hand dropped away from what she had been doing, but he understood.

"I know you told me not to, but the guys couldn't stop talking about it, so I replayed the whole recording. What Jackson did to you—his deception as a lover and his complicity in hurting you—it was all wrong, Kyra. That night wasn't about your ex-husband's changing sexual preferences—that was just about greed and control. You know that, right? All those men conspired against you when you were vulnerable."

"Yes. Intellectually, I know that's exactly what happened," Kyra agreed.

Peyton reached down and lifted her chin with one hand until she was looking at him. He used his other hand to guide one of hers back to his erection. "Your past makes no difference to me. Your hand is wrapped around the best proof. But mostly I'm glad you didn't let what happened break you. If you had, we wouldn't be here naked together and about to have shower sex for the first time."

Kyra laughed even as she sobbed. "You sound awfully sure about our sexual future in the next ten minutes or so, Captain Elliott. I don't like men very much right now."

"Good thing I'm still a cyborg then." Peyton smiled as he lifted her by the backs of her legs which he wrapped around him. "But I think from now on, we're going to call what we do *lovemaking* instead of *sex*. I'm ready to try making a more human type of connection. How about you?"

Kyra sniffled a little harder as Peyton backed her up against the shower wall, but she still helped him navigate his way into her. Instead of moving though, he held her completely still on him. She lifted her questioning gaze to his. "What are you waiting for? I feel you throbbing inside me."

Peyton put his forehead against Kyra's. "Well, that's the most amazing thing about doing this with you, Doc. I'm not waiting for anything anymore. I don't how it happened, but I found everything in you I'm ever going to need. Do you think what I'm feeling about you could be love? I'd like to say that to you, but I was waiting until I was sure. This feeling isn't rational enough to be defined and measured. It hurts my brain—but in a good way."

Kyra sighed and leaned forward for a kiss. "Maybe this is love. We're going to have to do a lot of research before I can be sure myself. Fortunately, I have some experiments in mind that can test your theory. Want to volunteer your services in my science lab?" She squeezed around him as tightly as she could.

Laughing at her metaphor, Peyton withdrew a little and slid home again. Every stroke was more thrilling than the last. It was complete acceptance. . .and yet also choice.

"How about I volunteer for the rest of our lives together—however long that ends up being?"

"Is that some sort of cyborg inspired marriage proposal, Captain Elliott?" Kyra heard herself panting heavily as she asked the question.

Peyton shook his head, slinging water off them both as he picked up speed. "No. We're already married. I just want us to stay that way no matter what kind of status change you manage to wrangle for Cyber Husbands who want out of their deals."

"Umm. . .if you're sure staying is what you want. . ."

"Doc—you're what I've wanted since I laid my cybernetic eyes on you."

Kyra nodded at her good fortune, closed her very human eyes, and gave her worried mind over to how amazing Peyton was making her feel.

Chapter 20

"Why can't I just wear my lab coat over regular clothes?" Kyra protested.

Peyton looked away to hide his grin. "Because you look badass in your apprehension gear. Wear the speak-through too. They'll think you're talking to someone about them."

"Why is black the color of our gear? Why not brown or gray? Those are the colors of most landscapes. You don't see black on anything except old pavement and there's not much of that left. Land vehicles are used only in third world countries now. Peyton? Are you still listening to me?"

Peyton laughed at her chastising tone. "Yes, Doc. You know damn well the Cyber Husband chip won't let me tune you out completely. Even without pain, it flashes lights through my brain every time you fuss at me. Now to answer your question—black clothing never gets noticed unless it's a short dress on a tall woman wearing four-inch heels."

Kyra sighed. He always answered her, but sometimes she still didn't understand what he was saying. But this wasn't one of those times. Sighing, she made a mental note to look for a short black dress and four-inch torture devices to match. Maybe she had some in her old closet. She didn't remember. At least she wouldn't have to dumb down her conversation for him.

"Okay, Captain Elliott. I get your point. I'll wear the black clothes."

She watched as Peyton stopped what he was doing and froze. Since the other five cyborgs had become a part of their daily lives, his freeze-ups happened often. But she'd learned it was just him centering his attention on their wireless communication.

"The guys are back with our hostages. Hustle it up, Doc. It's horror movie time."

Kyra rolled her eyes at the order, but pulled on the black boots that matched her pants with the twenty plus pockets.

She rolled her eyes again when Peyton insisted she wear her lab coat over the black t-shirt that showed way too much of her breasts. "Is showing cleavage really necessary?"

"Depends. Are you worried about dealing with these men?" he asked.

Kyra shook her head. "No. I'm looking forward to it. I even know exactly what I want to say."

"Then yes—showing cleavage is necessary. You don't want them to think they make you uncomfortable. This is the perfect time to use your femininity in your favor, Doc. Men are typically afraid of women as confident as you are—well most men. I'm not afraid, but I'm also not typical." He leaned down a little to kiss her lips when she stood. "But if reasoning doesn't work, I can always remove them permanently from the picture. We'll figure out another way to get the UCN to go along."

Kyra fisted a hand on her hip. "Way too dramatic, Captain Elliott. Did you ever consider that the use of force is ineffective at times? Two dead world leaders wouldn't be helpful. I want to use them and their power the way they used me. I know that sounds bad, but as you keep reminding me, I'm one of the good guys now. The end result will justify what I have to do."

"Damn straight it will, Doc. Now let's rock and roll."

"Do you have any idea what that slang phrase actually means, Peyton?"

"Not a clue. I'll have to look it up later. There—I just made a note. Now seriously, let's go."

Rolling her eyes for the hundredth time that day, Kyra walked reluctantly out the door. "I don't know why I bother trying to respond to you."

"I do. I'll show you later," Peyton promised.

Following the nicest ass he'd ever come across on a woman, he shouldered his pulse cannon and grinned as they headed to the cage room.

***

Kyra walked in with a frown in place, but had to fight back a smile when King winked and Eric made smoochie lips at her. Turning away from them she saw Marcus sitting in the operating chair they had brought in for a prop. He was idly flipping a switchblade he'd gotten from a source Kyra promptly decided she didn't need to know about. She was still worried about Marcus—more now since he'd discovered his wife had remarried. After getting the news, the man had just drawn a little bit more inside of himself. She nodded, relieved when Marcus nodded back to her.

"How's Gloria doing today, Marcus?"

"Impatient, but not any more dysfunctional than usual," he reported.

"Good. Thanks for keeping an eye on her. I think I'm getting closer to figuring out how to get her voice working again. I removed all the pain wiring I could find. The source of the pain she feels with each attempt is still a mystery, but I'll solve it eventually."

As she turned away from Marcus, one of their blindfolded hostages launched into a verbal attack.

"I recognize your voice, Dr. Winters. I don't know why you've brought us here, but I can promise you this deplorable behavior will not go unpunished."

Kyra felt no regret at all about having had Peyton's fire team abduct the chancellors from their homes. Their wives were still soundly sleeping off a blast of knock-out gas, sparing them from seeing their husbands being abducted. Both men were still in their bedclothes, but she'd send them home dressed later. They currently had restraining devices on each wrist and were tied with ropes that would just get tighter with every move they made trying to escape.

Amazingly for once Kyra felt absolutely no compassion for the predicament of her captives. Instead she was savoring her temporary revenge.

Eric pointed to the cloth shielding their eyes and Kyra nodded. Eric shoved Chancellor Owens's down and King shoved down Chancellor Li's. She had a momentary flutter of alarm as she studied the professionally familiar faces she now had to consider in a new way. Jackson had let these men do some incredibly horrible things to her body. Fortunately, Peyton's exceptional lovemaking dominated her thoughts these days. The memory of that awful night seemed surreal to her now.

Behind her, she heard Peyton clearing his throat—several times in fact—before speaking.

"What's up, Doc? You sure are taking a long time to decide what to do with these fucking asswipes—I mean—*bad guys.*"

Kyra ignored his dramatic ruse and caught herself before she smiled. True. If the wicked chancellors had broken her legs, she'd be nothing but pissed at them. She wouldn't let the horrible intimacy of what was done to her be a deterrent to her plans. Instead, she would use that knowledge to get what she wanted—or she would do to the chancellors what she had done to Brad. Maybe she should worry about why the power-hungry tech's cybernetic conversion had not cost her one moment of sleep. Maybe her lack of conscience about it meant she wasn't quite one of the good guys yet, regardless of what Peyton thought. She certainly had redefinition plans just as big and grand as anything Jackson or Brad had conceived in their sick minds. The only difference was her intensions. It was a fine line, but one she was no longer afraid to walk.

"This is no time for stupid rabbit jokes, Captain Elliot. We're being rude to our reluctant guests."

She didn't turn to look at Peyton, but she knew what he was really asking. And it wasn't about her cartoon deprivation. He wanted to know if she was going to have balls enough to dish out the retribution they'd discussed. Well, they were all about to find out.

"Hello, Chancellor Owens—and you too, Chancellor Li. Sorry for staring at you so intently. It's just that I'm enjoying the sight of the two of you blindfolded and at my mercy instead of the other way around this time. Or are you going to pretend you don't remember me being blindfolded while each of you took turns sexually assaulting me in some very degrading ways?"

Even after she saw the truth in their gazes, Kyra found it was much easier saying it aloud than she had imagined it would be. Maybe it was because she could see the bound Chancellors were spineless and fear-ridden men. They certainly were the kind of men who didn't get their hands dirty doing their own evil. No, they were the kind that paid men like Jackson to do it. That was fine with her—she planned for them to keep right on paying.

"I'll get right to the point. I intend to restore the rest of the Cyber Soldiers like I have Captain Elliott and his men, but I need you two to help me do it on a much grander scale. If you won't do so as cooperative humans, I'm going to turn you both into compliant cyborgs who will never complain about doing anything I ask. But don't worry, Chancellors. Only the first five hours of the conversion surgeries are actually painful, but I'm sure you've seen the demonstration films about the process."

"Someone will stop you, Dr. Winters. We know you're not the smartest cyber scientist in the world. That's been proven already," Chancellor Owens declared.

Kyra fought a mouth twitch when Eric whacked the back of Owens's head and ordered him to talk nicer to her.

"Since you insist on pretending I'm the one with a reality problem, let's review some facts. You traded assaulting me in exchange for covering up Jackson's madness and funding the Cyber Wife program. So if I'm an evil bitch for having once been your victim, what should I think about the two of you for what you've done to me. . .not to mention the rest of the world? Evil begets more and greater evil, and your evil is about to be turned back on you. It's time to either pay the price for your sins or become a victim of them. That is called justifiable retribution."

"We offered you money to continue your work, but you turned us down. What more do you want, Dr. Winters? Do you want an apology from us? If so, we are sorry for our actions and the harm they caused you. Tell her, Owens. Tell her, you're sorry too. *Do it now*," Chancellor Li ordered.

"But Chancellor Owens isn't sorry, are you, Chancellor? Even now Chancellor Owens thinks he's going to find some way to regain control of this situation. But neither of you will be able to do that because—let's just say it aloud here—you're both *genuine bad guys*, and everyone knows they never win in the end."

"Bad guys? We are not bad guys," Chancellor Li protested. "Perhaps we made some mistakes, but we are not evil."

Kyra snorted and shook her head at the interruption. "You're both lucky I'm a rational person with higher goals than making money. If vengeance for what you did to me was all I needed to be happy, I'd have already used Marcus's switchblade over there to cut off your man parts and laughed as you went back home to your wives without them. But I have higher goals and the satisfaction would be temporary. Besides—I already got my vengeance urge satisfied when I made a cyborg out of the first guy Jackson let have a go at me that evening."

"Vengeance?" Chancellor Li asked.

"Stop sniffling, Li. She's bluffing," Chancellor Owens declared.

"Bluffing?" Kyra repeated the word. Peyton had been right that they weren't going to comply without a lot of motivation to do so. "I assure you I wouldn't even begin to know how to bluff. How about I show you a sample of my latest cybernetic handiwork? You really need to see how I deal with bad guys who don't take no for an answer to their evil plans. This conversion was definitely a worthy use of my skills and I rid the world of one more evil mad scientist causing chaos. The personal revenge I got in the process was just a bonus."

Kyra tapped her speak-through. "Hey, Vincent. Send Brad in."

Moments later, a stiff walking Brad walked through the door. He looked warily at everyone in the room, including the bound captives, but finally nodded respectfully to Kyra. "Did you need something from me, Dr. Winters?"

Kyra nodded back. "Yes, Brad. I need you to tell Chancellor Owens and Chancellor Li how I dealt with your evil mad scientist plans to blackmail me into using my cybernetic skills to help you make customizable robots out of normal people."

"Can you please rephrase the question, Dr. Winters? My current processor is unable to understand your metaphors."

"Of course. I'm sorry, Brad. But you know why I couldn't give you a better processor. I had to give you one that your amazing brain would be less likely to overthrow when your human mind started to break free of the programming."

"Yes. I fully understand, Dr. Winters. All the assumptions made about the human mind being unable to conquer cybernetic brain implants are being proven false. You were correct about that in your theory. Many cyborgs are already building organic synapses on their own."

"Yes. I was right about that, wasn't I? Even now, many cyborgs are building organic bypasses that allow them to ignore large parts of their programming, particularly the fail safes that keep them submissive."

Kyra glanced at the men who were now staring at Brad in shock.

"And how is your mental illness resolving itself, Brad? Are you still as evil as you were last week? Oh wait—belay those questions. I forget. Your processor doesn't understand. Just give us your status and tell us about your current work," Kyra ordered.

"As you wish, Dr. Winters. My mental illness is now ninety-seven point three percent constrained. I wish no harm to anyone. By your choice, I have been programmed to assist you with research so my day can be productive. My current assignment is to find and locate all information associated with Chancellors Owens and Li. This includes the location of all family members, all financial holdings, and any links to nefarious activities that are outside their UCN roles. I have been compiling a list since you requested I start three days ago. The work should be finished later today. Shall I have the information sent to your portable?"

"Yes, Brad. Thank you very much. I just have one other tiny question for you."

Kyra walked to where Brad was standing and circled around him once while the chancellors watched and wondered what she was doing. She let them worry silently for a full minute. Brad stared straight ahead the whole time.

"Are you happy, Brad?"

"I do not understand the question, Dr. Winters. Can you please rephrase?"

Kyra patted Brad on the arm. "It's not necessary for you to understand—that's all for now. You can return to your tasks."

Brad nodded. When he turned toward the door, she watched Peyton hold it open for Brad to leave. She smiled at the cyborg she loved, and he smiled back. He pointed two fingers to his cybernetic eyes and then turned them to point to her. *"Be a good guy,"* he mouthed. It made her grin, thinking about the debate they were undoubtedly going to have later about how she was enjoying her control over Brad a little too much.

"Dr. Winters. It's apparent we did not understand how trauma could affect a mind as intelligent as yours. We're also deeply sorry for any emotional pain we have caused you in the past. We do not wish to become like Dr. Smith. How can we avoid his fate?" Chancellor Li asked.

She turned slowly away from Peyton to once again face the men who had damaged, but not broken her.

"What you did to me was bad, Chancellors. . .but selling the Cyber Soldiers and stuffing your pockets with the money was far, far more evil. There is only one logical course of action guaranteed to pacify my sense of justice. You must make swift, full, and immediate amends to every soldier Jackson and I converted."

Chancellor Owens squirmed as the rope encircling him got tighter. "Preposterous. You have no proof we're guilty of any wrongdoing to anyone. Who do you think people are going to believe when this blackmail becomes public knowledge? You'll never get away with this."

"Are you sure, Chancellor Owens? Dr. Smith proudly confessed to his sins and yours before we managed to apprehend him. Turns out, he was kidnapping and experimenting on young women whose families will probably believe me when I return their damaged daughters to them. Some of the women he abducted were put into the Cyber Wife program without even the most dubious consent being present."

"So? We knew nothing of his crimes. Dr. Smith did all that on his own," Chancellor Li declared.

"Who funded Dr. Smith's experiments? When his last victim gets her voice back, I'm sure she's going to have a lovely story to tell about being taken to Norton and how UCN funds and equipment were used to create her. It was the two of you who let Dr. Smith get by with his heinous acts—just like you let my power-mad ex-husband, who was lining UCN chancellor pockets at the galactic rate."

"You have no right to talk about Dr. Channing when it's obvious you're twice as crazy as he was," Chancellor Owens declared.

His grunt of pain when Eric leaned down and yanked on the rope made her smile. Kyra glared at the pompous ass of a man who deserved twice everything she was planning. But as much as she would like to turn him into a docile servant of good, that would not balance out what needed to happen.

"Maybe what I did to Dr. Smith was a little harsh, especially since he did me an enormous favor by programming Jackson's Cyber Wife to kill him. And yes—I have his confession to that crime recorded as well. But what I did to my amazingly gifted fellow scientist is nothing—*absolutely nothing*—compared to what I will do to you and Chancellor Li if you don't make things right for the Cyber Soldiers. The ends, of seeing you do the right thing, justify any means I choose to use on you because I'm one of the good guys. If you want to point your finger at real evil, go look in the fucking mirror and do it. I already hate myself for all the years I spent working for people like the two of you."

Kyra glared at both of them, ramping up her intensity.

"So the way I see it. . .*gentlemen*. . .you only have one choice, which is to do exactly as I ask. You can either cooperate as a morally responsible human or you can both become my personal UCN affiliated cyborgs. Utilizing that evil side you accused me of having, I'll redefine you over and over until you're perfectly reformed to my exacting specifications of what obedient chancellors should behave like. Do you want me to call back Dr. Smith and give you another sample of my immensely gifted programming talents?"

Kyra smiled at Chancellor Owens when he swore richly.

"Well, Chancellors? What's your decision? Cyborg creation takes more than a single day and I'd like to get started on one of you soon if that's what it's going to take."

Owens snorted. "Fine. Can you skip the rest of your theatrical threats and just tell us what you want us to do?"

Kyra switched her glare from Chancellor Owens to Li who also nodded vigorously.

"Glad we could find a point of agreement. I know how hard that is for global politicians like yourselves—but I digress." Kyra crossed her arms and stood straighter. "First—as much as it pains me—we're going to turn the evil pair of you into global heroes. You will begin by making a public announcement today that Norton and I have finally discovered a restoration process that will make the Cyber Soldiers normal again. Peyton, myself, and all the men in this room are going to be standing beside you while we make that recording."

"But. . ." Chancellor Owens began, only to be smacked in the back of the head again.

"Afterward, registered letters will be sent to each and every soldier's family to let them know their loved ones are being reactivated and restored. Once the soldier is cleared for release, restitution will be made, commensurate with the soldier's rank and time in service, *including* all time spent in the Cyber Husband program or any other trumped-up cyber slave job."

"The UCN will think we're as crazy as you if we ask for all of that," Chancellor Owens exclaimed.

"Maybe they will—or maybe they won't. Whatever the UCN or the rest of the world thinks, I still want you to tell the truth, Chancellor Owens. For once in your corruption-driven career, you're going to take the high road. I think you'll be surprised at how many good people will respond favorably to the news."

"What about newer cyborgs? Most of them were redefined prisoners. We can't turn all those prisoners loose into society," Chancellor Li protested.

Kyra nodded. "I agree that it's a messy problem and one UCN greed created. I think you should direct Norton Industries to put all its energies and manpower into seeking a viable solution. Think of all the great publicity you're going to get when that happens. For my part, I intend to oversee Dr. Smith's restoration personally. I might even restore his humanity—in a few years—after he's been redefined about twenty more times to get rid of his mad scientist complex. It would be a shame to waste a mind like his forever."

"When you tip over the evil science bitch ledge, who's going to redefine you, Dr. Winters?" Chancellor Owens demanded.

Kyra laughed and crossed her arms. "Insults again, Chancellor Owens? Well now that you mention my potential competition, I think I do want the lead scientist position you and Li offered me. And more than that—I want to sit on the cybernetic advisory board at the UCN. That way I can make sure you two keep your word. Hell—I'll even work at Norton for my old salary. You can keep the twenty million you tried to bribe me with and use it to pay off a few soldiers. You can start with your abductors. Be grateful. They saved you from the evil plans of Dr. Smith—your favorite UCN-funded mad scientist."

Kyra stopped pacing and stopped trying to be brave. She looked at them genuinely, her gaze insisting that they understand.

"I know this may surprise you, but *none* of this is really about money. One day the world will thank me for figuring this out in time to stop a worse world war than any we've had to date. It would be very bad for all those military cyborgs to free themselves without being put back in touch with their humanity. Am I being clear about the gravity of the situation? We need to treat them well so they won't hate us and use the prosthetics we gave them to hurt us. Do you get the edge we've all been walking, Chancellors? You're looking a little stunned by the news."

Their dazed nods made her happy, but she wasn't able to show it. Instead, Kyra turned on her heel and marched to the door. She stopped and looked back one last time.

"Even after our recording goes live, I'll be watching what you do and so will these fully restored soldiers who can come get you anytime they want. I wouldn't advise betraying them or me ever again."

She glanced at Eric and King. "Help the chancellors get dressed for their big hero scene, then take them to the conference room. I'll be there shortly. I need to go change into my evil science bitch clothes and put my lab coat on. I wouldn't want the world to get the wrong idea about me."

The last thing Kyra heard was Eric and King mock apologizing to the chancellors as they roughly pulled the complaining men to their feet.

***

Outside in the hallway, Kyra leaned against the wall. Within a minute, Peyton followed her out. She stared up at his grin. "Too over the top?"

Peyton rubbed his mouth. Kyra made him smile so often, he hoped his face never froze that way. It would play hell with dealing with his men.

"Are you kidding? Hearing you give those two that ballsy lecture was hot. In fact, I'm having a very strong physical reaction to knowing you're a real badass under that dorky lab coat you wear. Hell, you sounded so mean I even forgot for a moment that you weren't really an evil cyber scientist. How about I have the guys stop at your house and pick up those red high heels to go with your apprehension gear? I think the combination of dumb woman shoes and badass scientist could inspire me to keep you awake all night."

Kyra sighed. "Sexual mockery? Really? After all the hell I just went through? I'm wishing now that I hadn't taken off your wrist restraints. I'd be shocking the disrespect right out of you, Peyton Elliot. And by the way, your Cyber Husband rating just took its first serious nosedive."

Shoving at his chest, Kyra smiled as she heard Peyton belly laughing as she walked away. She wanted to put her real clothes back on, including her lab coat, before she went to confess her cyborg restoration work to the world.

Chapter 21

Five weeks after the recording aired, Kyra was hiding out and dressing in the master bathroom of her house. It was still a shock to her that she and Peyton had been able to move back in, much less into the master bedroom which he'd redone right down to painting the room trim.

Every day now she surreally went to Norton and performed a new cyborg restoration. So far only one had been a total failure, but they hadn't let the man commit suicide. Instead, they'd had to put him back the way he was before the restoration. While it had hurt to take that action, she was keeping a list of the failures. One day she'd find the answers for them as well.

"How's Marcus holding up?" she asked through the open bathroom door.

"Marcus at least got to see his sons. They don't remember him much after ten years, but their stepfather was pretty decent about it. He hung out to ease the way for Marcus and the kids to get to know each other again. Eric was keeping an eye on it from a distance in case it went badly. Eric said Marcus's wife. . .or ex. . .or hell whatever she is to him now. . .was clearly still in shock. He said she seemed incredibly afraid of Marcus. He said you could see it in her eyes. It may take another decade before all the lies about cyborgs are proven to be false," Peyton reported.

Kyra nodded as she pulled the short black dress on over her head. Then she laughed at herself because Peyton couldn't see her. She cleared her throat so she could yell again. "The rest of your team appears to be adjusting, but I can never tell how much turmoil they're trying to hide. How do you think they're doing?"

She sat on the toilet seat lid to strap the tall black high heels on. When she stood, she wobbled and had to catch herself on the sink. It took a few steps to get the hang of balancing her weight on them. It had been many years since she'd worn the sexy, but stupid shoes.

"Each man is identifying some quirks in his programming, but the average functional efficiency range stays in the ninetieth percentile for the ones I'm equipped to track. Their UCN pensions have made their adjustment as good as it can be considering normal people still tend to freak out when they discover they're interacting with a cyborg. No one is getting a hero's welcome home. In fact, most seem to have forgotten about the war, and that includes their families. Cyborgs will never be able to forget."

"Maybe the world the cyborgs are waking up into will improve in time," Kyra said, walking out of the bathroom. Peyton's genuine surprise over her appearance proved worth every painful moment she was experiencing trying to maintain her balance.

"I know my world sure just got a hell of lot better," Peyton declared, rising from his prone position on their bed. It had been his first purchase with his pension. The next had been the set of gold rings in his pocket. He walked slowly to where she stood.

"Damn, Doc. I can't take you out in public looking like that. I'll get arrested before the night is over just trying to keep the men off you. That includes *my* men—and especially King."

Kyra smacked a hand to his chest. "We're not staying home. King is expecting us to come to his restaurant's opening and *we are going*."

"Okay, but ditch the tall heels. There's no reason to be uncomfortable for anyone but your husband." Peyton stepped into Kyra and dipped to her mouth. His body went rock hard when he felt hers lined up so well with his. "My circuits are scrambling. You need an outfit like this in every color. You don't ever have to walk around in the shoes, just wear them to bed. Start with our honeymoon."

Kyra snorted. "*Honeymoon?* Is that suggestion your idea of a marriage proposal, Captain?"

"Yes. It is," Peyton said. Reaching into his pocket, he pulled out the box. "Wearing rings is old fashioned, but I want the world to know we're a couple. I figured if you enjoyed boiling water in a teakettle, you might like to wear matching wedding rings. These were artifacts that I had resized to fit us."

Kyra flipped open the jewelry box, instantly tearing up at the matching gold bands nestled inside it. "Peyton—what were you thinking? These are real gold. That metal is worth a fortune these days. We'll have to have body guards to keep from getting mugged for them."

Peyton nodded. "Well of course they're real gold. And they're worth a lot for other reasons than just the metal they're made of, but we'll talk about that later—much later."

Kyra lifted both rings from the box before tossing the empty container on their bed. She lifted Peyton's real hand and slipped the gold ring sized for him on his finger. After it slid home, Peyton took the other one, lifted her hand, and slid a matching circle of gold onto hers.

"How can I be so happy when there's so much left to do?" Kyra asked.

Peyton sighed before answering. "Even the good guys get a night off now and again, Doc. We'll go back to saving the world tomorrow. I promise. How about we enjoy a little reprieve this evening?"

Kyra wrapped her arms around him and hugged. "I say my husband and I are probably going to be a little bit late for dinner at their friend's new restaurant. I'm thinking maybe I need to try out my sexy new shoes in bed before I change back into my flats. What do you say?"

Peyton lifted a laughing Kyra into his arms. "I say—there's no maybe about what I intend to do to my incredibly beautiful wife in next ten minutes and fifteen seconds—give or take an hour—if it turns out she's in the mood for some serious lovemaking."

# # #

NOTE FROM THE AUTHOR: If you enjoyed this book, please consider leaving a positive review or rating on the site where you purchased it. Reader reviews help my books continue to be valued by distributors/resellers and help new readers make decisions about reading them.

You are the reason I write these stories and I sincerely appreciate you!

Many thanks for your support,
~ Donna McDonald

Excerpt from *THE TRACKER'S QUEST*

Book 6 of the *Forced to Serve* Series

Chapter 1

If Rena had still been alive, she would have called her naïve for having hoped for a better welcome. Seta hadn't expected her father to greet her warmly. It would have been foolish to let her mind indulge in such a fantasy. But the two giant males dragging her by her wrists were reprehensible treatment from the wealth-obsessed tyrant who had sired her. The phony escorts had met her Peace Alliance courtesy shuttle only to make her a prisoner the moment they'd driven away from the landing station.

Seta stumbled in her regulation boots as her father's two chief guards literally tossed her into a small holding room just inside the walls of her father's canton. Luckily she was still completely in uniform, so no Ethosian female drapery impeded her progress as she whirled around to face the traitors. Angry heat flooded her face over her disrespectful treatment. The power she hosted clawed inside her to be recognized. . .and used. But she feared doing so would mean her death as much as that of the males she faced.

"Chief Arghane, I demand to see Suzerain Trax immediately. I have come at his explicit request. Why have you taken me prisoner? He expected me to present myself to him as soon as I arrived. Your mistreatment of me will not go unpunished this time."

"We know why you have returned, errant daughter of Trax. This is where you will wait until the Suzerain is ready to see you. Be patient for his will and show your sire some respect. Your manner of dress is enough offense to earn a beating with the lash," Chief Arghane replied.

"My father is not the only threat you need to heed, Arghane. I am a Peace Alliance officer now. This clothing is my uniform . . .hey." The heavy metal door slamming loudly on her protests made Seta jump back a step or two. Curses flew from her mouth without regard for the fact that everything she said and did was most certainly being monitored.

In the Peace Alliance, she had been respected as an officer. She had almost forgotten what it was like to be insulted and treated so poorly. All Ethosian females were secondary citizens on Ethos, really no more important than any other possession a male could own. Males, especially those in higher positions like Arghane, had socially sanctioned power over her.

She thought of her dead sibling and how relieved they had both been to put Ethos and their lives there behind them. Anyone that had managed to obtain their off-planet freedom usually had the good sense never to return. It was doubly wise for females to heed that wisdom. So why had she felt so driven to come back when her father had asked?

"Do not haunt my thoughts from wherever you have gone, Rena Trax. Making right my foolish mistake is going to be enough torture."

Seta laughed as her words bounced off the metal walls of her cage. If she was lucky, the guards would think she was crazy for talking aloud to her dead sibling. Mental insanity might be a profound truth about her before she escaped again.

Her father's request had seemed genuine enough via com link, but given her immediate incarceration, that obviously had been a ruse to gain her presence. In her desire to avenge Rena and gain some measure of freedom for her mother's family, she had chosen to believe his words. If Rena's spirit was watching from wherever it had gone, she was no doubt genuinely furious that Seta had let herself fall into their father's trap so easily.

She strode to the single small mirror in the room. After her Peace Alliance training, she knew the mirror was a security surface behind which guards watched her every movement. The female staring back at her looked intimidated by the whole situation. Unwilling to accept that was her only choice for reality, Seta placed a hand on the glass and closed her eyes. She thought of her conversation with Ania Looren and of the secrets the other alien demon host had shared. It was as good a time as any to try some of it out. Arghane had taken her weapon.

"*Zorinda. Show yourself to me in the mirror,*" Seta said firmly. But when she opened her eyes, all she saw was the same frightened female. She tried to recall what it was that

Ania has said about needing to be firm when commanding the creature within her.

"*Demon Zorinda—I require your help. I command you to show yourself to me in any form you can,*" Seta said in a fierce whisper. Her hand slid from the glass as she felt the surface turn freezing cold beneath her palm. A misty swirl of black rippled over her own reflection until her face was no longer visible.

You have been misled by your abductors.

Seta frowned. The words appeared in her mind, but they were also given sound in her head by a strange female voice resonating within her. She now understood Ania's cautions about believing every whisper from within. It was virtually impossible to tell what commentary was her own inner dialogue and what was Zorinda speaking.

Seta stepped back, studied the surface, and then stepped forward again. "Yes. I understand the danger. Please explain what you know."

The mist danced and moved. Seta waited and watched until it had settled again.

Don't trust their words, the black mist ordered.

Seta snorted. "No worries there, but I need more than advice. How can I get out of here?"

Patience. The way out will come soon. His choice is made.

Seta felt Zorinda pull back her energy. It left her pondering the confusing statement as she watched the black swirl disappear rapidly from the glass. It hadn't been the kind of conversation she had hoped for with the powerful being inside her, but then again, Zorinda hadn't ignored her demands for communication either.

As she settled down on a chair to wait, Seta congratulated herself that Ania's introductory lessons about mastering the alien spirit within her were working. If Zorinda was right, the request from her father might have been no more than a ruse to get her to return so he could punish her for leaving. Maybe he intended to make her torture and death a public example of what would happen to those who tried to defect.

Her father and his guards would receive a surprise if he did try to kill her. Zorinda had done nothing to help during the attack on the Guardian, but then it had been Ensign Vetin at risk—not her. Ania had felt that was the only reason Zorinda hadn't intervened.

"How much of a fool was I in agreeing to this farce?" Seta asked the walls.

Disgusted at herself for feeling regretful, she marched to a cot and plopped down on it to wait. All her thoughts were focused on only one thing. She must find a means to escape the planet again. Having managed to do it once with Rena, she knew escape was possible. Doing it alone might prove more challenging, but she would still find a way.

Her last conversation with Ji came back to mock her captivity. Perhaps she should have taken her bossy former captain up on his offer to accompany her after all. Her greedy sire would no doubt have enjoyed trying to extort a high union price from the wealthy Siren.

***

Kelzar Hornex walked with his former captain to the shuttle's ramp as it lowered. "Are you sure you want me to just leave you here alone? Only small parts of this planet acknowledge the Peace Alliance. I don't know what kind of reception you will have among the majority of these unenlightened beings."

Ji shrugged. "I have studied Ethos, Kel. I know all the potential risks, but Seta Trax is here."

Kel snorted. "Yes—that is my point. I'm still finding it hard to accept you're putting yourself in danger because of the tracker."

"No one is more aware of the irony than I am," Ji agreed. Then he thought of Seta's complete surprise at finding her first pleasure under his hands and all doubt left his mind. He bowed his head respectfully even though the male who faced him still shook his in denial.

"Ji, the Ethosian is only one female out of so many you have known. You have but to walk near the most alluring of them to get an offer to their sleep space. It seems illogical to risk your life for someone so reluctant to have you," Kel insisted.

Ji let loose a frustrated breath, but there was no reason to be angry with his former commander. Kel was only pointing out the same truth his mind warned him about repeatedly.

"I understand why you would say that to me, Kel. The only explanation I have is that Seta Trax is the only person in my life who matters now. Since my decision about being here is not based in logic, I can't explain it well to you. Just know this action is necessary—and it is my choice."

Kel pondered the statement, then dipped his head in a bow. He was resigned but still determined to do what he could to help his longtime friend.

"For many years, I have owed you my life. I now know I owe you my captaincy as well. The High Council informed me it was your recommendation to offer me the commission as Captain on the Paladin. So I will now use that promotion to repay part of my increasingly long-life debt to you, Ji Warro of Rylen. In eight Earth days, I will come back into range of this desolate planet. Contact me with your location and I'll send a shuttle to retrieve you and your..."

Ji laughed at his friend's hesitation. "The word is *mate*, Kel. Seta Trax is my mate. This is the case whether she admits it or not. Sirens take that kind of connection very seriously. We have no choice."

"But is the resistant female, who never seemed to care for you before, worth giving up your life as well as your captaincy?" Kel demanded.

Ji shrugged. "Only time will answer that question. I'm barely over three hundred Earth years old in a life that may span a couple thousand years if I live as long as my Siren parents. Yet all I can tell you is the female is worth it to me at this time. My energy has chosen to align with hers. It is a life choice more compelling than any contract I could make with any organization—even the Peace Alliance."

"Very well then," Kel said, bowing his head. "I won't try to talk you out of your quest for your chosen one. May the Creators be with you."

Ji laughed. "Indeed. I may need their help to survive Seta's wrath for chasing her here, much less the normal hostility of this desert planet. I will gladly accept the offer of friendly transport out of here when we are done with her quest. If we are late, please try to wait a couple Earth days for us."

Since he knew Kel was not a male who hugged, Ji put a hand on his friend's shoulder and squeezed. Then he jogged down the steps of the ramp to meet the guards waiting for him at the bottom. Behind him, he heard the boarding ramp rising and the shuttle's engines revving again to leave. He pushed away the momentary panic of being without backup and hoped for the best.

"I've come to see Suzerain Trax about a mating union with one of his offspring. He is expecting me," Ji said.

One of the guards nodded and bowed his head. "Of course. My name is Chief Arghane. I am to see you to Suzerain Trax's canton gallery. It is rare that a union suitor comes from off-planet. How did you meet one of the Suzerain's female offspring?"

"We serve on the same Peace Alliance ship," Ji said.

"So it is true then. Seta of Trax fled Ethos to become a warrior. We did not believe her story," Chief Arghane said.

"Why would you not believe her?" Ji asked.

Chief Arghane shrugged. "Females lie to suit their purposes. They will manipulate what they can for personal gain."

"Are you sure we are talking about the same female? Seta is the most guileless female I have ever met," Ji said.

Arghane laughed. "Don't you mean *beguiled*, Siren? We don't see your kind often, but we know what Sirens do to their females. You can bend her will to yours. An Ethosian male would pay much to have that ability."

"Well some Sirens take those measures with mates, though it's not as easy as you make it sound. But I assure you, I have not affected Seta's will at all. My relationship to her is based on mutual agreement of our suitability. Why are you laughing at me, Chief Arghane?"

"Perhaps you will soon be wishing you had exercised your full Siren skills on that female. Seta of Trax denies the presence of any union suitor in her life. We've had the rebellious female in isolation since she arrived back on planet. Suzerain Trax wanted to speak with you before he met with her."

"I see," Ji said, working hard to ignore the rage rising inside him. It was illogical to feel he had failed her and yet that was exactly what went through his mind. Arghane's next words revealed how upset he must have looked.

"Relax, Siren. There is nothing to fear in the female's denial of your claim. If the Suzerain agrees to your union price for her, we will place the female in restraints for her transport to your destination. It is common practice here. Many of his female offspring are resistant to the union matches the Suzerain makes on their behalf."

Ji stared at the laughing male as he climbed into their land transport. "I was under the impression that Seta had returned for a quest her father wanted her to make for him. It was why I allowed her to proceed unaccompanied."

"A quest? Perhaps that is the case as well," Arghane said, shrugging. "We only do as the suzerain commands. Once you contacted him, he became focused on your satisfaction. His union eligible females are highly prized on our planet. Most of them are fair-haired and quite attractive. They usually bring high prices."

"Indeed," Ji said. "I trust Seta has not been harmed during her restraining process."

"We would never willingly damage a female with a bid on her," Arghane said quickly, sensing the Siren male's growing displeasure. If he upset the potential suitor, the suzerain would not be pleased. "Your female of choice is merely in isolation. Seta of Trax has been well cared for in every way she allowed. The most unfortunate circumstance is that we have not been successful in getting her out of the vile clothing she arrived wearing. She said she would rather starve than change her clothes. We accepted that challenge."

"Are you speaking of her uniform?" Ji asked, trying not to grind his teeth as Arghane nodded. The thought of them not feeding her had him picturing how best to kill the male beside him.

"A uniform. Yes, that is what she keeps calling her clothing. Is it true she was trained as a warrior?" Arghane asked.

Ji nodded tightly. "Yes. Seta was trained during academy. Why do you keep asking that question?"

Arghane shrugged as the land transport passed through the canton's outer wall. "She was easily subdued. Proof was lacking of her warrior skills."

"It is illogical to fight when you're greatly outnumbered," Ji said. "Her skills are not in fighting anyway. Seta is the best tracker in the Peace Alliance."

"Is that so?" Arghane said, huffing at the news. "Well perhaps the suzerain does have a task in mind for her as she claims. He keeps his own counsel on most decisions. Often I don't know his intentions until after the task has been completed."

"When will I be allowed to see her?" Ji asked.

"As soon as the suzerain agrees to your union," Arghane said.

Sensing further questions would only make the Ethosian male more resistant, Ji leaned back and studied the passing surroundings. Here and there males of all ages walked in the street, but he saw few females, not even in the market.

"Where are all your females?" Ji asked.

He watched Chief Arghane turn to him with eyebrows raised.

"Do you consider us barbaric, Siren? I assure you that is not the case. Our females are safe in their homes where they won't be abducted. Where else would they be?" Arghane asked in return.

Ji nodded. He had read that the females were kept in isolation until they were needed, but it was still unnerving to see proof of it in their most progressive urban area. The contrast with Rylen made him more appreciative than ever of the beautifully clad and smiling females on his home planet.

###

Coming Soon
*See **www.donnamcdonaldauthor.com** for more info.*

Connect with Donna McDonald

WEBSITE
www.donnamcdonaldauthor.com

EMAIL
email@donnamcdonaldauthor.com

TWITTER
@donnamcdonald13 and @scifiwoman13

FACEBOOK
Donna McDonald Contemporary Romances
Donna McDonald SciFi Romances
Risky Readers

CONTEMPORARY BOOK BLOG
www.donnamcdonald.blogspot.com

PARANORMAL/FANTASY/SCIFI BOOK BLOG
www.donnamcdonaldparanormal.blogspot.com

Other Books by Donna McDonald

Visit **www.donnamcdonaldauthor.com** to see a complete list of my books
including the following bestselling series:

NEVER TOO LATE SERIES
ART OF LOVE SERIES
NEXT TIME AROUND SERIES
FORCED TO SERVE SERIES

If you want to hear about new releases and planned books, subscribe to my newsletter at
http://www.donnamcdonaldauthor.com/Subscribe.html

Thank you for Reading my work! You are the reason I write.
~ Donna McDonald ~

About the Author

Donna McDonald is a best selling author in Contemporary Romance and Humor, and lately has been climbing the Paranormal Romance lists as well.

Paranormal readers are calling McDonald "a literary alchemist effortlessly blending science fiction and romance". Contemporary and humor readers often write to tell her that the books keep them up reading and laughing all night. She likes both compliments and hopes they stay true forever so she can write for the rest of her life.

Her idea of success is to be sitting next to someone on a plane and find out they are laughing at something in one of her books. She hopes that someone will be you.

Visit *www.donnamcdonaldauthor.com*. I love to hear from readers.

Made in the USA
Charleston, SC
31 March 2016